# DUE NORTH - A CONDUCTOR ACROSS TIME SERIES

# Due North - A Conductor across time series

Jason Harris

# Contents

To my incredible wife who encouraged me and kept
me company, not just on this journey but in life.
Love you always.

# Prologue: Savior

The whip cracked as it ripped through skin, leaving ripples of red flesh exposed to the cool night air.

The victim screamed in agony as he struggled to free himself from the straps binding him to the tree. However, the whip lashed out, easily finding its target sending pieces of flesh and blood splattered across his back. Again he cried out, a scream mixed with pain and rage.

The beating began just after night fall. The slave catchers found him and his family hiding in an abandoned barn on the outskirts of town. He initially fought back, successfully overpowering the older slave catcher. However, that momentary victory seemed only to further enrage the violent duo. After the long and arduous escape, the pair proved to be too much for his exhausted and frail body to overcome.

"Where did you think you were going?" shouted the older slave hunter. "You gonna hop on that Underground Railroad and ride to freedom?"

The whip handler laughed as he passed the large brown jug to the younger slave catcher. He too laughed deeply as he tossed back his head and turned the jug up, taking a long swig. Using his sleeve, he wiped his mouth allowing the excess liquor to dribble down his chin and onto his sweat-stained undershirt.

"You ain't never gonna be free," he shouted before striking the Negro in the back of the head. "We're gonna whip you, and after we're done, we're gonna have our way with your two females. Then, when we're finished, we're all gonna take a ride back to Alabama."

After another gulp of the rust-colored liquor, he passed the jug back to the older hunter before returning his focus to the beating. With a flick of the wrist, he unleashed three quick strikes with the braided leather whip. The Negro man, exhausted from the beating, slumped against the tree, seemingly unable to fight or even cry out with emotion.

Sensing the Negro had lost his will to fight; the old man reached into his boot and pulled out a large knife. Rolling the wooden handle across his palm, the long metal blade reflected the bright light radiating from the fire. "We're gonna show you what we do to Alabama Niggers that like to fight and run," spat the old man.

The woman, tightly clutching the young girl, screamed, "No Massa, please don't kill him. I'll do whatever you want, but please don't kill him."

The leader smiled as his eyes looked the woman up and down. Her long cotton dress, torn from the treacherous journey now exposed her leg and the upper portion of her thigh. Frantically reaching for his legs, she fought furiously while begging for mercy.

The aged bounty hunter looked down at her menacingly. With long exaggerated swipes, he ran the knife along his rough stubbled neck." Don't worry honey, we ain't forgot about you," he said as he turned his attention to the wide-eyed young girl sitting quietly, tears beginning to stream down her face. "We want to get to know the whole family," he added while kicking himself free from the mother's clinched arms.

As he reached for the young girl, her mother grabbed at his extended arms only to have her maternal instincts rebuffed with a quick backhand to the side of her face. Falling backwards, she clutched her jaw tightly as the pain radiated from her face to her outer extremities.

"I told you, we ain't forgotten about you!" he snarled. "Besides, there's plenty of this to go around," he added with a smirk before returning his gaze to the young girl. Her fragile body shivered in the cool night breeze as he reached down and gently scooped her up.

"Hello sweetie," he whispered while laying her down several feet from her mother. "Like I told your mammy, we ain't gonna hurt you. We just want to get to know you a little better."

***

Deep in the recesses of the forest, the large man sat on the mare as he watched the violent scene unfold before him. The dark hooded cloak coupled with his coffee-colored skin easily camouflaged him as he sat in the dim shadows of the forest. He had followed the bounty hunters for much of the day, riding along the forest's edge as they closed in on the runaway family. The clash occurred just before dark. He looked on as the mother and daughter helplessly watched the Negro man bravely fight off their captors before being overcome by the younger of the two slave catchers.

Watching the struggle and eventual beating triggered memories that instantly flooded his mind. Memories that took him back to a time where a question, a perceived slight, or even a look could result in the most severe beating. He shifted uncomfortably in his saddle, momentarily reflecting back on some of the childhood instances he and others had endured. Those memories and the beatings that resulted had proven to be useful reminders of what would happen if he were ever caught.

As a result, although it sickened him to witness the brutality, he would occasionally allow victims to experience a small measure of abuse. Although barbaric, it served as a fresh and sobering reminder of what would become of them if they were again captured. If they were going to make it safely to freedom, they had to fully understand the extremes to which their former masters would go to retrieve them. That was true for any captured Negro man however, that stopped when it came to women and children.

He continued watching as the hunters turned their attention from the man to the woman and young girl. Primarily motivated by money, most bounty hunters conducted their responsibilities with an understandable amount of civility. However, watching the pair, it quickly became evident that these two were different. Drunk and obviously enraged from the Negroes' resistance, they seemed intent on obtaining blood.

Reaching deep into his cloak pocket, he pulled out a cigar and a metallic colored BIC lighter. After a quick snip with his cutter, he discarded the folded cap. Holding the cigar barrel loosely in one hand, he firmly flicked the lighter's mechanical wheel with the other. After several firm strikes, the lighter ignited. The bright orange and blue flame instantly illuminated his face as he exposed the tip of the cigar to the bright flame. As it began to smolder, several quick puffs quickly filled his mouth with the peppery flavored smoke. Exhaling through his nostrils, the smoke slowly danced around him and into the night sky before slowly disappearing into the darkness. Closing his eyes, he listened to his breathing, his body becoming more relaxed with each breath.

The large mare shuffled nervously beneath him in anticipation of the coming charge. "Whoa, girl," he whispered while calmly stroking her neck. After another deep draw from the smoldering cigar, he extinguished the bright orange embers against a nearby oak tree and placed the remnants in his cloak pocket. A gentle nudge prompted the large horse's advancement, stepping out of the shadows and into the brightly lit night sky.

Lying in the dirty rubble, with the blade pressed firmly against the girl's tiny throat, the older slave catcher whispered calmly, "You be quiet, darkie. I'm about to make you a woman."

With one hand loosely gripping the blade, he slid his right then left arm out of the denim overall suspenders.

Standing over the young girl, he let his pants fall loosely to the ground, prompting a small smirk from the old man.

With eyes wide opened, she tearfully whimpered as he kneeled down beside her when the snap of a branch caught his attention. Startled by the unexpected appearance, he stumbled backwards, surprised to find the cloaked black man sitting on top of the large horse. Before the old man could speak, the rider pointed a small gun-like device and pulled the trigger. With a quick flash of light, metal tips sailed through the night sky before finding their target in the bare mid-section of the unclothed hunter. The electric leads dug deep into his bare flesh, causing his body to immediately erupt into convulsions as his nervous system reacted to the electrical stimulant.

The younger hunter turned and looked on in horror as his older partner's spine-chilling screams conveyed the pain caused by the electricity flowing mercilessly through his body. Abandoning the whip, he quickly unsheathed the knife strapped to his belt and looked up at the large black man still sitting on the horse. Defiantly tossing the knife from hand to hand, he motioned for the stranger to come down from the horse.

Peering down at the young man, he smiled as he slid out of the saddle. With surprising cat-like reflexes, he landed in a crouching position before slowly standing erect. Now, towering over the wide-eyed young man, his casual grin was quickly replaced with a serious cool anger.

The young hunter walked cautiously toward him before blindly charging, swinging wildly at the cloaked man's abdomen in hopes of finding flesh. With skilled anticipation, the black man parried the desperate charge and, using the young man's momentum, sent him plummeting into the nearby brush. Dazed and confused, the young man shook his head slowly before frantically pawing through the rocky soil in search for his knife.

The cloaked man smiled as he mockingly held the knife up for display. With a flick of his wrist, the blade sailed across the clearing before sticking innocently in a large pine tree.

The young man looked at him, the knife, and back again at the black man. After a brief pause, he again charged headfirst, desperately hoping to take down the much larger man.

Recognizing the strategy, the cloaked black man widened his stance and absorbed the young man's shoulder as he slammed into his mid-section. Swinging his left arm under the young hunter's neck, he locked his right hand on his left wrist and stood partially erect. The guillotine move instantly succeeded in cutting off the hunters' essential flow of blood and oxygen. His arms flailed wildly in a desperate attempt to free himself before his body calmed and went limp. The black man, still breathing calmly, released his grip, allowing the unconscious body to slump to the ground.

A few steps over to the large pine tree and he grabbed the knife's hilt. With a firm pull it loosened then easily slid from the tree trunk. Using the blade, he cut the leather straps binding the bloodied Negro to the tree and scooped up his lifeless body.

Laying the man in the rear cargo area of the hunter's wagon, he reached into his leather saddle bag and pulled out a plastic water canteen. Drizzling the fresh water on the wounds scattered across the man's back, he patted them dry before digging deeper into his bag to retrieve a simple white shirt and a small aerosol can. The two female slaves watched in amazement as small clouds of antiseptic sprayed from the device leaving white foam to bubble on top of the ribbons of open wounds. Digging around in the front of the wagon, he found several neatly wrapped napkins with biscuits, salt pork, and apples.

"Please hop in ladies," invited the large black man while picking up the young girl and placing her next to her father. "Give your daddy some of these and this," he added, handing her the supplies and simple cotton pullover shirt, "I'll be right back."

He reached into his saddle bag and retrieved a small black leather pouch with several plastic syringes. Holding the two vials in the moonlight, he gently tapped the liquid filled cylinders before walking over to the older bounty hunter still twitching from the electrical stimulant. After a quick jab from the hypodermic needle, he walked over to the younger unconscious hunter and repeated the injection. Slipping the empty syringes back in the saddlebag, he turned his attention back to the family.

"Thank you sir," muttered the father while attempting to sit up.

"No, please don't," he replied while helping the father lay back down in the wagon. "You need to rest. I will take you as far as the river," he said while strapping the black mare to the rear of the wagon. Climbing in he flicked the straps, and the two horses jolted forward.

The unlikely travel companions made their way west before gradually turning north. Guided by the brightly illuminated North Star, they traveled for several hours before stopping abruptly in front of a wooden bridge suspended over a fast-moving river.

The black man turned and looked down at three pairs of eyes anxiously looking up at him.

"This bridge connects Georgia and Tennessee. Take the food and keep heading north on the other side of that bridge. Every time you stop to eat, put some of this on his back," he added while reaching into his bag and producing a small tin can of cream and a metal object wrapped loosely in a cloth towel. Unwrapping the object, the mother examined the now exposed handle of the revolver.

"You must not be caught," the large black man asked. "Do you understand?"

"Yes...," she replied nervously while examining the gun and the metal jar. "What about those men? Won't they be looking for us?"

"Don't worry about them," he replied reassuringly. "They're going to be asleep for a while, and by the time they awake, they won't remember much. But let them serve as a reminder of what will happen if you are caught. Stay out of sight, keep north, travel at night and use these," he added while reaching into his bag and producing two small tin lanterns with a candle in the middle.

"About ten miles north of us, you'll find a barn with a symbol of a lantern etched above the doorway. Any time you see that symbol, know that you've found a friend."

The mother burst into tears. "Massa, is you an angel?"

"No," he said with a smile. "I'm just a friend. Now go, and may God be with you."

The family climbed out of the wagon and scurried onto the narrow wooden bridge dangling just out of the fast-moving water's reach. He watched as they crossed, then disappeared into the night. Hopping out of the wagon, he unstrapped the two horses and tied their reins to his horse. After a firm push, the wagon slipped into the rapidly rushing water. Climbing into the mare's saddle, he glanced over his shoulder before slipping the hood over his head and nudging her gently. She responded immediately by leading the two horses into the forest's cover of darkness.

# One

# Discovery

"Getting up for school that day, I never in a million years thought I'd be sitting here telling you this story. I was just another know-it-all kid confused about where I fit into the world. A lot has changed since that winter day. In retrospect, I should have told you sooner. Told you…told you and trusted that you'd understand."

Looking out the murky windowpane I whispered to myself, "Where to start? Where should I begin?"

"Maybe you should sit down. Let me start from the beginning."

It was late February 2018 in Atlanta Georgia. I peered down the long hallway leading to the gymnasium while trying my best to blend in with the wall of gray lockers. With the exception of the sole janitor slowly pushing a broom, the hallway was abandoned. Pausing briefly, I listened as his boots clinked on the linoleum floor, the keys jingled creating a melodic marching song as he moved. I had just finished my first class, government, which meant PE was next.

As a junior, I technically did not have to take it but considering coach gave me a "B" last spring, my GPA took a serious hit. After reviewing my options with the counselor I decided my only choice was to retake it.

Although we were already nine weeks into the semester, I had somehow managed to leave first period early every day. History taught me that the sooner I got into the locker room, the less likely I was to bump into the local douche bag, Marcus Rivers.

Every school has them, but Marcus was definitely our guy 'the leader of the gorilla pack' we called them. You know that loud group of guys regularly intimidating or engaging in practical jokes, seemingly intent on making every classroom a virtual combat zone.

Sliding my hand under the sleeve of my hoodie, I nervously ran my fingers along my forearm. The short ribbons of raised scars instantly took me back to a darker time. A time when the pressure to fit in and deal with people like Marcus, coupled with the anger that ensued, were at times too much to handle. Unable to work through the feelings, I had turned to what I thought was my only outlet.

"Focus," I thought as I pulled the sleeve over my now exposed arm.

Glancing at my watch, I followed the hands as they slowly made their way around the watch face. The four-year-old device had been an elementary graduation gift from my grandmother. In the beginning I had to use the first hole on the band just to keep it from sliding off my wrist. Since that summer, I had loosened it on two occasions, once during the summer after 8th grade, and another during my sophomore year. But standing there waiting for 2nd period I found myself twisting my hand in a circular motion.  I was surprised to discover how tight the band had gotten. Unlatching the band I moved it over one hole.

"Maybe I'm going through another growth spurt," I thought while latching the band.

Considering I had always been smaller than most of my classmates, any growth really amounted to more of a "catch up" rather than a spurt. I chuckled as I thought about my mother's generic response to anything related to my size: "What you lack in physical stature, you more than make up for it with intellect and wit!"

I had personally never viewed my grades or advanced classes as anything special. Whenever kids asked about the Physics or Calculus classes I took as a freshman, I usually compared it to the kid who can throw a perfect pass or dunk a basketball, "it just kind of came naturally." Oddly enough, my comparison usually annoyed people like Marcus and his friends. At least, that is the excuse I made for my run-ins with him.

Adults call it bullying or intimidation, but my friends and I simply referred to it as being an ass. I think we all thought that once we became juniors it would stop. Unfortunately that optimism was short lived when earlier in the school year Marcus posted pictures of several of us getting dressed before gym. Since then, I had tried everything: ignoring him, being the bigger person, even anonymously reporting incidents; all to no avail. As a result, most of us resorted to our last line of defense, evasive maneuvers.

Clumsily twirling a random locker door padlock, I stood in the hallway waiting for the bell to ring. As the alarm sounded, kids began flowing out of classrooms and into the narrow hallway. Slipping across the hall, I wove my way through the throngs of over-sized football players exiting the locker room. Once inside, I immediately executed my tried and tested 'in and out routine'; T-shirt on, double shorts with my phone tucked safely in the under short pocket.

Stepping onto the parquet floors, I could see other athletically challenged classmates, kids of all sizes and shapes scattered throughout the gym waiting for the whistle to blow. And there, leaned against a rack of assorted dumbbells, was my best friend of 10 years, Justin Anderson.

If I was undersized, Justin was definitely the junior class runt. Standing at an unimpressive five-foot-one inch he was a physically small guy but his mind and personality always assured he was the biggest person in the room. A wizard when it came to computers and technology, he had always been there to help me build or fix any issues with my system. However, because of his size and the same advanced placement classes, he too got his fair share of unwanted attention from the likes of Marcus and his gorilla friends.

Looking at Justin amongst the various ethnicities slowly flowing into the gymnasium, I was again puzzled by Marcus's attacks. Having been raised in a diverse multi-racial downtown Atlanta neighborhood, virtually all of our junior class was raised in or around African American homes. During those early elementary years, we were part of a large group of guys that played with or hung out together. That was until something changed during our first year of middle school.

My mother being of Irish descent and Justin's mom being born in the Philippines, gave us both a different twist on the African American experience. Although all of us identified as black, our bi-racial roots earned Justin the nickname 'Pho-gro' and I, a lighter shade compared to most, became known as the 'Half-Rican American.'

Explaining Marcus's erratic behavior, my mother attributed it to jealousy of our complexion.

"Sometimes people are jealous of people that look different. Even within the black community, some people think it is better to have a lighter complexion like you, rather than your father's beautiful chocolate color."

I smiled as I replayed her words in my mind.

"Hey, you sure got dressed fast," I said with a smile.

"No shit! I don't have time to be messing around with those dam gorillas!" Justin replied with his trademark dramatic anger.

"Dude, what's up with the rage?" I said, laughing at the words coming out of his little body. "You look like a miniature Stephen A. Smith."

Justin had recently taken up swearing as my mother called it. It had started off as a deliberate attempt to sound hard or tough, but now it appeared to be more of a bad habit.

"My bad! I don't have time to fool around with those darn gorillas. Is that better?" he replied while over emphasizing each word.

"Besides, I see you got dressed pretty fast too."

"Yep. In and out," I replied while reaching into my short's elastic waist band to retrieve my phone. "Did you find that app?"

Justin held up his phone and smiled.

"Text me the link. I've gotta figure out how to get to that next level."

"This will help, it gives you all the cheat codes," Justin replied while sending the text.

As the final bell rang, kids continued flowing into the main gymnasium, the girls on one side and the guys on the opposite end. Justin and I shook our heads as Marcus dramatically chased down a basketball in a blatant attempt to navigate his way to the girl's side of the gym.

Coach Brown blew his whistle indicating he was about to begin his ritual of dividing the class into groups.

"123...123...123," he called out while pointing to kids, sending them scattering into smaller groups.

Justin and I performed our customary "in-line shuffle" to ensure we were placed in the same group.

"Number ones, you're working upper body today, hit stations 1-5," he barked. "Number twos, lunges and squats, stations 6-10. And all of you number threes, get those knees up, four laps around the gym."

Coach Brown, focusing his attention on Justin and me, gave us a stern warning, "You two ladies better move it today. I'm gonna get some muscle on your tiny frames if I have to work you before and after school this semester." Justin and I started with a slow trot, just long enough for Coach Brown to resume his conversation with Ms. Sanders, the girls' coach.

When it was clear his focus had changed, we returned to our slow stroll tech discussion. It was during our second pass on the girl's end of the gym when Jennifer Tran stepped in front us.

"Hey, Dante," she said while leaning in and hugging me tightly. "Hey, Justin," she added with a friendly wave.

All three of us had been friends since elementary. In fact, during the summer before 6th grade, she and I had even 'dated' over the summer break. Back then, she was that skinny girl with her nose buried in a Harry Potter book however, the years following elementary had been kind to her. Now, as a junior, she was fully grown. Originally from Vietnam, her frame had not changed much since elementary, but the combination of southern living and year-round gymnastics had suited her well. She was without question a dime, a perfect 10 in my book. Struggling to lower my ever-changing alto voice, I nervously mumbled a response,

"Hey Jen, what's up?"

"Nothing just wanted to see if you might be going to the mall after school. I am getting a new phone and was hoping you could help me pick one out," she asked while twirling a thick lock of hair around her finger.

I watched in a trance as the jet-black hair wrapped around her index finger leaving temporary ringlets draped over her shoulder. I must have frozen mid-sentence because Justin spoke, snapping me out of my momentary trance.

"Yeah, we were planning to go," he replied with a nudge to my ribs. "Right, Dante?"

Considering my mother was super overprotective, I knew there was no way she would let me hang out at the mall, especially on a school night.

"Of course…of course we'll be there," I replied, pushing aside reality and any hope that I would actually be able to go.

"I was planning to be there about 7. Maybe we can meet at the Food Court?" she asked with a smile.

"I guess I'll see you at 7," I replied without hesitation.

"Awesome," she added before giving me another hug and jogging back over to the group of waiting girls.

"Of cou…cour…. course," Justin mocked before laughing out loud. "What happened to you? I thought you we're going to lose it, right there in front of her."

"Shut up. I was thinking about my mom."

"Dude, that's gross. Thinking about your mom, really? I mean she's hot, don't get me wrong."

"You know what I mean. I was trying to figure out how I can convince my mom to let me go."

"Well, you better figure it out, because she wants you dude. And just so we are clear, I'm talking about Jen."

"Shut up! I replied while giving Justin a firm shove. "Besides, it's Jen. We have known her for years. I mean, don't get me wrong, she's definitely one of the hottest girls we know."

Justin looked at me with a puzzled look.

"Ok, the only hot girl we know. Actually, the second hottest, if I count your mom."

"Dude, I told you to stop checking her out. That's gross," Justin said while throwing a flurry of playful punches at my arm.

I laughed while returning the swipe. "It's not my fault she's hot. You need to have another sleepover so I can accidentally walk in her room again."

"Dude, that is so messed up! I knew you did that on purpose," snapped Justin. "You're a freakin Perv."

We laughed as the coach blew the whistle indicating it was time for everyone to change stations.

***

The rest of the morning was a breeze. After fourth period, I tossed my books into my locker and grabbed my lunch and phone.

I'm not sure how or where it originated but Justin and I always brought our lunches.  I'm not sure if it was the complaints, the urban legends kids told about the food, or if we just felt safe keeping our lunch with us.  After all, we reasoned, if there was any place in the school that we would hate to bump into Marcus and his friends, it would have to be the lunchroom. An unlimited supply of food, a group of distracted teachers, combined with Marcus and his gorillas, made for a regularly scheduled 'incident' waiting to happen.

As a result, Justin and I could usually be found hanging out in the hallway next to the teachers' lounge. Not only was it the safest place in the school, but the computer science teacher set up the lounge Wi-Fi spot using the same password as she had used for the computer lab. Which, for those of us that knew the difference, meant an unbridled and unfiltered Wi-Fi connection.

As lunch wore on, teachers began slowly strolling out of the lounge signaling lunch was quickly coming to an end. It was during this exodus that a familiar deep voice instantly grabbed my attention.

"Good afternoon, Mr. West. I need your assistance. Are you in the middle of your dinner break?" I turned to find Dr. Stillwell standing behind me, looking over the tops of his thick dark rimmed glasses.

Dr. William Stillwell was without a doubt the oldest teacher at West View High School. His gray hair was combed backwards into an old school-styled afro, matching his neatly trimmed gray sideburns and beard. Rumors circulated that he was a former high-profile attorney with several of his early clients being amongst Atlanta's Civil Rights Trailblazers. However, rather than speaking about his pre-teaching years, he instead chose to focus on what he described as his passion, history.

"No, sir. I am all finished up. Can I help you with something?"

"Yes, son. Please grab those books," he said, pointing to a stack of shrink-wrapped textbooks sitting on the hallway floor, "and follow me."

I walked slowly, pausing briefly after each step to allow Dr. Stillwell to lead the way. His age, combined with the antique wooden cane he heavily leaned on, increased the short thirty second stroll to several minutes as we made the hike from the lounge to his classroom.

Out of all my teachers, Dr. Stillwell was hands down the most interesting. Most instructors seemed to rely on handouts or busy work to fill the hour-long class periods; some were visibly bored by the idea of teaching, while others did not seem qualified. The doctor was none of those. He loved to teach, and it showed.

As the door swung open, I was greeted by two life-sized mannequins standing erect at the front of the classroom. Each was adorned with iron masks, rusty colored chains, and shackles.

"What in the...what is that Dr. Stillwell?" I asked.

"We are starting a new unit today. Those are replica restraints African slaves would have worn during the 18th and 19th century. They're on loan to me from a former client out of South Carolina."

Dr. Stillwell walked up to the mannequin while staring at it intently.

"Imagine it's 1861. A mother and her young boys are free, living and working in New York, maybe Philadelphia. While returning from work or an errand, they unknowingly cross paths with a Slave Bounty Hunter.

Without proof or due process, she and her children are seized and shipped in the middle of the night to Georgia or Alabama. The boys, being healthy, are ripped from their mother's arms and placed in chains like this before being sold at auction. Their mother, in a desperate attempt to free her children, is brutally beaten before she, too, is sold and led away."

I stood, silently imagining a mother, beaten, bloodied, and bound before being taken away.

"That, son, will be the basis for our discussion this semester. A stain on mankind's history, one of the greatest atrocities ever committed against a people." After a long pause, he snapped out of his momentary trance before hobbling to his desk.

"Stolen and shipped...even if they were already free?" I wondered. As I examined the metal contraptions and chains, I began to feel uneasy. The idea of slavery and the brutality it represented had always bothered me. At times, while reading or watching movies on the subject, I had wondered, "What I would do?" If it were me, my family, or someone I cared about, how would I respond? Would I fight or submit?

Focused, I stood motionless staring at the mannequins as I replayed the questions in my mind. Thoughts began to rush through my mind before being abruptly interrupted by the buzzing of the school bell. I turned to find the doctor frantically pressing buttons on the overhead video control panel before motioning for me to take the controls.

Students began filing into the room, pausing to examine the life-sized mannequins on display. The final bell rang, and the chatter ceased as Dr. Stillwell made his way to the front of the class. As he began to speak, Marcus and his entourage stumbled into the room.

"Welcome! We're glad you gentleman could join us," Dr. Stillwell said mockingly. "Please come in and find your seats."

As the last of the group closed the door, Dr. Stillwell waited patiently as one by one they shuffled to their seats. I braced myself as Marcus collapsed into the seat behind me and performed his customary kick to the back of my chair.

"I believe we've had recent conversations about your tardiness and disruptive behavior, gentlemen. Mr. West, please grab that attendance ledger from my desk and tell us, how many times has Mr. Rivers and his associates have shown contempt for punctuality this month."

"Shit!" I thought as I made my way over to his desk. "That's the last thing I need is to get involved with these idiots."

"It looks like it's happened six times this month, sir," I replied before quickly sliding into my chair in a futile attempt to lean forward out of Marcus's reach.

"Six in such a short span of time? It appears as though I am going to have some afterschool company for the remainder of the week. Let us say, 4:15, gentlemen. And if you choose to show the same lack of appreciation for punctuality, I'll increase your visit by an extra week."

Marcus and his friends mumbled a unified, "Yes, sir" through forced robotic smiles.

Leaning in, just within arm's reach, Marcus whispered loudly, "This isn't over, Yella Pet," before flicking the top of my ear.

"Great," I thought while grimacing in pain. "Another reason to look over my shoulder."

"Dante, please go ahead and queue up the video," instructed Dr. Stillwell. "This is a PBS special produced by famed historian Henry Louis Gates, "Many Rivers to Cross". We'll watch this then begin our discussion of the 19th century US Slave Trade."

The video flickered before displaying the opening credits. As the program began, I once again found myself lost in thought, enthralled by the mannequins peering over us.

"What would I do if I saw someone enslaved and in chains?" I again wondered. "I would definitely fight! I couldn't allow anyone to be kept in chains." My thoughts were again interrupted as Dr. Gates began his commentary.

The remainder of the afternoon was painfully slow; Advanced Calculus with Coach Thomson followed by Literature Appreciation with Ms. Franklin. After the final bell, I made my way down the hall to retrieve my skateboard for the ride home. Normally, I would take the back stairwell to avoid Marcus however, considering he and his gorilla friends had an "appointment" with Dr. Stillwell, I felt free to go down the main staircase. Looking around, everyone seemed at peace and relaxed knowing he and his goons were not loose in the hallways.

Walking down the stairwell, I paused as I looked up at the large white hallway clock and immediately thought about Jennifer. Picturing her in those gym shorts and my appointment later that evening made me quicken my pace until I thought about my mom. If I had any hope of convincing her to allow me to go, I would have to get home quickly in order to finish my chores and homework.

Passing Dr. Stillwell's door, I curiously peeked through the glass window, hoping to catch a glimpse of Marcus suffering through his detention. After a quick scan, I found him, in the back row, sitting amongst his buddies. I exhaled deeply, relieved to know that at least for a couple of days I would have some peace. However, the momentary celebration was short lived. Before I could duck out of view, Marcus caught sight of me spying through the window.

With an angry smirk, he looked directly at me and mouthed the words, "You're dead!" He amplified the threat by running his finger along his throat, making a slashing motion.

I tried to look away, pretending as if I had not seen him, but I had, and he knew it. And my experience with Marcus taught me one thing: he never made idle threats.

***

"Dad...mom...I'm home," I yelled while tossing my bag on the chair by the front door.

"Stop yelling Boobie," quipped Trisha as she appeared out of the kitchen, pausing briefly to pinch my cheeks. "They're not home yet, although they may have heard you from work."

Trisha, although only a year older than me, routinely acted as if she were my mother. She had on more than one occasion confronted Marcus and his friends about bothering me. Once, her then boyfriend Jonathon "Scooby" Wilson roughed him up a bit. Scooby, who earned his name for his love of snacks, was last year's starting outside linebacker for the varsity football team. After the hazing, Marcus stayed away for a while, but after Trisha broke it off with Scooby, he eventually resorted back to his d-bag ways.

"I'm not yelling and stop calling me Boobie!" I yelled.

As long as I could remember, my family had called me Boobie. My mom said it was because as a baby my cheeks were full like a woman's boob, thus the name. Despite the 17-year tradition, my parents had recently stopped using the childhood nickname. But not Trisha. As far as she was concerned, I would be Boobie for life.

"Hey, how about you give me a ride to the mall tonight? I'm meeting Justin...for some...research on an economics project."

Trisha looked at me and immediately began to laugh hysterically.

"Boy, you'll need to do better than that. Mom isn't letting you go to the mall on a school night, especially with that weak excuse."

"Ok...well...help a little brother out. What's a better one?" I asked.

"Hmm...let's see," Trisha said while rapidly popping her gum. "It's a Tuesday, so we can't use just any excuse. It is March, and mom and dad's anniversary is next month. So...let us say we are going to go look for a gift. And the key is, we are doing it together. Mom and dad love when I do stuff with my little brother," she said as she again pinched at my cheeks.

"Wow...you're good. How did you get to be so devious?" I asked.

"Years of practice, little brother," she said, laughing. "Let us not celebrate yet. Just to be on the safe side, be sure you finish our chores before they get home. We don't want any excuses."

"Ok...good idea. Wait, 'our' chores?" I asked.

"To be so smart, you're pretty slow little brother. If we are walking around the mall, I need to look fab. And mom and dad would never believe us if I went looking like this. So... I need to get dressed."

"Which means...?" I asked.

"Which means, I don't have time for 'our' chores, silly." Walking out of the room, she repeated her boast before pinching my cheek, "Years of practice, Boobie."

I spent the next hour finishing up homework and washing the last of the dishes when my dad and mom pulled up. As if scripted, Trisha came in from the kitchen 'drying' her hands on a dish towel.

"Hello, mommy and daddy. Perfect timing, I just finished up the dishes. Can I help with those bags?"

"Sure, honey, you're so sweet," replied my mother as she gave Trisha a kiss on the cheek. I looked on in amazement at her blatant lie. Yet, at the same time, I was equally mesmerized by her ability to carry on the charade. I could not do anything but laugh.

"Hi, mom and dad," I added. "Can I help with anything?"

"Sure, Dante," my dad said while tossing me the keys. "Please bring the bags from the back seat and trunk."

I unloaded the bags and put the last can in the pantry before slipping into the dining room. Pulling out my phone, I began calculating how many minutes I had until my appointment with Jennifer. Peering at Trisha in the kitchen, I watched and waited for her cue to bring up our planned excursion. However, despite my steady focus on her she appeared to have forgotten about our earlier conversation. Rather than discussing our plans, she continued offering a blow-by-blow description of her day. While she continued her updates into dinner, I flipped through my phone while thinking about my meeting with Jen. That is, until my mother noticed me.

"Got somewhere to go Boo...I mean Dante?" she asked. "It's like you're miles away."

"Uh...no. I was thinking about..." I looked at Trisha, not sure if this was the right time to mention the mall.

"He was probably thinking about school," Trisha interrupted while popping a carrot wedge into her mouth. "I saw Dr. Stillwell this afternoon, and he said Dante was super helpful in class today."

"Oh, that's nice," my father added while gobbling up a few carrot wedges. "I wish they had teachers like Dr. Stillwell when I was kid. Back in my day, you listened, or the principal whooped your..."

"Honey...really?" my mother asked while interrupting his 'go to' expression. "What did you learn today sweetie?

"Well...we started a new unit on Pre-Civil War Slavery and the Fugitive Slave Act," I replied while smiling at my father's gentle rebuke.

"Oh, and we watched a video narrated by Henry Louis Gates. Dr. Stillwell showed us two mannequins with chains and shackles illustrating the types of restraints slaves would have worn during the 19th century. We then discussed how free blacks or even former slaves living up north were often stolen and brought to the south to be sold as slaves."

"Ahh...and the government didn't do anything to stop it," my mother added while spooning some of the popular carrots onto my half empty plate. "Nineteenth century slavery is a subject that's always intrigued me. As a white person, I could never relate culturally or racially, but I can understand how it would feel having your children taken from you. It would be devastating."

"That's because you love us mommy," Trisha added in a not so clever attempt to change the subject.

"Speaking of love, it's March, which means you two lovebirds have an anniversary coming up next month."

"Oh, yeah, thanks. I mean, not in the sense that I didn't remember," replied my father with an awkward smile.

"So...we finished our homework and chores," continued Trisha. "We thought about spending a little time at the mall looking for your anniversary gift."

"Hmmm…. I don't know," replied my mother. "It's a school night."

"Yes, but I will be studying all weekend for my SAT and before you know it, school will be over, and I'll be off to college," Trisha added while launching into what we referred to as her 'rapid fire of facts'.

A masterful debater, Trisha had the innate ability to quickly list an overwhelming amount of information or arguments until her victim was forced to yield. I had seen her use it on both my parents and most often with guys she was dating.

"This could be the last time Dante and I have to shop for your anniversary together!" she concluded in her usual dramatic fashion.

My father popped another carrot in his mouth and gave my mother the, "come on, lettem go" look.

"How long are you gonna be gone?" he asked.

"We'll be back before nine. You won't even know were gone," Trisha replied while trying to suppress a smile.

"Ok. But not a minute later," my mother replied reluctantly.

"Sounds great! I had something I needed to discuss with your mother anyway," my dad added while reaching for her waist and offering an exaggerated wink.

"Eww daddy. You're gross!" Trisha replied while grabbing the keys and nudging me to follow her out of the kitchen.

***

Considering it was a weeknight, the mall was oddly busy and bustling with activity. I looked at my phone and quickly calculated how much time I had before returning to meet Trisha. She had dropped me off at the main entrance while her and some friends made their way to the opposite side of the mall.

Looking up at the movie start times my eyes quickly focused on the large red digital clock located above the ticket booth: 6:25 PM. I made a mental note of the time and started making my way up the escalator to the Food Court when my phone rang.

"Hey, where the hell are you?" whispered Justin.

"I just stepped on the escalator, making my way to the Food Court. Why, what's up?" I asked.

"It's Marcus. He is looking for you. Whatever you do, don't go to the Food Court," Justin whispered before hanging up abruptly.

The escalator hummed as it slowly climbed up to the second floor. Approaching the second level I could make out the different smells of the Food Court. Fresh baked pretzels, pizza and Chinese stir fry immediately awakened my senses. For just a moment I forgot about Justin's warning, that was until I spotted them. Peering down the long corridor of food court stools and benches, my attention instantly refocused. It was Marcus and his buddy Leroy. Marcus smiled as they started walking, then running toward me. Looking around for a quick escape, I hopped across the rail separating the two escalators and started making my way down.

"Excuse me, pardon me," I offered while weaving through the unsuspecting shoppers patiently traveling down to the lower level. Leaping from the escalator my tennis shoes screeched against the lower lever linoleum floor. A quick glance up confirmed Marcus and Leroy were standing above me, peering down over the banister. I began to run left, then darted back right however, regardless of my direction, the pair quickly mimicked my movements. Pausing, I looked around for a possible escape route when I noticed two large cabinets sitting just inside of the 'Bright Light Shoeshine Store.'

A quick sprint across the open lower level put me directly in front of the store's entrance. Leaning against the large ceramic pillar, I watched as the single employee finished up with a customer and walked to the rear of the store. After a brief pause, I looked at the escalator then casually walked in the store and stepped into the first of two large armoires. With the door slightly open, I peered through the narrow opening and watched as Marcus and Leroy stepped off the escalator. Standing around awkwardly, they looked in various directions before focusing their attention on the Shoeshine Store. Closing the door, I stepped toward the back of the cabinet and huddled quietly hoping they hadn't seen me. Surrounded by darkness, I stared blindly into the direction of the cabinet's door, carefully listening to their approaching voices as they stood in the store's entryway.

"He had to come this way," Marcus snapped "There's nowhere else to go."

My breathing began to increase rapidly as I took another step to the back of the cabinet. Leaning firmly against the rear panel, I shifted my weight against the solid wooden wall. Pausing briefly, my eyes blinked rapidly as I began to feel my body falling backwards. In an attempt to stand erect I grasped at darkness in an attempt to catch my balance. With nothing to break my fall, I twisted my body just in time before slamming into the ground with a thud.

Face down with eyes closed, I froze, afraid to make a move for fear that any motion might leave me exposed to those pursuing me. When the anticipated response didn't come, I slowly opened my eyes and found I was lying, not on the mall's industrial textured carpet, but atop a floor composed of dozens of narrow wooden planks. Through the decks narrow gaps, I watched as bugs crawled on the exposed earth beneath the structure.

I twisted my body and looked up at the small, vaulted ceiling supported by large wooden beams. And there, towering above me, was a large wooden Armoire. My nose wrinkled as I fought to adjust to the unfamiliar musty smell of the rustic room. I cautiously looked around for Marcus and Leroy however, as I panned the room, I discovered I was very much….alone. Alone, but not in the same large, carpeted Shoeshine store I had taken refuge.

It was a single room, simply decorated with two small windows. In the corner sat a small black potbellied stove with a hefty supply of wood stacked neatly against the wall. On the opposite side of the room was a single bed, a small wooden chair, and a matching table complete with a wooden bowl and plate. And there, along the main wall, sat a large wooden armoire. I paused, listening for the hustle and bustle of the mall, however despite my best effort all I heard was silence.

"I must have fallen and bumped my head," I thought.

With tightly closed eyes, I rubbed them firmly with the backs of my closed fists however, after opening them, nothing had changed. I was still standing in the same room with nothing but silence. A couple of steps across the single room I peered through the murky windowpanes.

"Trees, in the middle of the mall?"

A couple of steps to the other side of the room I gazed through the adjacent window and again, nothing but trees. Pausing momentarily, I turned to the single door to the room and, with a gentle twist of the metal doorknob, I slowly opened the door and stepped through the entryway.

From on the porch, I was once again shocked by the number of trees surrounding the small structure. Rows upon rows of tall pine trees towered above the simple shack. The large trunks swayed slowly in the gentle breeze giving the illusion that at any moment they might be overcome by the wind and topple over. I stepped off the porch onto the sandy soil and picked up a rock. Tossing it into the wall of trees the rock sailed through the air before colliding with a thud into a large tree trunk. I picked up another rock, and before I could throw it, something about the color and texture caught my eye. Rolling the shiny stone in the palm of my hand, I looked around and again wondered, "How the heck did all of this get in the middle of the mall?"

After a brief walk around the structure, I confirmed the entire perimeter was surrounded by walls of trees. The only exception was a narrow path leading away from the building. Rubbing the stone between my index finger and thumb I stood there in front of the small, elevated house while examining it.

"This doesn't make any sense. I've got to be dreaming?"

I slipped the stone in my pocket and collapsed on the step. Determined to figure out the puzzle, I refocused my attention on the path. Looking through the trees the wooden fence was slightly visible as it ran parallel to the winding path. It was narrow, but I could clearly see that it curved through the woods before eventually disappearing in the tall pines. Curious about the paths destination I followed the fence line until, looking back, the small house was barely visible through the brush and trees.

Following the path for another 40 or 50 feet the thick forest began to slowly thin before revealing a large green pasture. The grassy field spread over several acres was oddly familiar to me. Deep breaths of the fresh air combined with the beautifully sloping hillside prompted me to pause as I took in the scenery. That is when I felt it. Standing there on the fence line I froze as the ground beneath me began to rumble in a way that was instantly familiar.

In the distance I could now see a group of horses galloping towards me. The dozen or so horses trotted along the top of the hill before descending downwards toward the fence line.

There are a lot of things in life I am clueless about; sports, girls, maybe even fighting however horses was not one of them.

My sister and I had taken equestrian classes for years, spending our weekends riding along rural country roads. It was only in the last year that I had stopped. A late summer accident left my horse, Ebony, lame. After consulting with several specialists, my mother and I made the tough decision to have her put down. Since then, I had lost my motivation to visit the stables.

Balanced on the wooden fence, I could instantly see the group of horses was well cared for. Their coats and manes were brushed, and their lean bodies showed they were well fed. However, the lead horse, the large black mare, was by far the most beautiful.

She boldly walked up to me and gently rested her head in my open palm. I rubbed her head just above the eyes and between her ears as she neighed in appreciation. Looking back at the path, I could vaguely see the small wooden house through the brush and dense tree trunks.

"What are you guys doing out here?" I asked while hopping off the fence. "Hell, what am I doing out here?" I thought while my eyes fixated on the spirited mare lead the group in their trot around the clearing.

I spent what seemed like hours watching and talking to the group of horses until the setting sun reminded me that time had gotten away from me.

"Oh crap! I was supposed to meet Trisha at 8:30," I shouted out loud while pulling out my phone. "No signal and how could it still be 6:31? I have been out here for hours. She's gonna kill me." I climbed back on top of the fence and looked at the path leading back to the house.

"Retrace your steps," I thought as I hopped off the fence. "I ran into the Shoeshine store, climbed in the cabinet and closed it. The next thing I know, I am here looking up at another cabinet. That's gotta be it! The cabinet."

I bolted down the path and up the single step leading into the one-room building. Standing there in the doorway, my heart pounded as I struggled to catch my breath while examining the cabinet. Unlike the plain table and chair, the cabinet was large and well crafted. Along the front, deeply etched into the cabinet's door, was a pattern. Gently following the grooves, the pattern began to slowly come into view. A step back was all it took. A lantern with a candle burning in the center was deeply carved into the doorway. I focused on the image and immediately realized where I had seen it before, it was the same design as the logo at the "Bright Light Shoeshine Store" in the mall.

I opened the door, stepped in, and began examining the dark empty cabinet. As the door closed, I began groping along the wall's joints, searching for a handle or an opening. As I bent down, pressing firmly on the floor of the cabinet, it happened. The rear wall opened, and a sudden flash of light illuminated the closet. Cutting through the bright light, a pair of powerful hands reached in and immediately began groping for my throat. I in turn struggled, desperately grasping at a hand or finger, anything to loosen the iron-like grip, however, the more I fought, the tighter the hands seemed to clamp down on my throat. Despite my weakening body, I continued fighting until darkness overtook me and my body went limp.

*** 

My eyes opened widely as the cold water crashed against my face. Prompting me to sit up, startled by my instant consciousness. Now, fully viewable I immediately identified the source of my momentary unconsciousness. A tall dark muscular man stood over me holding an empty glass. He was older however I could tell from the way he carried himself that escape was not an option. The sleeves on his white button-up shirt were neatly rolled up exposing scarred muscular forearms while his clean-shaven head and focused eyes reinforced his no-nonsense persona.

Kneeling next to me, he spoke in a clear deep voice.

"What are you doing here?"

The accent was not easily recognizable. It was definitely English but something about it screamed foreign, maybe even proper. The shack and horses immediately came to mind however, I searched for the words to explain what I had just experienced and thought, "Hell, even if I could explain it, he'd never believe me."

"Who sent you?" he repeated calmly as he sat the glass down on the linoleum floor next to me.

"No... no one, sir. I came to the mall with my sister.... these two guys...they were following me, so I hid in that cabinet. I swear!"

The man stood quietly, staring at me as if considering my story.

"Was it two Negro youths?" he asked.

"Yes. I was in the Food Court, and they chased me down the escalator. I was just trying to get away."

"They were here a few minutes ago, looking around my shop. My name is Simon," he said, extending his hand to me.

I looked at him for a moment, unsure if I should accept his outstretched hand. Sensing my hesitation, he held up his hands signaling he meant no harm before again extending his hand.

Reluctantly I reached up and accepted his assistance.

"My name is Dante."

"It is nice to meet you Dante. Sorry about the choking thing," he said while miming a choking motion. "I've had some problems with kids vandalizing my store. As a result, I have had to be careful regarding who I allow through my doors," he explained while adjusting my hoodie. "The bigger kid, your friend, asked me if I'd seen a small kid wearing a hoodie. My guess is he was referring to you."

"That would be me and neither are friends of mine," I replied.

"I told him this wasn't a playground and instructed him to find an alternate place to hang out. He replied with a few obscenities before returning to the escalator. Look, I understand you were trying to get away from your mates, but you cannot take sanctuary here. If I find you back in here without shoes to shine, I am going to be very irritated," he said while again miming a choking motion. "Do we have an understanding?"

"Yes, sir," I replied.

I began walking out of the store when I saw a gently worn riding saddle. Looking back, I asked, "Do you ride?"

"On occasion," he responded. "However, that one is being repaired for a customer."

"Oh," I replied. Looking at the saddle instantly reminded me of the time spent with Ebony as well as the horses I had met that evening. "Nice to meet you, Simon," I added when my phone rang.

"Dude, where the hell are you?" Justin yelled through the phone. "I followed Marcus down the escalator, but I lost you. Come up to the Food Court."

"Where is he?" I asked.

"Don't worry about them. Mall security is walking them out now. Those idiots were apparently banned from the mall because of some fight last week. You should see how stupid they look," Justin added with a chuckle.

"Cool. It is 6:35. I gotta meet Jennifer at 7. I'm coming up the escalator now."

The ride home was quiet, at least for me. Justin and I hung out before I met up with Jennifer. I thought about explaining to Justin my experience in the Shoeshine Store; however, after I thought about it, I decided it was not worth it.

Besides, what would I say? Where would I even begin?

I slipped on my headphones and thought about the evening I had spent with Jennifer. I looked down and smiled as I re-read the text she had just sent me. Maybe Justin was right. I had only thought of her as a friend, but it was becoming apparent this might be more. Driving along the dark roadway, the brightly lit streetlights redirected my attention back to my excursion in the shoeshine store. I pulled the rock out of my pocket and rubbed my thumb over the smooth stone. Although I had not put all the pieces together, I was certain it was not a dream.

"I spent hours in that...that....place," I thought, "and by the time I came out, only a minute had passed. And Simon, 'Was it two Negro youths?' Who talks like that? What did it all mean?"

The more I thought about the evening, the more questions popped into my mind. However, one thing was crystal clear: if I was going to find answers, I only had one choice, I had to go back in.

# Two

---

# Fortitude

The remainder of the week was painfully slow. I followed my normal routine of avoiding Marcus and his friends while relaxing after school knowing he and the gorillas were spending time with Dr. Stillwell. The rest of the day, I occupied my time by hanging out with Jennifer.

After school I would walk her to her bus and stand outside until it pulled away. Then as I walked home we would spend the entire evening talking or texting. But that was during the week and today is Friday. Although Jennifer was a pleasant distraction, I hadn't been able to get the Shoeshine Store out of my mind. As soon as Simon pulled me out of the armoire and threatened me about returning, I knew I had to go back. I had to fully understand what I had experienced. It was only by climbing into the wardrobe that I would find answers to the questions racing through my mind.

I made the short walk to the city bus stop, collapsed on the bench, and began mentally planning how I could slip back into the store.

"Maybe I could cause a distraction," I thought as I stepped onto the bus and tossed my coins into the bus fare coin machine. "A small fire… maybe a spilled drink in the entryway." No, that was stupid.

My thoughts bounced between the images I had seen and the effort it would take to get back in. As the bus reached the mall parking lot, I hopped out and walked through the automated doors. Casually buzzing across the ground floor, a mall security guard made his way towards me on his motorized Segway. Looking around frantically for any kind of entry point, I ducked into the service entrance behind the stores. The metal stairs echoed loudly as I made my way to the top level and, after a quick peek through the swinging mall double doors, I casually walked through and collapsed on a bench directly above the Shoeshine store.

Looking down at the people busily walking in and out of stores, I quickly realized how much busier the mall was this evening compared to earlier in the week. I watched as customers, one after another, came in to either pick up or drop off shoes or handbags. After carefully watching several transactions I noticed a pattern.

If someone arrived with a pair of shoes, the shop owner would put the contents in a box and neatly stack it behind the counter. Then, when all the customers were gone, he would carry the stack of boxes to the back. I watched my phone's clock and timed the transactions: just shy of a minute. But I also noticed if customers came in without any merchandise, they were there to pick up. Those transactions took twice as long to complete, upwards of a minute and a half. The difference, of course, was on the pick-up, it left the customer waiting in the store lobby. I would have to wait for a customer that was somehow preoccupied if I had any chance of slipping into the armoire. Either way, I felt like I had the information I needed. I made my way down the escalator and casually walked into the jewelry store next door.

"Can I help you, sir?" I looked around, surprised to find the saleswoman was speaking to me.

"Uhh....no...I'm just looking for something for my mother."

"Oh, how nice.  What's the occasion?" she asked.

"It's her and my father's anniversary," I said while eyeing customers leaving the Shoeshine store next door. "I was thinking about a bracelet or a pair of earrings."

"That sounds like a perfect choice. I have both over here," she replied while pointing to a cabinet on the opposite side of the store. "These are very pretty. Can I show you something specific?"

"Umm, how about that one?"

"That's lovely. It is one of my favorites. Let me get my keys," she replied as she began frantically looking for her keys. "I'm sorry, I just had them," she said while digging through a row of drawers.

I waited patiently as I noticed a woman pass the jewelry store digging through her bag until she pulled out a pink claim ticket. Turning the corner, she disappeared behind the tall ceramic pillar dividing the two stores.

I began a mental count down from 100 seconds as I started walking toward the same dividing wall.

"Sir, I'm so sorry. I have a spare set in the back. I'll be right back."

"No problem...I'll be right here," I said with a smile. "89, 88, 87...." I walked out of the store and leaned against the exterior pillar dividing the stores. "66...65...64." A quick look around the corner found the woman chatting on her phone next to the empty counter. I took a deep breath and casually walked into the Shoeshine store careful not to speak to or make eye contact with the woman. I stood by the armoire for a moment waiting to see if I had been detected. After a quick glance over my shoulder, I opened the door, quickly slipped in, and gently closed the door behind me. I exhaled as I leaned against the side of the cabinet.

"Now what?" I thought. I had been so focused on getting in, that I had not thought about what I had originally done to get through to the other side.

I thought back to the old cabinet I had re-entered while in the shack. Feeling along the side and the back panel of the cabinet, I began searching for a latch or hinge. Leaning back, I looked at the panel and imagined I was standing inside of a closet door without a handle. I reached to where the handle would normally be and gently pushed. As I did, the door swung open, exposing the wooden cabin. I stepped out of the armoire, and the door swung shut. I smiled, pleased with my cleverness in finding my way back to the cabin.

After a quick examination of the armoire, I again ran my finger along the etched pattern of the lantern and reaffirmed my recollection, it was identical to the sign and cabinet in the Shoeshine store. With a step backwards, I looked around from the center of the room hoping to find any signs of life. The bowl and plate were still sitting on the table however, I noticed this time, the bowl was now stacked neatly on top of the plate. Someone had been here.

The realization that someone might be here made me resolve to keep my eyes and ears open. Wherever I was, the owner was likely not going to appreciate some black kid strolling through his house or yard.

I twisted the front doorknob and pushed open the wooden door. Now on the porch I took a deep breath of the fresh air and exhaled deeply. From the elevated vantage point of the porch the yard seemed untouched since the last time I was here. "How long ago was that?" I wondered. I had spent several hours here, but only a minute had passed 'on the other side'. I stepped off the porch and began the stroll down to the fenced pasture. "What about the horses? Were they just a cruel part of my imagination, a rehashing of memories spent riding and competing with my horse? Or were they like the little shack, as real as the stone I'd been carrying in my pocket all week?"

The weathered wooden fence was a good 5ft tall with a standard three horizontal cross beams. I climbed to the top and swung my leg over the top beam straddling the fence. Placing my index finger and thumb in my mouth I whistled. As if anticipating my call the horses came, aggressively galloping toward me.

"Hey pretty girl. How are you doing?" I said enthusiastically while rubbing the black mare's muzzle. "What's your name?" I sat rubbing and talking to the black mare for several minutes until I noticed some of the horses were heading back up the gentle hill. One by one they slowly disappeared over the small crest on the hill side. Standing first erect and then stretching to where I was partially standing is when I first saw it.

There, just over the hill was the rooftop of another small structure. The previous time I had visited, the horses simply appeared over a small ridge however this time I noticed the peak. The roof appeared to be wooden shingles however the structure was wood painted bright red.

I hopped down from the fence and walked up the grassy slope. With each step, the hill gradually exposed a multi-stalled red barn sitting against a backdrop of densely packed trees. Out front was a large watering trough next to a metal bin full of fresh hay. I unhooked the latch and swung open the large barn door, exposing a fully functional barn. My fingers ran along the leather saddles sitting on the stall fence.

There had been saddles like these at the ranch, but they were usually on display considering they were over a hundred years old. But these were different. The leather was not worn, nor did it show any signs of wear. It was almost as if they were newly made. And the tools, everything looked like it belonged in a museum. Either a museum or someone purchased them but didn't get a chance to use them. Opening a large wooden trunk, I found more pristine looking relics and gadgets, all brand new and never used.

"How could this be?" I wondered as I sifted through the items in the trunk.

As I redirected my attention to a series of closets, I was interrupted by the neigh of the large black mare. She had come into the stall and was attempting to get my attention. I closed the trunk and hopped on the gate connecting the barn to her stall.

"Hey you. What are you up to?" The mare stomped her foot and nudged the saddle sitting on the fence. "You wanna go for a ride?" I asked, mockingly reaching for the saddle. And again, she stomped her foot and snorted her approval.

"Ok. I guess it wouldn't hurt to give you a little exercise."

I hopped off the gate, slid the saddle from the fence and gently nudged it on top of her. After securing the saddle and bridle, I slid into the fresh new leather seat, rubbed her neck, and patted her broad smooth chest. She neighed her approval as I grabbed the reins and, with a click of my teeth, moved her in motion. Leaving the barn, we started off at a slow walk. I couldn't help but smile as she moved effortlessly beneath me, prancing like a show horse in a competition ring. Then, with a gentle nudge of my heels, she began a nice trot before quickly transitioning to a swift gallop.

It was hard to imagine I was back in the saddle. Two years had passed since I had lost Ebony. After her passing I could not have imagine sitting on another horse, let alone one as beautiful as this. Slowing to a walk I led her to the forest's edge and explored the fence line and the surrounding hillside pasture. Glancing over my shoulder I could see the other horses had followed every step we had taken. It was like a ranch sponsored trail ride. I laughed as I thought back to the dozens of rides my sister and I had participated in, but most of all, I remembered how much I enjoyed riding.

The remainder of the day was spent riding around the hilly pasture. As the sun began to set, I made my way back to the barn and slid out of the saddle. Peering out of the barn window I watched as the sun slowly slipped over the horizon.

"It looks like it's time for me to go," I said, rubbing her back. After removing the saddle and giving her a good brushing, I put away the tools and started making my way back to the hillside fence. Climbing atop the weathered boarded barrier, I paused and looked back at the pasture. "See you soon," I said to no one in particular before hopping down.

I began the short walk back up the narrow path leading to the shack. It was dusk and despite my lack of visibility you could clearly hear the animals moving and darting through the underbrush in preparation for the approaching nightfall. The woods and surrounding area were eerily silent however it was refreshing, almost relaxing, to hear the silence. Stepping through the doorway I paused momentarily to reexamine the cabinet door. Rubbing my finger along the etched wood outlining the picture of the lantern.

Despite now seeing it several times it still intrigued me.

"What does it mean?" I thought while rubbing the smooth wooden door face.

I took one last look around the room before gently pulling the door handle and stepping inside. There in the rear of the cabinet, I gently pushed on the right-side back panel allowing a narrow slither of light to fill the cabinet. Looking for any signs of activity I peered through the opening.

"Mom, I told you, on the tv remote, press source until you see HDMI 3, then hit ok. You cannot watch Netflix until you change the HDMI. Where are the instructions, I left you?" she asked exasperated.

I continued to watch as the customer turned her back to the armoire, still engrossed in her conversation. A quick glance to the rear of the store confirmed the shop owner was still preoc-cupied with the customer's order. With a gentle nudge of the door, I gently stepped out of the cabinet allowing the door to close softly behind me. With a relaxed but brisk walk I strolled out the open door. A quick left turn took me by the jewelry store and a wide U-turn put me back on the up escalator destined for the ground level. Stepping off the escalator I glanced left then right before letting out a sigh of relief.

From the food court entrance, I could not see the shoeshine store, so I followed the handrail until I was standing directly above it. Collapsing on the bench I peered through the glass window attached to the handrail and watched. The woman was still talking on her phone when Simon returned from the back of the store with two large packages. After paying for the items, she too left the store and turned right.

With a satisfying smile plastered across my face, I leaned back against the rail and exhaled. Riding the large black mare in the fresh air brought back memories of times past. Despite the threat from Simon, I had managed to step through the armoire for a second time. My second visit was productive however I still had a host of questions; the most pressing, what time will I go back in tomorrow?

***

The bell rang signaling the end of 3rd period. I stood up and slowly made the walk down to the lunchroom. I was never a morning person, but considering it was a Monday, I was ex-ceptionally slow. This was especially true after a full weekend of exploring an 'unexplainable world found via an armoire in an Atlanta Georgia shoeshine store'. I laughed as I realized how crazy that sounded. After my second visit to the store on Friday, I could not help but to go back Saturday and again on Sunday. In all, I had managed to step through the armoire's door four times over the last week. But I was not done.

Normally my mother wouldn't allow me to go to the mall during the week but tonight was different. She needed to pick up my new suit being altered. Somehow, I had managed to convince her that the smarter plan would be for me to meet her at the mall. That way, I explained, I could try on the suit before she arrived. After giving me that, 'what are you up to' look, she reluctantly agreed. The plan was to take the city bus after school and wait for an opportunity to get back in the cabinet. Even if I spent the majority of the day exploring the ranch, I would still be out well before I planned to meet my mother. What could go wrong?

Over the course of the weekend, I managed to go in and out of the cabinet without even so much as a glance from a customer or Simon. He had warned me about coming back, and although I initially took his threat seriously, it had not taken long for my curiosity to overrule my momentary fear of his threat. After all, I thought while strolling into the school cafeteria, what was he going to do, tell the police he was being harassed by a kid curious about his antique time traveling armoire? I laughed as I imagined the local mall cop notating the complaint in his little black notepad.

"Hey Dante. What took you so long?" asked Jennifer, "And what are you doing with your books?"

I looked down and realized I had walked straight by my locker without dropping off my books or picking up my lunch.

"My brain isn't here. Long weekend, I guess. I am going back upstairs to drop off my books and grab my phone. I'll be back." I turned around and started the climb back up the stairs.

By now, the main halls were relatively empty except for several groups sitting in small circles eating lunches or chatting about their weekend escapades.

I walked down the hall and noticed a group of kids playing Yu-Gi-Oh. Each of the kids crouched closely together holding their cards as they prepared to do battle. Justin and I had been heavy into the game back in Middle School, but as we got more into games and game systems, we did not have much time for anything else. I paused and stood behind a kid named Winston as I looked at his cards.

"Use your Monster card," I whispered loudly. The group of players paused and glared at me with disgust. "Sorry," I said to several blank faces. "Just trying to help."

I continued down the hall, passing the rowdy band kids energetically practicing their marching routine while eating Lunchables and drinking juice boxes. Turning out of the main hallway, I stepped over the drama kids sitting in a semi-circle practicing lines while nibbling on fruit and Cheezits.

They were by far the most outgoing group in the school. Seemingly uninterested in what others thought about them, they dressed and acted however they felt on any given day. I looked at their bizarre and colorful vintage clothing and momentarily admired how comfortable they seemed at being themselves. Stepping on the first stair step, I paused and thought about the way we segregated ourselves into groups. "Why was that?" I wondered. "Just four years ago, most of us were playing tag or football on the elementary playground. And now we don't even speak to each other."

Reaching the top of the stairwell, I entered the locker wing of the top floor. With the exception of one single kid sitting quietly in front of his locker eating his lunch, the halls were empty. I did not readily recognize him but judging from his size he was small, likely a freshman. Although I did not know everyone around the school, I was certain I had not seen him before. I smiled and gave him a quick nod before continuing to my locker.

A quick spin through my locker combination and the door swung open. After tossing my books into the locker is when I heard him. Pausing, as if my lack of motion might help me hear more closely, I listened. It was Marcus, he was coming up the nearest stairwell. I gently closed my locker and began looking around frantically for somewhere to hide, but the only exit was the stairwell on the opposite side of the floor and the stairs hosting his obnoxious laughter. I momentarily thought about making a run for the stairwell farthest away from me but quickly realized I would never make it. The only option was to duck into the bathroom and wait it out.

Leaping across the hallway I slipped into the bathroom and settled into an empty stall. Standing on the porcelain seat, I closed the door and crouched in silence while Marcus and his gorillas emerge from the stairwell. The words weren't recognizable, nor could I physically see what they were doing, but they seemed to be standing directly in front of the restroom. After a couple of minutes, I heard Marcus say something that ended with a "Let's go."

I relaxed for a moment, relieved that whatever they were doing, they were about to do it somewhere else. As I prepared to take a step off the toilet seat, I heard one of them say, "Hold up, I gotta take a piss." I paused for a second, not sure if I should continue to huddle on top of the commode or open the stall and make a run for it. Frozen, I paused as I heard the rubber of his shoes squeak against the polished concrete floors.

He made his way over to the urinals, each step identified by a loud echoing squeak before the steps stopped briefly at the sink. The water ran briefly followed by another brief stop at the hand dryer. I waited, hoping to hear the steps resume until they were no longer audible but all I heard was silence.

"Had they spotted me?" I wondered.

Squatting on the bowl I listened intently until the steps continued. First one step, followed by another and another. Rather than walking away from the stalls, the sounds were getting closer until they passed my middle stall and stopped abruptly at the far end. The silence was instantly and abruptly shattered when the door flew open and clashed against the tiled wall sending shards of ceramic tile over the stalls and along the floor. I immediately jumped down from the commode, opened the stall and bolted out of the restroom. As I turned to sprint down the stairwell, I ran directly into Marcus and quickly stumbled backwards before collapsing to the ground.

"Look what we got fellas…it's the Yella pet. Where you running to Half-Rican?" he asked while nudging me with the heel of his foot. "We've been looking for you."

I scrambled to my feet, frantically looking for an opportunity to run around or through the group of guys.

"Yeah," mimed Leroy, "Thanks to you, we got detention last week."

"All because of the Yella Pet. Always kissing Stillwell's ass," spat Marcus as he shoved me against a group of lockers. "I told you it wasn't over. You and your smart-ass honor's classes….you think you're so dam smart?"

Marcus ended his rant with a quick jab to my gut. The blow instantly sucked all of the air out of me, forcing me to double over before finally collapsing to my knees.

Putting his foot on my shoulder, he pushed me backwards then collapsed on top of me. Leroy and the other gorillas cheered him on as he began smacking then punching at my face. I struggled to wiggle from beneath him while at the same time attempted to deflect his blows, but it was no use. His weight kept me pinned down, and although my hands were free to shield my face, I could already feel the stinging effects of my failures. It felt like an eternity had passed before I heard a voice down the hall, "What are you kids doing?"

Uncovering my face, I looked down the hallway and saw the school Security Guard coming out of the stairwell. Marcus and his friends immediately jumped up and bolted down the stairway closest to us. Laying there looking up at the ceiling I listened to the rhythmic sound of the guard's keys jingling combined with his boots crashing against the concrete as he ran towards me. Sprawled out on the cold concrete floor I could see the sectioned ceiling tiles above me. In that moment, laying there, I thought, "Did that really just happen?"

***

The office bustled with kids and staff coming and going. Outside the 11th grade Vice Principal's office, I sat with closed eyes in an attempt to focus on something other than the pulsating pain ringing through my ears or the salty taste of blood oozing from my lip. I reflected again on the beating I'd just received, "What could I possibly have done to deserve that? Marcus and his gorilla friends made the decision to be late. What did any of that have to do with me?"

Although I did not understand why it happened, my history with Marcus assured me it was almost certainly going to happen. What I also did not understand was how the Security guard got there so fast. It was rare anyone was ever on the top floor during lunch, which made the fact that a security guard would be in the area even more odd. I ran through different possibilities as, one by one, kids came and left the principal's office. Some appeared to be genuinely sick, walking slowly or coughing loudly, while many of the same sick kids would then exit the office in preparation for leaving for the day.

Peering out of the glass window leading to the hallway, I instantly recognized a face. It was the kid sitting in the hallway eating his lunch. He walked by the door and gave me a quick thumbs up before slipping into the sea of people crowding the hallway. That is when it clicked; it was him. Sensing the possibility of trouble, he must have gotten the security guard's attention. As I stood up to follow him, the door swung open, and Mr. Johnson's secretary stepped into the lobby.

"Mr. Johnson will see you now Dante," she said smiling.

Stepping into the office I found Mr. Johnson leaned back in his office chair. He continued his phone call while casually nodding toward a pair of chairs sitting empty in front of his desk. Shuffling across the room, I collapsed into the wooden seat and looked around the room.

It was no secret that Vice Principal Johnson was a proud retired Marine. Although older, his gray-haired buzz cut, and stocky frame served as a constant reminder that his military roots run deep. That and his custom of addressing everyone by their last name. I looked around at the wall of pictures displaying men and women fully adorned in military uniforms. Other pictures had Mr. Johnson in various parts of the world, also in military fatigues. As he spoke, I could see him eyeing my injuries while discussing a pending suspension to what I imagined was an upset parent. After several minutes, he hung up the phone and looked at me.

"Hot Damn West!" he exclaimed with a chuckle. "Did you get the license plate of the truck that hit you?"

"No sir…it's nothing," I replied, trying to avoid making eye contact.

Mr. Johnson stood up, closed the door, and sat in the chair next to me. Looking through the bottom of his thick, dark-rimmed glasses, he quickly inspected my injuries.

"Does this hurt?" he asked while poking my cheek with the eraser end of a pencil.

I grimaced in pain from the poke. "Nope," I said through clinched teeth.

"Nothing huh?" he said, poking another spot on my temple. "Look son, I can't help you if you won't tell me who did this to you."

I sat quietly looking at the ground while he sat patiently waiting for an answer.

"The Security officer saw several kids run down the stairs. Did you ever think about what would have happened if the guard were not there? What would those guys have done if he'd gotten there maybe 2 minutes later?"

"I said I don't know who it was."

Mr. Johnson looked at me and let out a long sigh.

"These guys aren't going to simply leave you alone West. Eventually you are going to have to show some courage and take a stand," he paused while waiting for me to respond.

I looked at him and replied, "I told you..."

"I know," said Mr. Johnson interrupting me, "you don't know who they were." Mr. Johnson sat looking at me for a moment. "Ok West. You win. Just remember, they aren't going to stop." He pointed to a slogan on a poster, "Fortitudine." "You took Latin, do you know what that means?"

I looked at the word, breaking down the core word, fortitude. "Strength or Resolve."

"Exactly! It's a term we Marine's use," explained Mr. Johnson. "It means courage. You are going to have to stand up son, Fortitudine!" he added before standing up and opening the door. "You're free to go, Mr. West."

I stood up, still woozy from the blows and walked out into the steady stream of kids going left or right in the busy hallway. Navigating through the crowd, I slipped into a restroom to survey the damage.

Turing my head left and right I instantly thought, "It's not that bad. Besides the one black eye, swollen cheek, and busted lip," I concluded, "it could have been worse."

After a deep breath, a splash of cool water, and a quick wipe with the coarse brown paper towels, I made my way down to the lower-level school cafeteria.

Passing through the long corridor leading to the lunchroom I thought about Justin and Jennifer and what I would tell them. Then I thought about my mom. "She's gonna lose it," I thought.

"How the hell did I get into this?" I thought again as I walked into the lunchroom.

Entering the cafeteria was like walking into a crowded football stadium. Kids were sitting everywhere, talking, and eating while the administrators stood around doing their share of talking. Spotting Jennifer and Justin at a large table in the center of the room, I made my way over to them. As I approached Justin saw me first.

"What the hell happened to you?" he asked through nervous laughter.

Jennifer turned around and from her expression I immediately knew she did not agree with my injury assessment.

"What happened? Are you ok?" she asked while frantically examining my injuries.

"I'm fine…seriously," I said through a forced smile. "It was the Douche.' I was putting my stuff away when I bumped into him and the gorillas. If it had not been for some kid grabbing a security guard, it could have been worse. I spent the last 20 minutes being interrogated in Master Chiefs office."

"Did you tell him what happened?" Jennifer asked seemingly annoyed by my casual recollection of events.

"No, he didn't because my boy aint no snitch!" replied Justin. "Plus, it won't make a difference. They could get suspended, maybe even expelled, but Spring Break is coming up. Being suspended does not do anything when school's out. We could be at the mall or just hanging out around the neighborhood. It would just make things worse. Who was the kid, did you recognize him?"

"No. I'd never seen him before. I saw him briefly while waiting for Mr. Johnson, but I did not recognize him.

The bell rang signaling an end to lunch. Justin and I headed upstairs while Jennifer went to her afternoon classes. As we walked up the two flights of stairs, Justin broke the silence.

"You know this isn't over, right? We can't keep running from these guys. We gotta do something," he said.

I knew he was right, but I did not say anything. My thoughts had already focused to my parents and what they were going to say. Although my mother would freak out, my dad, being a police officer, wouldn't allow me to simply ignore his questions the way I did Mr. Johnson. I knew something had to be done, but what? The bell rang, and I looked at Justin.

"You're right. We will figure it out. I'll give you a call tonight," I said as we parted.

The afternoon ended painfully with Marcus and his gorillas stopping me in the hall to ask what happened to my face before erupting into hysterical laughter. Hoping to block out the afternoon I immediately made my way out of the school and hopped onto the waiting city bus. Tightly clutching the buses metal bars,

I navigated through the crowded afternoon bus traffic before collapsing in the rear seat closest to the window.

The bus engine revved as it stopped and started while navigating through the residential neighborhoods before merging onto the highway. Bouncing around on the bus I spent the majority of the 30-minute ride slumped in the seat reflecting on the day.

Justin was right, something had to be done. Although I could not imagine hurting anyone, I had often thought about taking one of my dad's guns to school. It would be a simple 'show of force', something to let Marcus and his goons know I wasn't playing around. I knew it was a stupid idea, but I also agreed with Justin, something had to change.

The bus pulled into the mall parking lot and just seeing the large entryway immediately made my thoughts switch to the armoire and the beautiful black mare. Despite my rollercoaster of a day, I had been looking forward to revisiting the ranch. The last few days of riding and breathing the fresh air had been more than relaxing. It had become the only place I could really escape to and block out everything, school, my parents, Marcus, and his friends.

Entering the mall, I assumed my normal perch on the bench above the shoeshine store. Customers strolled up and down the mall's lower level, casually walking by the store's entryway. A quick glance at my watch and I realized several minutes had passed since anyone had entered or left the store. Simon too walked casually from the front to the rear of the store moving packages while repacking others. After grabbing several boxes left on the counter he disappeared into the rear of the store. That was my cue.

Navigating down the escalator I once again paused in front of the jewelry store. Looking around the corner, I confirmed the front counter was still empty. After a quick countdown I slipped through the store entryway, but something was different. Before I could get completely through the glass doorway an unfamiliar doorbell-like chime greeted me. The sound echoed throughout the store, reverberating on a loop as if the goal were to alert any-one within a five-store radius that the shoeshine store had a cus-tomer.

Uncertain if the alarm had alerted Simon, I took a running jump, and in one motion, opened the armoire door and hopped in.

Slamming the door tightly behind me I sat quietly crouching in the cabinet waiting for Simon to reach into the armoire and pull me from the cabinet floor once again.

After a moment of silence I exhaled, opened the rear panel, and stepped into the small wooden cabin.

# Three

# Reality

As I glanced around the room, I was surprised to find it clean and undisturbed. I stepped through the doorway, onto the porch and inhaled my now customary gulp of fresh air. The sun, peeking over the large pine trees, told me it was early afternoon. The warm air immediately reminded me that I was still wearing my flannel hoodie. Back home, it was a cool winter afternoon however, the difference in temperature here made me uncomfortable. Slipping out of the cotton jacket, I tossed it on the porch and stretched widely in my white T-shirt. Looking at my jeans, I thought back to a conversation I had earlier in the week with my mother.

*"What happened to your jeans?" she asked while sorting the laundry. "It's like you're five years old again playing in the dirt. If you come home again like this you will do everyone's laundry for a week," she threatened.*

I smiled before rolling up the bottoms of my pant legs and hopped off the porch.

The path down to the pasture was a skillfully carved out walkway built amongst the thick underbrush. Rounding the final bend, I noticed movement off to the right. Pausing I spotted a large buck. Startled by my appearance, he ran across the path. Rather than leaping the fence, he fled down a separate path leading deeper into the woods.

By now, I had visited on almost five separate occasions however, it wasn't until now that I had realized the existence of this alternate path. Unlike the footpath I normally followed, this one was more rugged. Using the direction of the deer as a guide, I plunged deeper into the wall of trees until a new trail appeared amongst the brush. Two narrow parallel dirt trails wound through the woods disappearing into another thick cluster of trees.

"That's odd" I thought. "It's almost like a tractor was driving through these woods."

The path continued for another 100ft or so, gradually twisting and navigating between and alongside large pine and poplar trees until it ended abruptly. Both trails appeared to have stopped where a large object was wedged in between two large pine trees. After a close examination, I decided it resembled a large hot tub turned upside down. Rubbing my hands along the inside, I felt the rough hardened plaster that created the 'tub.'

"What the hell is this?" I thought as I walked along the tree line. Discovering two pine trunks evenly spaced, I squeeze between them and stepped into the clearing.

Once on the other side, I could see a dirt road loosely running parallel to the thick wall of trees. No paved roads, just open country, and trees as far as the eye could see. I walked along the overgrown tree line when I first began to see it, a large plaster dome protruding above the brush. Initially, from a distance, it appeared to be a large boulder or rock. But as I got closer, it appeared to be the same plaster material. A quick knock on the surface and the hollow echo confirmed my suspicion. It was much like the rock walls you see at a water park. Every water slide I had ever been on always had those fake plaster rocks lining the path of waterway. This was obviously constructed for the same purpose, to give the appearance of something natural, but why? "Who would build this out here?" I wondered out loud.

While standing erect and looking at the plastered structure, I heard the unmistakable sound of nearby voices. The words were not easily discernable, but I could make out that there were not just one but two voices, and they were slowly becoming clearer as they got closer. Scurrying along the thick tree line, I frantically searched for an opening hoping to get out of sight of whomever was approaching. Once through, I crouched behind some low hanging branches confident the thick underbrush would shield me from sight. There quietly crouching in silence I could hear the voices grow increasingly louder until finally they were directly in front of me. It was a sight that will stay with me forever.

Two men on horseback led a convoy of nearly a dozen black men and women bound together in chains. Their size and shades of brown varied however, the chains that bound them were the constant. Thick iron bands clasped around their necks, while smaller shackles connected shorter chains to their ankles. A few wore tattered leather shoes, however most walked barefoot, all seemingly exhausted by the forced march. They moved slowly and silently while one of the horsemen, the younger of the two, rode alongside them while barking orders and issuing threats. I started to stand and run, but before I could become fully erect, I noticed one of the women turn. It wasn't clear where exactly she was looking, but I could feel her eyes reach out to me as if crying for help.

"Had I been spotted? If she saw me had others?" I laid motionless on the forest floor as the convoy continued down the dirt road. After some time had passed, I pushed myself up on my elbows and peered through the tall grass anxiously looking for a sign that the coast was clear.

When I concluded I couldn't see anyone I stepped into the clearing and began walking, then jogging. Frantically looking for the original opening I had slipped through. Just as I located the large plaster rock, I heard a galloping horse. Looking over my shoulder I was shocked to find one of the horsemen had somehow split off from the group, back tracked behind me and was now, club in hand, quickly galloping toward me. Sprinting toward the entrance I dove to the ground in an attempt to quickly slide through the lower and wider portion of the opening.

Unfortunately, before I could crawl through the wall of trees, he was already on top of me. I jerked free from his grip, sacrificing my shoes and socks in an attempt to break free but he continued undeterred. I kicked wildly in all directions until I made contact with his chin. Falling backwards, he cursed loudly as I rolled over and instantly began crawling for the opening.

Reaching the tree, I clawed desperately at the base in an attempt to pull my body through the opening however the horseman quickly recovered, determined not to allow me to escape. I fought frantically to pull the rest of my body through the gap, but the horseman was relentless. Desperate for any separation I rolled over onto my back, resolved to resume my defensive kicks for any type of an opening.

Now on my back I could clearly see my pursuer. He looked much like any man I would meet in the mall or at school. His graying beard and mustache gave him a grandfatherly look, but as he fought, I could tell there was no frailty in him. In the midst of my wild thrusts, I landed another solid kick that seemingly bounced off his chest. Rather than deter his aggression, I seemed only to antagonize him. With a smile on his face, he pulled out the wooden club. Holding it high over his head, he ferociously swung the wooden baton aimlessly before colliding with my left temple. The pain immediately radiated throughout my body. The fluid surrounding my eye instantly flared and the resulting pressure caused my vision to instantly blur. I continued to kick however, the lunges were less focused and effective. Peering up at the thick line of trees, I realized this was my last chance.

"If I have any chance of escaping," I thought, "I have to get through the trees."

I mustered my strength and made one last attempt to pull myself up when I felt another strike to the back of my head. My eyes fluttered wildly before everything went black.

***

I opened my eyes and looked up at the evening sky. Although blurry, the bright luminaries seemed more radiant and livelier than I recalled ever seeing. It immediately made me think about chronicles of the afterlife.

"Had I died? Is this heaven?" I thought as I looked up at the night sky.

Any question of my mortality was immediately confirmed as I attempted to push myself up on my elbows. The sharp pain shooting through my head confirmed I was very much alive. I reached up to massage away the discomfort but instead struck myself with a thick iron band strapped to my wrist. Examining my hands, I discovered both hands were shackled with cold rusty colored iron cuffs. Those metal bands were then connected to another chain linking the two iron clasps. I tugged on the chain but quickly confirmed it was locked. Fear immediately overtook me as I tried to sit up, but a hand gently pushed me down.

"You need to rest boy."

I turned to find a black woman, also bound in chains, sitting next to me. Wearing a simple cotton dress with no shoes, she sat next to me with a gently flowing creak flowing behind her. I closed my eyes as she gently pressed a moist cloth against the side of my face. The cool refreshing water instantly soothed the sharp pain pulsating from my head. After several gentle pats from the cloth, she submerged it in the creek, squeezed it tightly, then once again gently dabbed it along my temple.

"Who are you? Where am I?" I asked.

"My name Bethany Whitaker, yous in Georgia. Massa dun hit you real hard. You been sleep for mos da night."

Thoughts and questions immediately flooded my mind, forcing me to close my eyes in an attempt to force the pain to subside. "How could I explain who I was or how I got here?" I thought, "Would anyone understand or even believe me?"

"I don't belong here," I replied. "I need to….I need to go home to my family. "

"We all goin' home. Massas men takin' us back to Alabama. Ima be back in the field. What you do for yo Massa?" she asked.

I looked at her with a confused blank look. "Massa? Alabama? What is she talking about?" I thought.

"Young yella boy like you gost to be a house Negro."

She pulled on my jeans and shirt inquisitively then turned her attention to my feet and hands, rubbing them firmly.

"Yo clothes sho is funny. And yo feets and hands, they softer than a baby's bottom! You ain't never done no work have you? Where you from, Boston or Canada? Is you free?" she asked with wide eyes.

"Of course I'm free," I said, pulling my foot from her grasp. "What are you talking about??"

"Isa slave. Just like my mammy and her mammy. She cames from Africa 20 years 'fore the Stars Fell'. We all belong to Massa Whitaker. My daddy and I tried to escape to Il nois but he dead. Fell into a creek and drowned on account he did not know how to swim. Massa's men found me and the others hiding in an old chicken pen. He paid these here men to bring us back to Alabama. He gon' be mighty angry when we get back. Don't know what he might do when he sees me."

"Slaves? I said." I again tried to rub away the fog. "I gotta get home," I said while attempting to stand. Standing partially erect my vision immediately began to blur forcing me stumble backwards.

"You need to sit down boy. Massa hit you real hard. You need yo rest. Wes gonna to be walking soon as da sun come up. You gotta be strong," she added while submerging the cloth and again dabbing my face.

I closed my eyes and let the cool water run down my forehead and the front of my shirt. Resting the damp towel on my forehead she pulled out a small bowl and scooped out a large ball of yellow mush smeared on her fingertips.

"What's that?" I asked anxiously.

"Dis corn, you needa eat," she explained while smearing the salty corn paste into my mouth.

The granular raw cake-like batter instantly made me want to heave however she was right. I could not remember the last time I had eaten. Despite my knowing I needed to eat, my gag reflexes fought with my mind as my insides twisted and turned in an attempt to expel the yellow paste. Sensing my discomfort, she held a small metal cup to my mouth and gave me a sip of water. I laid back, looked up at her and smiled as my eyes began to slowly close.

"I'll just close them for a minute," I thought. Before I knew it, sleep overtook me, and I fell fast asleep.

***

"Boy, you betta wake up. Wes leaving!"

I opened my eyes and sat up quickly. The sharp pain I had felt earlier had gone, but the numbing pain around my temple remained as it slowly pulsated with each silent heartbeat. Through squinted eyes I could see the camp was busy with activity. Whips cracked and threats were hurled throughout the encampment as the white horsemen ordered the slaves to get up and ready for their continued march.

Peering up at the eastern sky, I could see daylight was quickly overtaking the night sky signaling another day lost to my captors. Looking up at the large pine trees I thought back to the dense tree line I had fought to climb through while being pursued.

"How will I ever find that rock, my landmark to the shack? It's like looking for a needle in a haystack."

My thoughts were abruptly interrupted by a loud piercing scream.

"Get up ya lazy nigger," the head horseman growled while striking the defenseless old man lying on the ground.

"Please Massa, he very sick, he can't stand," pleaded the young woman.

"He should have thought about that when he ran away from his Master. Now get up!" screamed the horseman as he again struck the man with the long wooden switch.

I continued to watch the savage beating until it was too much. Seeing the lifeless body continuing to be beaten now oozing with blood was too much. The simple corn mash fed to me earlier in the evening immediately came rushing from my insides. Leaning forward I collapsed to my knees as I continued to gag at the gruesome sight. The woman, in an attempt to protect the old man, used her body as a protective shield however the other horseman pulled her away kicking and screaming.

The verbal and physical intimidation continued for several minutes until everyone's gaze instantly changed. No longer focused on the rantings and violence of the bounty hunters, their eyes all appeared to focus solely on me. I looked myself up and down in an attempt to understand why everyone was looking in my direction when I realized what had caught everyone's attention.

Atop a large black mare sat an immense man draped in a long black hooded cloak. In the dim morning light, it was impossible to decipher his identity however I could easily see the silhouette of his chiseled facial figures. He raised his hands close to his face and lit a small flame revealing a partially smoked cigar protruding from the corner of his mouth. In slow deliberate movements he lit the cigar, took a few puffs, and inhaled deeply. The embers began to glow brightly as he fueled the small flame with each puff. After examining the remaining piece of cigar, he flicked the remnant into the creek and sat motionless as he slowly exhaled the smoke.

Watching in disbelief I immediately thought of the stories of the black cloaked Grim Reaper of Death. For several years, Justin had dressed up as the Reaper for Halloween. He'd become obsessed with the character, even dressing in black and demanding we refer to him as Grim.

My eyes quickly moved over his body looking for the mythical scythe. Before I could complete my search, he raised his hands to the hood of his cloak and slowly pulled back the covering exposing the unlikely travelers. He was a black man wearing dark colored fatigue pants and a dark colored turtleneck. In the stirrups I could see tightly laced dusty black boots. He looked oddly familiar however, the morning glare partially masked his identity. Refocusing on his face, while squinting in the morning light, I wondered, "Who is this and how could I know anyone from this…this place?"

Then, in a clear deep voice he spoke.

"What kind of a person hits a defenseless old man while he's lying defenseless on the ground?" he asked.

As soon as I heard the voice, I instantly understood why he looked familiar. It was Simon, the shoeshine store owner.

He slid off the large black mare and again questioned the Bounty Hunters but this time his words were more forceful.

"What kind of a man hits a defenseless old man while he's lying and dying on the ground?" He turned his back to the now captive audience as he slid the cloak off his shoulders and draped it across the saddle. The tightly fitting turtleneck exposed the muscular build I had witnessed firsthand when he ripped me from the floor of the armoire. Simon turned to see the group of slaves had parted leaving a clear path between him and the slavers. He looked at them with an angry smirk and growled, "A coward!"

The two slavers looked at each other and slowly started their advance.

"But he's not a man," said the most vocal and older of the two Bounty Hunters, "He's just runaway property. Property that don't know its place. I's guess we gon have to show you what we do to niggers that don't know they place."

As he began talking, the other hunter slowly eased his way to Simon's right. Raising his club waist high, he sat waiting for a cue from his companion. Just as the other stopped speaking he lunged at Simon, swinging wildly. Simon easily sidestepped the lunge and in one seamless motion pulled a small pole from a pocket on the back of his shirt. With the flick of his wrist the small 8-inch pole expanded to a 3-foot rod.

The Hunter spun around just in time to find the pole speeding towards him. Before he could react, the rod slammed into his exposed jaw. The blow sent him stumbling backwards screaming in pain as he spat out blood and shards of teeth.

The younger Bounty Hunter looked on in amazement, his gaze bouncing from his fallen friend to Simon. Glancing down at the small knife in his hand he immediately dropped it and selected instead an axe wedged into a nearby tree stump.

Holding it firmly in front of him, he grasped the handle tightly with both hands and slowly advanced toward Simon. Inching closer, he got within a few feet and immediately launched into several high chopping motions. Simon easily sidestepped the initial lunges before expanding the metal rod and blocking the last lazy lunge. Using another shorter rod he jabbed at the hunters midsection. This time, the rod shot sparks as it collided with the unsuspecting victim. The force of the sparks sent him flying backwards, his body twitching as his cotton shirt smoldered from the contact.

Pushing the pole together, Simon collapsed the rod and placed both devices in their respective pockets. Walking over to the smoldering trader Simon patted him down and discovered the large ring holding several metal skeletons keys.

"Take the keys and free yourself then free the others. When you are finished toss the keys into the creek

By now, the sun had fully risen in the east. Simon walked over to his horse and reached into his saddlebag. Pulling out a small black pouch, he walked over to the severely beaten old man. The young woman who had frantically fought for the beatings to end sat next to him now cradling his lifeless body in her arms. The camp and all of its inhabitants sat quietly as Simon rested his ear against the man's chest while gently holding his wrist between his thumb and index finger. After a couple of minutes, Simon spoke softly to the young woman. Tears began to slowly stream down her face as she held the old man tightly. Pulling out a single syringe he tapped the vial before gently grabbing the man's arm and calmly injecting the clear colored fluid.

Walking over to the smoldering young slave trader he took off his burnt clothing and shoes and tossed them in the direction of the slaves. Using another syringe, he injected him. I looked on as his twitching movements slowed until he lay motionless. Then, focusing his attention on the remaining slave trader he pulled out a third syringe. Although badly beaten and bloodied he too had witnessed the events after being struck with Simon's pole.

"No.. no. Don't…. kill me" he mumbled as Simon walked toward him.

The words gurgled out of his bloodied mouth as he stood and began to stagger away. I looked down and saw the club he had used in his unsuccessful attack on Simon. Now, free from the chains I felt the newly formed knots on the front and side of my head and instantly recognized him as the club swinging slave trader who had captured me the previous day. The anger I felt for his attack combined with the brutal attack on the old man began to bubble up feelings inside of me. Compounding that anger was the years of abuse and recent beating by Marcus. It was at that moment when my anger turned to rage.

Grasping the club and holding it firmly in my hand I watched as the hunter staggered out of the camp. I slowly and calmly walked behind him as he turned and attempted to again plead his case.

"Please, don't kill me" he repeated frantically.

I looked him in the eyes and for a moment imagined what thoughts were running through his mind. Was he sorry or was it simply an attempt to garner mercy? Despite his desperate cries all I could see was him standing over the beaten and bloodied old man, pushing away the young woman desperately trying to protect him. It was at that moment that I realized it was the latter. He had not shown any mercy when he chased me down or when he beat the old man.

My grip immediately tightened on the club. After twisting my hips, I reached back and with all of my strength swung the short wooden baton directly at his head. The club instantly found its target and delivered a thud as the slaver collapsed to his knees. His eyes rolled back in his head but miraculously he remained upright. My breathing became heavy as the rage continued to well up inside of me. I again wound up for another swing, the rage preparing me to deal the necessary fatal blow when that same familiar hand grabbed my arm. Turning around I could see Simon looking down at me.

"I'm not like them. You are not like them," he explained calmly.

I turned to see the old man slowly fall forward and collapse face first into the red sandy soil. Simon rolled the man over and checked his pulse and after a few minutes pulled out his black pouch and gave the man the final injection. Turning around I could see all of the slaves had congregated behind us as they watched the last few minutes unfold.

Simon tucked his pouch into one of his pants pockets then stood up to address the small audience.

"My name is Simon. Your masters have sent many men like these to find and bring you back to their farms and plantations. You are not far from freedom, but there are too many of you. You must split up into smaller groups. Take as much of the food and supplies as you can carry. Hide in the forest by day and when it becomes night, continue following this path north" he added while pointing north. "The first barn you find, you will see a lantern painted on the door. If you need help or a place to stay, they will help you."

The group stood silently looking at Simon in amazement, likely frozen with indecision and fear.

Simon, now yelling, barked more forcefully, "You mustn't delay. Leave now!"

The group instantly jumped into action, ransacking the contents of the saddlebags, clothing, and shoes of the remaining slave trader. As they gathered their supplies one by one they scurried into the woods. Looking on I watched as my rescuer too gathered her supplies and quickly ran into the thick brush. Before walking into the foliage she turned and smiled before disappearing into the dense forest.

Simon walked toward the two horses and checked them over before turning to me, "You can ride correct?"

"Ye...yes sir. I can ride," I said.

Simon strapped the larger of the two animals to his horse and handed the other set of reins to me. I pulled my body into the saddle and waited for Simon. After securing the animal, he hopped onto the waiting black mare and looked at me and said, "Let's go."

***

We rode for the better part of an hour with only the sounds made by the four horses. I sat quietly until I could not take it anymore.

"What was in the syringes you pulled from the black case?" I asked, breaking the silence.

"Excuse me?" Simon asked.

"You took a syringe out of the black case and injected something into those men. What was it? Did you kill them?" I asked.

"Benzodiazepines or Benzo," Simon responded. "It's a strong sedative that makes them unconscious. Doctors use it when they want a person to remain unconscious because of an injury."

"Did you kill them?" I pressed.

"No. Like I told you, we're not like them. I gave them just enough to help them sleep for a little while. By the time they wake up they won't know what's real vs what was a dream."

"What about the old man?" I asked.

"He had a lot of injuries and his pulse was very weak. He is not gonna make it. I gave him an extra dose to make him comfortable."

Simon and I continued riding in silence. I am not sure what thoughts ran through his mind, but I could not help but think about the old man and the young woman. And how it must feel leaving your loved ones behind uncertain of their fate or well-being.

How did you know where to find me?" I asked continuing the conversation.

"Your foot prints. I don't get many….visitors and I saw your prints in the yard. And although you are the only person I have seen around the store, I was not certain it was you. That's why I ultimately installed a security system."

"That was the chime I heard when I walked in the store?"

"Correct. I didn't see anyone in the store so I checked the video footage. I figured you must have found your way through the armoire which led me to your jacket and later shoes and socks. I continued south through the night until I caught up with you."

"I guess it's a good thing I got half undressed," I said smiling.

Simon laughed, "It helped but that's not the only clue you left behind. Any time something moves, it leaves behind a trail. Broken branches, footprints, all of that helps in locating something. "

"Wow so you're some kind of tracker?"

"Sort of. Let's say I've been trained to survive in the outdoors. Maybe a Survivalist is a better term."

"Combined with a little Mixed Martial Arts! I saw you handle those guys like rag dolls. Where did you learn that?"

"Where I am from it's important to know how to take care of yourself. As a result, I have studied multiple disciplines of self-defense."

"Yeah, tell me about it. By the way where are you from, where are we? Slavery's been outlawed for over 150 years. Where in the hell could this still be happening in the 21$^{st}$ Century?"

"You're right. Slavery was outlawed in 1865 but here it's still very much an ingrained institution. When you stepped through the armoire, it took you back in time."

"You mean I, or we traveled back in time?"

"Yes. We're about 20 miles from downtown Atlanta. It's 1861," responded Simon.

"I knew it!" I responded gleefully. "It all makes sense. The barn, the brand-new antique tools, and the slaves.

Oh my god the slaves."

"Oh, so you're familiar with time travel?" he asked.

"Yes, well not exactly. We have almost weekly debates in Physics class about the Theory of Relativity and the existence of Closed Timeline Curves. Up until now, we did not have any conclusive proof. It's just been a theory."

"It still is just a theory," said Simon. "What you've seen here can never be discussed with anyone."

"You've got to be kidding!" I responded. "This is breaking news! Scientists all over the world will want to know. This will change modern science forever."

"That is why it must never be mentioned Dante. Can you imagine the harm, the irreversible damage men could do if they had confirmation time travel existed? Who would manage the science? Who would ensure that past generations weren't exploited for financial or military gains?"

I thought about the questions and the potential consequences. "Our government can't even regulate financial markets to ensure people don't abuse insider information when it comes to stocks and investments," I thought.

"What would the world look like if people today could go back and manipulate world events or discoveries just to benefit certain segments of the population?" I wondered out loud. "Wow, I guess I didn't think about that. In the wrong hands, the knowledge could be disastrous."

"Disastrous is an understatement! African Americans are already having a tough time here in the 1860's.

Have you learned about a new law passed a few years ago? Maybe you've heard of it?" asked Simon. "The Fugitive Slave Act."

"Yeah, we just started talking about that in history class. Slave owners could go up north and bring their escaped slaves back to the south."

"Unfortunately no one wears a sign identifying themselves as fugitive slaves. And even if they did, laws up north do not protect blacks, free or enslaved. As a result, slavers or bounty hunters like those guys," he said, pointing over his shoulder, "go up north and steal black people, both free and runaways. Then, once they have a group they bring them back south to sell at a profit. It has really become an issue for runaways in border states like Pennsylvania, Ohio, and Indiana. But it's a problem for all black people, free and enslaved."

"Oh, so you're like a Time Traveling Cop, upholding justice throughout the universe," I said with a chuckle.

"Not exactly. Have you ever heard of Araminta Ross?" asked Simon. "You probably know her as Harriet Tubman?"

"Yeah, she was one of the conductors of the Underground Railroad. She helped dozens of slaves escape the South to freedom up north. Every kid learns about the Underground Railroad."

"Yes. Well I was one of those slaves she helped escape. It was 1851. I was 15 years old that year. With her help, my mother and I made it all the way to Fort Erie Canada.

"So…you're twenty-five years old?"

"Close. I'm twenty-six." At least, when I am here. When I am in your world time goes much slower. I would say if you add my twenty-six years plus the amount of time I have spent in the 21$^{st}$ Century, I would be about 50 years old. But when I come back to my time…"

"It's like time stops while you're gone because time is relative. Einstein's theory of Space-Time, someone moving through Space-Time will experience it differently at various points. That explains why when I'm here, my phone won't work, and when I return, it's like time moved but very slowly."

"Exactly. The Conductors made Einstein's same discovery over a hundred years before he even proposed it as a theory," explained Simon.

"What do you mean?" I asked.

"Scientists have always theorized about time travel. The discussions date back hundreds of years. However, the conductors as we later became known here in the US, used those ancient theories to discover black holes or portals that could be used for time travel. Going back as far as the 1830s the first conductors were able to map out those portals to use them in our fight to end slavery. They were able to discover many of the portal's locations and ultimately, even map all of their destinations. To keep track of their locations and monitor their security, they crafted the armoires and placed them in front of the portals. Now, we use them as doorways to and from the past. All for the sole purpose of…"

"Fighting slavery," I said.

"Yes. We use them to fight slavery, to guide slaves north or to fight any kind of injustice," explained Simon. Many like Ms. Tubman and I focus on freeing slaves and only resort to violence when necessary. But other abolitionists, like John Brown, are becoming increasingly frustrated. They have begun engaging in violent retribution toward slave owners. Unfortunately, the number of conductors subscribing to that ideology is growing however one thing we all agree on is that slavery must end. So, many of us have spent hundreds of hours in your world learning and collecting technology that helps us in that fight."

We continued to talk until we rounded a bend where the tree line began to look oddly familiar. Soon, we paused in front of the large plaster rock. After looking around, Simon pulled out a small controller and held it up. "Garage door opener powered by solar panels," he explained. He hit the button, and the plaster rock opened inwardly, exposing the parallel dirt trail leading through the forest. As we entered, another click of the switch again moved the large plaster structure closing the opening to the outside world.

We rode up the path and dismounted close to the large red barn where Simon opened a gate and led the large black mare and the two new brown colts into the barn. After unbuckling their saddles, he led them to the barn door where they both sprinted into the field to join the other horses.

"She's beautiful," I said. "What's her name?"

"Misty. I took her from a slave trader in Tennessee. She was abused and malnourished but she is hands down the smartest horse I have ever seen." As if on cue, Misty came back into the stall where I had recently met her and once again gently pushed her muzzle against me.

"I had a mare just like her. Name was Ebony. She was beautiful."

"What happened to her?" asked Simon.

"She took a fall and had to be put down. I haven't been able to ride another horse for the last two years, that is, until I met Misty here. She's definitely a special animal." I rubbed her again and looked back at Simon where he was leaned against a post watching me interact with Misty.

As I turned his brow immediately wrinkled and his eyes squinted while looking at my face.

"We need to look at those cuts. Follow me."

Simon walked back to a long wall and stopped in front of a large oil painting. Sliding the painting over, he exposed a small thumbprint scanner. After placing his thumb on the pad a section of the wall instantly slid open exposing a fully functional lab. On one side of the room was an assortment of weapons, guns, and body armor, while the other had exercise equipment, mats, and punching bags.

"You gotta be kidding me! Are you serious? This looks like the Bat Cave."

"Not exactly, but I do use it as my home base. Hop up on the table," he said, pointing to a metal exam table in the center of the room. "Let's take a look at that face." Simon turned on the exam light and navigated it around my face. "Interesting. I can see the two knots, one on your temple and the other on the back of your head, but what happened to the rest of your face? Did those guys do all of this?" he asked pointing to various parts of my face.

"No it was a kid at school," I said reluctantly.

"Those two that were chasing you last week?" he asked inquisitively.

I nodded my head. "They were just messing around," I said, hopping off the exam table and walking in front of the weapons displayed neatly on the wall.

"You know, my father is a police officer," I added. "He's part of an anti-gang unit in downtown Atlanta. He has a lot of guns like these. Sometimes I think about taking one of them and…." I said while staring at a silver revolver.

"Taking a gun and doing what Dante?" Simon asked.

"I don't know. Sometimes I just think about scaring them." My eyes were beginning to well up. "I thought if I could scare the guy and his friends maybe then they might leave me alone."

"I saw the anger in your eyes when you hit that man. It does not take much to lose your temper and really hurt or even kill someone, trust me. You've got to learn to control your anger."

"Hey you know to handle yourself," I said while quickly wiping my eyes with the backs of my fists. "Maybe you can teach me how to fight?"

"No. I said you need to learn how to control your anger and emotions," Simon replied.

"You also said everyone needs to know how to defend oneself. You can teach me to do both. And I can help you around the shop and here with the horses."

Simon reached for an ice pack sitting on the shelf and twisted the blue bag until it popped. "Here," he said, tossing me the cold compress. "Put this on your head," he said while staring at me as if he was considering my offer.

"If I say yes, you're going to have to work hard. I am not going easy on you. And it is more than just learning moves. It involves how you live both mentally and physically."

"I can do it, I swear," I said.

"Ok we start today. First things first, let's get you cleaned up."

# Four

# Quest

Getting back to normal went smoother than I anticipated. As expected, my mother lost it when she heard about my run-in with Marcus but introducing her to Simon, my new boss, took the edge off. She was so excited about my first job that negotiating my workdays was a breeze. My father, he was a different story.

After mom went upstairs, Dad sat me down to discuss the fight. I didn't have to tell him who it was or how it happened.

My run ins at school had generated several father-son conversations. Marcus would do something to me, my father would talk to the school, followed by a tense conversation with his parents. Marcus would then avoid me for a few weeks, and we would pretend like nothing ever happened. That was the pattern for the last few years. However, this time my father said something I wasn't expecting.

"Son, sometimes a man has to stand up for himself. For people to respect him, and more importantly for him to respect himself, he has to stand up."

I thought about that as I was getting on the city bus. Marcus and I had had virtually no interaction over the last six weeks. He appeared to go out of his way to avoid even bumping into me. I, of course, played along with the charade. The truth is, I didn't care. Any spare moment I had was being invested into my chores and grades. Both fulfilled the only two conditions my parents put on my new work schedule.

Since my rescue and eventual job offer, I had been a regular fixture at the Shoeshine Store. Three evenings a week and all-day Saturday, if the store were open, that was where you would find me. Re-stitching leather handbags or refurbishing designer high heels and boots. Over the last several weeks I had learned all aspects of leather repair and maintenance. But when there was no work, that is when the true lessons were given. We would put up the 'Be Back Soon' sign and step through the portal. There, Simon would patiently answer all my questions about the portal, time travel, and stories about life in the 1800's.

In between my barrage of questions, we would also find time to spar and train on various forms of weaponry and fighting styles. Simon would constantly say, "You're not a big guy, so you're going to have to be fast and surprise opponents with your power." He would then end every training session by giving me an axe, "It's going to be a cold Winter, chop!" I would then spend the next several hours chopping wood until my hands blistered.

As the bus pulled into the mall, I looked at the long rows of trees lining the parking lot. Winter was winding down, and the trees were blooming with brightly colored flowers and leaves. When the bus came to a complete stop, I stood up and grabbed my bag from the overhead rack.

With the change in weather, I did not have my usual hoodie I'd worn since entering high school. Stepping down one step of the bus I paused and looked at the reflection in the bus stop window. Where once a narrow frail boy would have peered back at me, now stood a much larger guy. My shoulders were broader, and the usual loosely worn T-shirt was now fitting snugly against my chest and biceps. Even my forearms were larger and beginning to look sculpted. I paused and turned slightly, amazed at my body's two-month transformation, I began rolling up the short sleeves to expose my shoulders when the honking of a horn caused me to look up.

"Hey boo boo…I have a schedule to keep," shouted the bus driver while tapping her watch.

"I'm sorry," I said before hopping off the bus. Peering at my reflection in the bus stop shelter I quickly reaffirmed the changes. The workouts and incessant chopping of wood, all suddenly validated the work. I could see the results and it felt good. Turning toward the mall door I began to walk, shoulders back, chest out, feeling confident for possibly the first time in my teenage life.

Descending down the lower-level escalator I found Simon pulling the large metal gate down and placing the "Be back soon" sign on the glass door. I hurried to the store's entrance, catching it just before the door closed.

"What's up?" I asked while Simon pulled the door open allowing me to slide under the large metal gate.

"I just got word of an assignment," he said while closing the gate. "One of the conductors is running low on supplies. I need to sell some of those horses and take the proceeds to the safe house. Would you like to assist me?"

"Of course!"

"Ok. Go ahead and lock up. I'll meet you in the back room."

After pulling the gate shut and double checking the padlock, I made my way back to the shop area. Simon had changed from his usual work uniform to a dirty and tattered shirt with equally dirty overalls. Sitting down, he laced up a pair of old leather boots.

"We're headed into town this time," he explained before tossing me a similar pair of overalls and boots, "So we need to blend in like the locals."

Simon began digging in a drawer, sifting through various leather and metal objects. "Ah...here they are," he said, holding up several leather strings with badges attached.

"What are those?" I asked.

"Slave tags. Sometimes, when slaves were being loaned out to neighboring slave owners or if slaves were running errands for their masters, they would use these as ids or badges."

He tossed one to me. "Masterson - Field Hand?" I read aloud.

"Yep. So, the holder of that badge belonged to someone named Masterson, and that slave was a Field Hand. I keep several of these just in case I run into trouble.

"Knowing when to fight is just as important as knowing how," I recited from my training sessions.

"Glad to hear something sank in," he said with a smile. "Leave behind your phone and wallet, anything that might identify us."

I looked at my phone and confirmed the time: 5:11PM before powering it off and placing it on the table. After a re-check of our equipment, we stepped through the armoire's portal.

I took my customary deep breath of fresh air as I stood on the porch of the small wooden shack. No matter how many times I stepped through the portal, the fresh air was always a refreshing treat for me.

"We need to saddle up Misty and Blaze, the brown colt, and then make sure the other five are tied in tow,"

Simon said as he hopped off the step and into the dirt yard.

By the time we loaded up and made our way out, it was well past dusk. With the horses ready and all necessary supplies loaded up, we made our way down the path and out of the plastered rock gate entrance. Once clear of the thick line of trees, we turned left and headed north, staying close to the tree line.

It was a cool spring night, and the road was void of any activity. The few signs of life scurried in and out of the forest chirping and screeching in preparation for the evening. Looking at the clearing I was reminded that just two months earlier, I was spotted by the slave traders and temporarily detained in route to Alabama. I stared into the woods and imagined where the other runaway slaves were and if they had made it to freedom. And the two slave traders, where were they? The anger I felt after the beatings stayed with me for weeks after the incidents.

Since my training began, I had found myself replaying the abduction over in my mind. "If I could do it over again, how might I have handled this or responded to that?" I tormented myself with the 'woulda-shoulda' game for what seemed like hours until I noticed we had gradually left the cover of the forest tree line.

"Where is this meeting place?" I asked.

"Not far from here, just a couple of miles south of the Tennessee border. I normally meet them just on the other side of the river."

"And how do you know them?"

"They buy anything of value I confiscate from slave hunters. It could be horses, wagons, supplies, anything of value. They, they sell it to settlers heading west," Simon explained. "They pay me, and I pass the money on to those Conductors in need."

"Ok. Sounds easy enough," I said.

"Yes, but that's the very reason you must always be careful and alert," Simon warned. "Just when you think something is easy, it inevitably turns out to be quite complex. The kind of people we'll be dealing with would just as soon slit your throat or sell you as do business with you."

We continued north until well past midnight. As we traveled, I could begin to see a faint glow on the horizon. The closer we got to the source, the clearer the picture became. A bright fire glowed in the darkness highlighting two silhouettes huddled close to the flames. Tied off to the side were three horses.

"What's wrong with this picture?" Simon asked.

I looked at the two figures, the horses and back again at the two figures. "How many men are we planning to meet?" I asked Simon.

"Two," replied Simon.

"So why are there three horses with saddles?" I asked.

"That's the question. Sometimes people take liberties when dealing with Negros. 'We's scared as mice and don't know nothing'."

I smiled at what I perceived to be a joke however, as I looked at his face, I could see that same cool anger I first saw when he rescued me from the slavers nearly two months ago.

"Keep your senses about you," Simon repeated. "We're heading into a trap."

We continued forward with the five horses in tow until we arrived. The two figures, now standing directly in front of us, smiled widely as we approached.

One was noticeably shorter than the other while his companion was significantly rounder. The shorter of the two extended a greeting.

"Good evening boys my name is Andy, and this is my partner, Willie. We've been expecting you."

Andy walked away from his partner while keeping a safe distance from Simon and me.

"My, my, my, those are some beautiful looking animals," he said while eyeing the five horses. "My customers sho gonna be pleased with these animals," added Andy. "Why don't you two come on over here and have a drink of whiskey with me an ol' Willie. You know, celebrate our doing business together." Andy held up a brown jug and two metal cups.

I paused, refusing to take my gaze off the odd pair when Simon spoke in a way I had yet to hear.

"We's sorry boss. Our Massa wouldn't take kindly to us drankin' whiskey with you gentleman. He expects us to be back by mornin' wit his money for these here horses."

"I understand that boy," replied Andy while attempting to hide his annoyance. "You come on down from them horses so we can give you Massa his money."

Simon looked at me and gave a slight nod indicating it was ok to comply.

Lifting my leg over the saddle horn I slid from the saddle and slipped to the ground. Both Misty and Blaze stomped nervously as I dismounted. Simon dropped from his saddle and joined me as we took the remaining steps to the partners.

Both men smiled exposing rotten and missing teeth.

Holding the jug and tin cups, Andy again offered a drink. Simon began his protest when we heard footsteps in the shadows next to us. Before I could turn, a third man leapt from the darkness and stood behind Simon with a knife pressed firmly against his neck.

"Hello boy. Don't you have any manners? Andy here invited you and your nigger friend to have a drank. Are you too good to drink whiskey with us boy?"

Simon stood relaxed with his hands held slightly above his waist. Then, with lightening quick speed, he reached up with his right hand and grabbed the man's arm holding the knife. Before the man could respond, Simon's left hand disappeared behind him, finding the tender part of the man's inner thigh. The knife wielding man's eyes doubled in size as he let out an audible gasp while slowly releasing his grip on the knife until it innocently dropped from his hand.

Simon turned to face his would-be attacker while repositioning his tight grip on the man's crotch.

"You were saying something about manners?" Simon asked as he increased his grip on the man's genitals. The attacker stood motionless as tears began to stream down his face. Finally, after continuing the pressure, Simon released his grip allowing the man to crumple to the ground.

Andy stood, mouth wide open, watching in disbelief as Simon turned toward him. Slowly reaching in the fold of his jacket he pulled out a knife. Holding it uncomfortably between himself and Simon, his hand and voice trembling nervously.

"Dammit boy….what you go do that fer? Now we gon' to have kill you boys."

Simon looked down at the wobbling knife in his dirty pudgy hand and let out a thunderous laugh as he turned his back to the quivering knife wielder. Unlatching the blanket strapped to his saddle bag Simon apologized profusely.

"I'm sorry you feel that way. I thought we might still complete this transaction and be on our way…"

Simon turned, now loosely holding a double-barreled sawed-off shotgun. Pulling back both triggers, he locked the hammers in place. "…however, it sounds like you would like to renegotiate our terms."

Andy immediately dropped the knife as he stammered a response.

"No, no, no, no, sir. Th-that won't be necessary. I would very much like to buy those horses from you and your nigg…I mean, your friend. I believe I mentioned they're some fine-looking animals…fine indeed," he stammered through an uncomfortable smile.

"Are you sure? Just moments ago, your friend here seemed pretty determined to slit my throat. Are you sure he wouldn't have a problem if we continued with our agreed upon terms?" Simon asked sarcastically.

"No sir. That idiot brother of mine is most definitely in agreement with the sale as agreed!" replied Andy.

"Then it's settled. We will finish the sale based on our original terms," Simon looked at me and said, "Please pour a drink so we can celebrate our doing business together."

I grabbed the jug and the two tin cups. After filling both with the brown liquid, I gave one cup to Simon and one to Andy.

"To business," said Simon. He held up his drink and started to take a sip but stopped. Andy watched while he too held his cup close without taking a drink. "You're not drinking. Is there a problem?" asked Simon.

"No sir. I..I.. I," stammered Andy.

"Spit it out sir, is there a problem?" demanded Simon.

"No sir," repeated Andy.

"Then drink," ordered Simon as he again raised the shotgun. Andy looked into the cup, at Simon, then again at the cup. Lifting the cup to his lips, he tilted his head back and nervously swallowed the contents.

Simon looked at me and said, "Let's not leave out our friends," pointing to Willie and the man still crumpled on the ground holding his manhood.

Uncorking the bottle, I poured a cup and gave the other two men a full helping of the brown liquid. After pausing momentarily, they both tipped their heads and drank the cups contents.

Simon smiled as he poured his cup's contents and tossed the empty cup at Andy's feet.

"What did you put in it?" asked Simon.

"Nothing. I don't know what you're talking about," replied Andy as he began to blink repeatedly, "I didn't do anything".

He spent the next 2 or 3 minutes bouncing between prolonged moments of silence and adamant denials, until finally collapsing back into a seated position.

"What did you put in it?" Simon asked patiently.

The man looked up through partially closed eyes and whispered, "Passionflower."

"See…..that wasn't so hard. How long do you have?" asked Simon.

The old man let out an audible sigh before answering, "…about ten minutes."

Simon stood up and unlocked the hammer on the shotgun.

Sometimes you can trust a thief, but you can never trust a liar." Simon explained before grabbing the barrel of the bun and swinging the butt directly into the center of the Andy's face. Cartilage crunched under the pressure of the blunt object as his nose instantly erupted into a bloody geyser. Already limber and easily pliable, Andy's lifeless body fell back into a fully reclined position.

Simon looked at Willie and walked over to where he was now sitting.

Willie held up his hands and began shaking his head, "Please don't kill me, I wasn't going to hurt you, I swear," he begged.

I am not gonna kill you Willie. I'm going to let you finish this transaction then take a nice long nap.

"Where is the money?" Simon demanded.

"In the saddlebag of the brown horse."

"Thank you sir. My friend and I are going to get the money and tie these horses off," said Simon.

"I can…I can…" Willie stammered before beginning to blink repeatedly.

The blinking, followed by a seemingly uncontrolled episode of swaying side to side, continued until Willie mumbled some unrecognizable expressions before he too collapsed backwards and passed out. Simon kneeled to check the third man. After confirming he too was out, he stood up.

"I'll grab the money. You tie those horses off."

I walked over to where the horses were temporarily tied up and gathered the reins. As I took my first step, I heard a voice. I immediately crouched behind a small bush, but again, the muffled voice called out, this time sounding more desperate.

The three men had cleverly used darkness to lie in wait, so I was determined not to fall victim to the same trap. Estimating where I thought the sounds were coming from, I circled around the location and slowly pulled back the long woody branches. That's when I saw him.

His long black hair initially made me think it was a girl, but as I got closer, I could see him. Through the dirt and soot caked on his face, hands, and feet I could clearly see the strong features of a young man.

Even though he was tied and bound, it appeared as though he was young, possibly 15 or 16. He was visibly weak, but I could see his chest slowly rise and fall as he lay looking at me through dazed eyes.

"Howatsu," he mumbled more clearly.

"My god!" Simon exclaimed looking over my shoulder. Handing me the reins, he knelt beside the boy. Pulling out his knife, he cut the ropes binding his hands to his feet and after a brief examination, effortlessly scooped up the boy and laid him next to the still roaring fire.

By the light of the flames I could now see he was not only dirty, but the cuts and bruises appeared to cover his arms and neck. Simon shook his head as he examined the injuries before standing up.

Looking left then right, he pointed left and instructed me, "Take those two pots and just past that clearing you'll find an inlet to the river. Fill both up with water and bring them back."

Without asking any questions, I grabbed the two pots and quickly made my way in the direction I was instructed.

Just as Simon predicted, the thick underbrush gave way to a large pond just out of sight from the campsite. I quickly filled the pots and slowly made my way back to the camp.

By the time I returned Simon had taken most of the boy's clothes off exposing more filth and even more cuts and bruises.

"Put both pots over the fire and check their bags for food and fresh water," Simon instructed, pointing to the lifeless trio lying nearby.

Patting down each of the three men I quickly found bread, cured meats and a couple of apples, I found a large knife and leather holder strapped to Willie's hip. Unlatching the holder I slipped it into my waist band before making my way over to Simon.

"I found some food, water and this knife," I said pointing to the knife hanging from my side.

"Nice looking bowie knife!" Simon replied before returning his attention to the young boy.

"These animals! It's not uncommon for men like this to use that same passionflower to kidnap children and women, both black and Native American, in order to sell them off. He is Cherokee. Probably kidnapped from a nearby nation or township.

They are mostly peaceful people who like to trade their pipes and jewelry for tools and clothing. But even the most peaceful people have their limits."

Simon tore a piece of Andy's jacket and handed it to me. "Take these and wash them off in one of the pots. We are going to clean his wounds and maybe do a couple of stitches," Simon said as he rolled up his sleeves.

We spent the better part of the day cleaning up and caring for the young man. I would clean the wounds, then Simon would add a couple of stitches before disinfecting the wound with his aerosol spray. It was not until mid-afternoon that the boy sat up, seemingly startled by his surroundings.

"Edoda!" he cried out, looking around frantically. "Edoda," he repeated as he stood before collapsing back on one knee.

"Ulihelisdi. Gado detsadoa," Simon responded.

The boy looked at Simon with my same amazement at hearing him speak in his native tongue.

"Mohe," he responded extending his arm.

"Simon," he replied embracing his extended arm.

"Grab him some water and some of that corn mash in the pot," Simon instructed as he again began speaking with the man.

I returned with the water and mash. Looking at the yellow-colored mush, it closely resembled what I had eaten while held captive a couple of months earlier. The young man quickly drank the water and spooned finger loads full of the warm corn mash while continuing to speak with Simon. Their conversation continued until late in the afternoon when he once again attempted to stand. After slowly balancing himself, he stretched out his arms and stood fully erect.

He had originally looked small lying tied in the bushes however, now that he was fully erect, he was at least three or four inches taller than me. At first, he walked in small circles, seemingly re-establishing his balance. After a couple of minutes, he turned the small steps into a light trot, followed by a quick sprint. I watched as if he were a young mustang being let loose on a wide-open plain.

"It looks like our friend is feeling better," Simon said walking up behind me.

"Yeah, I think so. What did he say?" I asked.

"His name is Mohe of the Cherokee nation. He was trading supplies near Chattanooga when these three men approached him. After trading with him, they offered him a drink, a cup of whiskey. That was the last thing he remembers. He woke up and has been captive ever since. That was almost one week ago. Simon and I watched as Mohe ran towards the river and disappeared into the thick brush before we heard a loud splash.

"I'm thinking he'll be ready to ride tonight," Simon said with a smile.

"Is he going with us to the Plantation?"

"No. His tribe resides west of Knoxville," Simon explained while drawing an imaginary map in the air above us. "We are here, and this is Chattanooga. We will ride up this way and by the time we get here or so, Mohe will break away and go the rest of the way alone. I was thinking we might need to take him all the way but I think he'll be fine."

Mohe walked toward us and again embraced Simon before turning to me and speaking.

"He's telling you his name and thanking you for helping him," Simon explained while interpreting. "Tell him your name," Simon instructed.

"My name is Dante" I said extending my arm.

Mohe repeated what must have sounded odd to him before taking my arm and embracing me.

"Dawntee."

He immediately began speaking again, this time pointing to the three men still lying motionless by the now dwindling fire. He looked at Simon and paused, allowing him to translate before continuing.

"These men have done unspeakable things to me and others. According to the laws of my people, they should be beaten for their crimes," explained Simon. Mohe continued to speak before pausing briefly to allow Simon the opportunity to translate. "However, the spirits smile on us today. Me for being found and assisted by you. And them for also being found by the two of you. The compassion and mercy you have shown is truly a gift. And for this, I'm forever in your debt." Mohe spoke to Simon while pointing to the Western setting sun before nodding his head and walking over to the horses.

"It's almost dusk," Simon said turning towards me. "We need to start heading north. We'll ride in ten minutes."

I packed the remaining supplies and climbed atop Blaze while surveying the campsite. It had been over 18 hours since the men drank the tainted whiskey, but they were still lying motionless around the now smoldering fire. I wondered what they would say to each other once they were awake.

"Outwitted and overpowered by two niggers!"

I laughed at the thought and imagined it might be easier to pretend like it never happened. With a flick of the reins, Blaze jolted into a trot in pursuit of Mohe and Simon.

Just two months ago, I would have been terrified at the idea of someone holding me or a friend at knife point. But now, it barely seemed to faze me. I replayed Simon's lightning quick moves in my mind and thought about several alternate moves he'd taught me. Moves that would have done far more damage than a simple nut grab. Looking at Simon sitting atop Misty, I thought, "That guy was actually lucky." Simon obviously used just enough force to get what he needed. It could have been worse.

I then looked at Mohe. Despite his horse being slightly shorter than mine, he still towered above me. Since I began working with Simon, I had developed the habit of analyzing people, looking for any kind of weakness or advantage I could exploit if the need arose. It could be an old injury, a disability, anything that might give me an edge. I looked Mohe up and down, searching for any such weakness. He had to be close to my age however, his broad shoulders and large physical stature revealed no apparent weakness. After another quick assessment, I quickly decided my best offense was to keep him as an ally.

"What's passionflower?" I asked while pulling alongside Simon.

"It's a sedative. Much like the Benzo I use in my syringes. It will knock them out for a while. Just to be safe, I gave them a small Benzo dose. They should be able to ride by morning,"

"What now?" I asked.

"We will continue north until we get close to Nashville. At some point, Mohe will head north east, while we continue north, that is where we will find Ms. Jackie Carter, another Conductor. She runs a safe house where runaways can stop on their way north."

"Does she know where you're from?" I asked.

"You mean does she know about the portal? Yes. But she is the only one. Ms. Carter is actually from your universe. She's originally from Chicago but spends all of her time in Franklin where she helps out with the cause," Simon explained. "We'll drop off the money and spend a day or two helping with a few things around the plantation."

"What about everyone else. Where do I tell them I'm from?" I asked.

"Tell the truth. Well, a version of the truth. You're originally from Atlanta, but now you work with me," Simon said smiling. "You'll be alright. The people you are going to meet are from all over the south. And they're not big on asking or answering a lot of questions."

I looked back as the campsite began to fade into the dark horizon, then I looked at the large Cherokee riding alongside us. "People from all over the south, what have I gotten myself into?" I thought.

# Five

# Introductions

We continued north for the remainder of the evening. In between his conversations with Simon, Mohe and I spoke with Simon serving as translator. Despite our language barrier, we talked about our homes and families, as well as things we enjoyed doing. I watched as he mimed shooting a bow while pointing to a leather pelt tied to his waist. I spoke in general terms, cognizant that some of my hobbies and family dynamics might be difficult to understand. After each expression, Simon easily translated my words in a way that appeared to be easily understood. Our conversation continued for several hours until Mohe paused and looked at Simon and me. After speaking briefly with Simon and engaging in a momentary embrace, he turned and spoke to me.

"He wishes us well in our travels and reminded us that he's in our debt," Simon translated. I smiled and awkwardly nodded my head. After a momentary arm embrace, Mohe turned toward the east and departed.

Simon and I both sat and watched as he rode erect, never once stopping to turn around.

"That's odd," I said. "No goodbye or anything?"

"The Cherokee don't believe in goodbyes. In fact, the word does not exist in their language," Simon explained as he turned Misty and resumed our trek north.

"For them, a goodbye conveys an ending or finale. And that is not how they view departures. They use the word 'Donadagvhoi.' It conveys more of a 'see you around' philosophy rather than a 'goodbye,'" explained Simon.

I looked back at what remained of Mohe's dark shadowy silhouette riding off into the darkness and thought about the phrase, 'Donadagvhoi.'

"See you around Mohe. Nice meeting you," I mumbled to myself.

***

We continued north on a compacted red colored dirt road. It was not until we got further north that the road turned into an even more crudely constructed dirt path. Wagon wheels and hoof prints left their deep impressions in the impressionable soil. I shifted uncomfortably in the saddle, feeling the discomfort of the long uneven saddle ride. I had participated in several two, four, or even six-hour rides however, this leg of the trip was already approaching 10 hours. A gentle pat on the side of Blaze's neck reaffirmed my appreciation for the lift while navigating over the dried uneven ground.

After a couple of hours, we passed a small wooden sign, "Franklin 5 miles." The news of our imminent arrival caused me to perk up in my saddle. Since the run-in with the would-be-thieves and the brief introduction to Mohe, I was looking forward to meeting some regular people. It was just before dawn when we reached the small country town. Gazing around I immediately thought of an old, abandoned Hollywood movie set. Wooden signs swung from small wooden shop doors, Barber, Bank, Saloon.

Although dawn was quickly approaching, the streets were still dark and largely abandoned. Positioned along the dirt road leading through town were dimly lit kerosene lamps hanging on iron rods. The light exposed unidentifiable bodies sitting slumped against walls while others walked down dark alleys or narrow walkways between buildings.

"Is anyone going to say anything to us?" I asked.

"No. People out at this time of night aren't worried about us. Most are drunk or looking for company. We have another couple of hours before honest folk start moving around. And if we do get stopped, we have the slave tags."

We continued into the middle of the town, turning down a dark street as we approached a small wooden courthouse complete with jailhouse windows on the second floor, everything you would expect in a small country town.

Simon continued winding his way through the dark narrow streets until the spacing between houses began to grow. I looked back and watched as the town began to shrink behind us. The small buildings started to give way to large well-manicured pastures.

Looking out over the moonlit fields, I could not make out much but you could tell a lot of work was underway.

Simon saw me looking into the immense emptiness.

"They are getting ready for the planting season. Over the next month, hundreds of slaves will be out here preparing the land and planting this year's crops."

We crossed a bridge and followed a path that ran along the bank of the river. The trail wound its way up a gentle slope with more neatly prepared fields on both sides of the dirt roadway. Approaching the top, we were greeted with a high arching sign, "Apple Mountain Plantation." It had that same lantern icon etched in the far corners of the sign.

The sun was now peeking through groves of neatly manicured trees separating the tilled fields from the large house at the top of the hill. As we got closer to the structure, we could see people bustling to and from smaller wooden homes. Greyish white smoke billowed from small, bricked chimneys dotting the land surrounding the hilltop. Most people passed, heads down focused on their task, while others, with the tip of their hats, acknowledged Simon. Other, brave young onlookers stopped, stared, and pointed, only to be nudged along by their older counterparts.

We rode down the long pathway leading up to the front of the house when the door swung open. An attractive white woman stepped onto the large wrap-around porch. She could not have been any older than thirty, her blonde hair pulled back in a gray scarf that matched her night dress. Beside her stood a younger black woman who also wore a simple yellow dress however hers appeared to be more of a nightgown with a scarf or shawl draped loosely across her shoulders. I smiled a greeting, but she looked away, disinterested.

We dismounted our horses and turned our reins over to a young man, possibly my age or slightly younger. Simon unhooked his saddle bag containing the recently obtained money and nodded for me to follow him up the stairs leading to the house. We walked up the short path to the house and quickly climbed the stairs. Simon approached the two women and awkwardly nodded then shook the hand of the nicely dressed white woman.

"It's a pleasure to see you again Jackie, I mean, Ms. Carter," he said nervously. "This is my friend, Dante West. Dante this is Ms. Carter, the owner of the Apple Mountain Plantation."

"Hello Dante. It is my pleasure to meet you. I've heard so much about you," she said, extending her hand. "I understand we have several things in common. We've both traveled great distances to be here," she said with a smile and a wink.

"It's my pleasure," I replied while a smile.

"Dante, this is Yolanda. Yolanda you know Simon. Dante is his new traveling companion."

"Hello Simon," Yolanda replied before stepping in front of me to give Simon a welcoming hug. "It's so nice to see you again. It feels like ages since we saw you last."

Seeing her up close, I was certain she was the most beautiful girl I had ever met. I watched as she nervously twirled her braids and laughed while catching up with Simon. Her long white nightgown danced gently around the porch as the stiff breeze lifted the dress, momentarily displaying glimpses of her lower legs and ankles. As she turned, the morning sun illuminated through the sheer thin material, exposing every curve and angle of her body. I had seen girls in school, particularly at the pool or in gym class, but none were built like her. I looked her up and down imagining her...

"Excuse me! Did you find what you're looking for boy?" spat Yolanda as she wrapped the scarf around her midsection and stormed into the house.

I looked up, startled to find both Ms. Carter and Simon fighting back laughter as I mumbled an awkward apology to the slamming screen door.

"It's ok Dante," said Ms. Carter smiling. "I'm sure she will find your...curiosity.... flattering once she has had a bit of breakfast."

Simon opened the screen door allowing her, then me, to walk through.

"Nice job blending in," he said sarcastically before playfully elbowing me in the ribs.

***

Simon and I spent the first half of the day catching up on some much-needed rest. The room was small with two little beds with feather filled mattresses. Next to each bed was a small wooden table with a small candle lantern. After an initial inspection of the room, I collapsed in the bed and quickly fell fast asleep. By noon, I heard a soft knock on the bedroom door. Peeking through partially closed eyes I could see Simon was already dressed, slightly worn overalls and a basic white button up shirt.

Leaning over he opened the door to find Yolanda waiting patiently in the doorway. Unlike the night before, she was wearing a long cotton dress. Rather than the two long braids, her hair was pulled up neatly in a bun with two curly ringlets hanging over each ear. Looking directly at Simon she spoke casually without acknowledging me.

"Ms. Carter will see you in the dining room Mr. Simon."

"Thank you Yolanda. We'll be down momentarily," he replied.

Yolanda smiled, turned, and quickly walked out of the doorway before disappearing in the long dimly lit hallway.

Simon closed the door and turned toward me.

"Looks like she's starting to warm up to you," he said with a chuckle. "Here are some clothes. Get dressed and meet me downstairs."

I watched Simon walk out of the small bedroom and close the door behind him. Collapsing backwards into the bed I looked up at the discolored plastered ceiling and thought about the plantation and the variety of people we saw earlier that morning. And Yolanda, who was she? I started thinking about our initial meeting and the thin night gown she wore. Burying my face in the pillow I thought about how crazy I must have looked.

Then I thought about Jennifer.

"What are you thinking? You have a girlfriend!" I thought as I slid toward the edge of the bed. "You're here to help Simon. Stay focused," I thought as I grabbed the overalls Simon had tossed on the bed and quickly got dressed.

Making my way downstairs I navigated through the narrow hallways while being careful not to collide with workers coming and going. Stepping through the large doorway adjacent to the front door I immediately saw the long wooden table with possibly a dozen chairs neatly arranged along each side. Then, on the far end sat Simon and Ms. Carter.

"For such a large table they sure are sitting close," I thought as I watched them looking at each other with wide smiles. Something was happening and I was not sure that I wanted to witness it. Clearing my throat, I immediately launched into a loud exaggerated cough.

"Oh...hello Dante. Good morning" said Ms. Carter as she awkwardly swallowed whatever Simon had just popped into her mouth.

"Hello. Glad you could join us," added Simon. "We were just going over the supplies we need to pick up in town."

"I see. It looks like we might need some more fruit," I added while leaning over and peering into the empty wooden bowl. Simon quickly pushed the bowl to the side while glaring at me behind a barely recognizable smile.

"Yes, well preparations need to be made for this trip," explained Ms. Carter. "I was thinking you could help Victor ready the horses and buggy for the ride into town. Simon here says you are an experienced rider."

"Yes ma'am. I've spent some time around the stables," I replied with a smile.

"Well splendid," exclaimed Ms. Carter. "Yolanda. Could you come in here please?"

Yolanda gracefully entered the room through two swinging doors.

"Yes ma'am," she said to Ms. Carter with a smile.

"Can you show our friend here to the stables? And please be sure Victor helps him ready the buggy for a ride into town."

"Yes ma'am," replied Yolanda. "Follow me boy," she said dryly before walking through the same wooden doors.

Yolanda navigated her way through the large kitchen bustling with activity before slipping through a rear screen door. I followed behind her like a child trying to keep up with his mother as she continued off the porch, down the hill, and passed the small wooden slave shacks evenly spaced throughout the plantation. By now it was mid-day and just beginning to warm up. People milled about doing chores or chatting, completely oblivious to me following behind the young lady of the house.

"I'm sorry about last night," I announced awkwardly.

"Don't worry, it's not your fault."

"What do you mean?"

"You are just a dumb mixed-up nigger" she said matter-of-factly. "These parts are full of dumb niggers that don't know no better."

"Is that so?" I replied, slightly curious by her quick characterization of me. "So, how are you and I different?" I asked.

"Are you blind and dumb? You're yella. Your daddy was probably your Master. Didn't your momma teach you anything?" she said while shaking her head.

"My father is actually…" I replied before stopping myself. I wanted so badly to tell her my father was black and my mother white, but she would not believe me or understand if she did. It was hard to believe I was having the same conversation I had with people like Marcus and his gorilla friends. I'm in a place where 90% of the world hates us yet we're still judging one another based on our complexion.

"What difference does my color make?" I asked. "Aren't we all still black just different shades?" Yolanda continued walking in silence as we approached the stables.

Walking into the stables I instantly recognized the boy from earlier that morning. Standing next to the wall, he was fixated on a piece of paper nailed to a wooden post.

"Ms. Carter wants you and this…boy…to get the buggy ready for a trip into town" announced Yolanda.

"Yes ma'am," said Victor. "I was just reading this paper. It says there's a rewa…rewa"

I leaned over his shoulder and read the phrase. "There is a reward for two escaped slaves. $100 dollars each for their capture," I read aloud.

Victor turned around with wide eyes that bounced from me to Yolanda then back again to me. Looking at Yolanda she too was staring at me in amazement.

Snapping out of her momentary trance she redirected her attention to the young stable boy, "What you need to do is stop fooling around with that paper and get the buggy ready for Ms. Carter. She and Mr. Simon will be waiting for you." Yolanda paused while briefly staring at me before quickly hurrying out of the stable.

"How you do that?" asked Victor.

"Do what? I asked.

"Read this here paper. You read betta than any white man I've ever met."

"Oh that. I learned when I was younger and have been…practicing for several years now," I said.

"Most Mastas would whip a negro for doing what you just did although Missy Carter different. She even tries to teach some of us negroes how to read and write words. But I ain't never seen nobody read them words like you."

I started feeling uncomfortable with the direction of the conversation. Simon had warned me about the importance of blending in, "Time to change the subject," I thought.

"So..what buggy are we preparing?" I asked.

"We're going to use da big buggy," said Victor, pointing to a large wagon with two rows of seats and room in the back for storage. "Missy Carter always likes to take the big one when we's fetchin supplies."

"Ok and what do you use to pull the big buggy" I said smiling.

"That'd be Big Jake and Peanut. They out in the pasture. We need to get 'em strapped up."

Victor guided me through the barn on our way to the pasture. Just in front of the large wooden gate leading to the pasture, I found the stalls holding Misty and Blaze. Hopping up on the railing, I gave them both a good scratch.

"Those sure are some pretty animals," said Victor. "I can tell you takes good care of 'em."

"Thank you Victor," I said as we continued to the pasture gate. Victor hopped up on the gate and placed his two index fingers in his mouth before letting out a loud whistle.

As he did, two large quarter horses came galloping toward the barn. Victor hopped off the fence and introduced me to the two big males.

"This here is Big Jake and his boy Peanut."

Big Jake stood patiently waiting for Victor to open the gate while the younger Peanut nudged Victor's hand for attention. "I've known Big Jake my whole life, even helped my pa bring Peanut into the world," he said proudly while rubbing between the horse's ears.

"Sounds like you know a thing or two about horses," I said.

"My Pa, Jim...Jim Turner, takes care of all of Missy Carter's livestock. Even makes all of their straps and shoes. He teaching me, and one day I'm gonna take care of 'em."

"Is your Pa a slave here?" I asked.

"Nope, he a free man. We live right here on the plantation. Been here 15 years, all my life."

Victor and I spent the next hour talking as we got the horses ready. I learned a lot about the area and his family while watching him skillfully display his command of the immense animals. I thought about the idea of free slaves and concluded I did not recall learning about free slaves living in the south, especially before the Civil War. Or that some were able to buy their freedom if they had the money and support of their owners. And others, like many living at the Apple Mountain Plantation, were perfectly happy living here. They had homes, families, and careers. And those constants were not guaranteed to them if they left the protection of the farm. However, there were others, like those two girls posted on the wanted poster, who made another choice. They were heading to freedom, even if it cost them their lives.

We hopped in the buggy where I witnessed Big Jake and his boy effortlessly pull the oversized wagon. It stopped in front of the large house where we found Simon and Ms. Carter waiting on the porch.

"Thank you Victor. You may assist your father for the remainder of the day," said Ms. Carter with a smile.

Victor turned to me and smiled, eyes looking downward. I stepped toward him and extended my hand. "It was a pleasure to meet you Victor. Before I leave, how about we spend some time practicing on that poster?"

"I'd like that very much sir, I mean Dante," he replied with a large grin on his face.

Simon stepped off the porch and extended a hand to Ms. Carter. After settling her into the rear bench, he closed the door and swung up to the front seat next to me.

"Looks like a nice kid."

"Yeah. Kind of reminds me of myself a few months ago."

I did not have to say anything more. I knew Simon understood what I was talking about.

Since I had met him and found the armoire, I had changed. Yeah, I was still the geeky kid from the ATL that liked school and video games, but the time over the last two months had made me wiser and more confident in how I interacted with others. I had also grown physically, but more importantly, I had grown mentally.

Simon flicked the reins and with the click of his teeth, the horses jumped to a start.

The three of us sat quietly as the buggy bounced along the dirt hill leading out of the plantation gate. Crossing the creek, I watched as the swift current swept away anything in its path. After several minutes of silence I turned to Ms. Carter and asked, "How can you own slaves?"

"Be careful Dante," Simon warned.

"No Simon, it's ok," said Ms. Carter.

"I'm sorry," I said, "I don't mean to sound disrespectful. It's just, I was talking to Victor and he explained that while his dad is free, he is still a slave and I just can't imagine how a person can own someone. I mean, I know you're not like the others, but doesn't it bother you?"

Ms. Carter laughed. "Honestly, it drives me crazy! I look around at men, women and even young children working hard for no pay or no home to call their own.

Calling me Master or Missy. Sometimes the guilt I feel is so overwhelming that I just want to scream. It's very difficult."

Ms. Carter sat quietly for a moment, deep in thought. Seconds later she snapped out of the momentary trance.

"Victor is a fine young man. A hard worker and very talented. I know he told you he was a slave, but he is not. He is actually free. In fact, most of the workers on this plantation are free. For example, Jim Turner, Victor's father, he has been free for over 20 years. Actually, Victor, like Yolanda and several of the young ones, were born free."

"What?" I asked perplexed. "Then why do they think they're still slaves?"

"Can you imagine the reaction of the townsfolk in Franklin if they knew over 25 slaves on this plantation were free men and women? One or two, maybe, but dozens of black men and women, free to collect wages and come and go as they please?"

I thought about the question then replied, "I guess it could be a little confusing for some."

"It could get outright dangerous," added Simon. "People would feel threatened and fearful that their slaves might demand similar treatment. They would hang every one of us, starting with Ms. Carter. "

"I moved to Nashville from Chicago several years ago. Jaquelyn Veratelli is what my mother calls me," explained Ms. Carter.

"I was working part time for an antique dealer while attending medical school at Vanderbilt University when I met a conductor, Dorothy Setterwhite. It was while working for her that I learned about the armoires and their connection to the portals. From my first visit to Franklin I knew I was home. Ms. Setterwhite introduced me to a wealthy abolitionist couple from Ohio, Phillip and Melanie Carter. I visited them off and on for several years until Mr. Carter and later, Mrs. Carter died.

By then the community and workers had accepted me as their daughter, a recent graduate of Wesleyan Female College in Macon Georgia. With Dorothy's help, I learned how to manage the plantation. That is where I met Simon and the others. In the beginning, I was just like you. All I ever talked about was freeing the slaves."

"Yeah, forget about old honest Abe's plans for America. We had Ms. Carter here, ready and willing to emancipate all of the slaves," Simon said with a chuckle.

Ms. Carter smiled at the thought. "If it were not for Simon explaining why it could not happen, at least at the time or how I would have liked, I might have ruined all of the good work we have been able to do over the years. Teaching people to read and write, helping others to learn a trade or escape to freedom."

"So, why don't people just leave? I mean, if they're free, why not just leave and go north?" I asked.

"Things up north aren't easy," Ms. Carter explained. "There aren't many jobs or homes. And although slavery is illegal, the idea of equality for all, women, or those with handicaps, won't happen for another 100 years."

"And for many, they do whatever is natural, what they're accustomed to doing," added Simon. "And for most, that is caring for their families. As far as they are concerned, they have everything they need."

The conversation continued with Ms. Carter explaining her experiences while learning to manage the plantation and her family back home in Chicago. I explained how I found the armoire and my subsequent meetings with Simon. He listened intently, quick to correct or clarify the story when my version conflicted with his recollection of events. I watched as Simon continued to turn around and smile at Ms. Carter, seemingly hanging on her every word. I thought back to the awkward meeting the previous night and the intimate breakfast I had interrupted that morning. I laughed as I thought about the two of them. Why hadn't I noticed it earlier? They were a couple, or at least they were interested in being a couple.

My thoughts immediately shifted to the attitudes of people of the 1860's. I knew white men often slept with female slaves, but I could not imagine the attention an interracial couple would attract during this time period. I thought about the stares and comments my parents still receive in the 21st century and the attention was not always from white people. I remembered my father's sister jokingly calling my mother Snow White or Penelope during family reunions. Or comments we regularly hear while walking through the mall. Things were at times uncomfortable however, things here were completely different.

The truthfulness of those words came to reality as the wagon pulled into Franklin. Those large empty fields we had seen earlier that morning were now full of black field workers. On both sides of the road, in any open pasture, slaves could be seen busily preparing soil, moving rocks and brush, or planting seeds. And never far away was the overseer. I rubbed my temple as I thought back to the slave catcher that had callously slugged me only to later be struck with the same weapon he had used against me. We rode in silence as we started to pass the small shacks leading into town.

Simon leaned over to me and whispered, "Don't speak or look at anyone. Keep your eyes down. Remember, we are here to get supplies and any information we can gather. Understand?"

I quickly nodded in agreement.

As we made our way into town, we discovered the activity had increased dramatically from the night before. The shops and dirt-covered streets were now filled with a steady stream of people bustling in and out of stores. The mill had wagons lining the street with each wagon holding slaves ready to load lumber or other supplies. I watched as the slaves sat, eyes down, in tattered clothing, looking miserable with their lot in life. Other slaves, women, and children followed behind their masters holding packages or tending to children. They, too, kept their eyes down while completing their tasks.

We pulled up to the general store and hitched the horses to the post. Ms. Carter stepped down onto the wooden deck and entered the store while Simon and I sat in the wagon waiting for her to complete the necessary transactions.

"A day in the life of a slave," Simon whispered as we watched a young black girl carrying a small white child and several packages while struggling to keep up with the older white woman. "They're completely dependent on it," he continued. "Everything from field hands, to cooks, to caretakers for their children. The southern economy would come to a screeching halt if it were to end."

"That's why they're prepared to fight, even go to war to defend it," I added. "It's funny. We watch movies or read accounts in history class but seeing it in person is completely different. Every part of their lives and their children's lives are so dependent on a single man or woman. A lifetime of servitude," I thought aloud.

"Yep. As a matter of fact, this year, in just a few days, that very war will begin. We are already behind schedule, so we need to handle our affairs and get back home by mid-week. The war won't immediately affect these parts, but it'd be best if we avoided it altogether."

We continued to watch the throngs of people shuffle in and out of the stores and shops until an older white man approached the general store. He moved slowly, taking small deliberate steps while strongly leaning on his wooden cane. Behind him, three young slaves walked awkwardly carrying several wooden crates. As the smaller of the boys stepped on the platform, his foot caught on the wooden step, sending the crates flying across the deck.

Now empty-handed, the young man smiled as he looked up at the older white man.

He was significantly smaller than the other two slaves, and judging by his child like expression, he had a disorder, possibly Down Syndrome. The other slaves put down their boxes and quickly began scrambling to gather the contents now littered across the platform. The old man turned slowly, surveying the spilled goods, and while still relying heavily on his cane, hobbled over to the young boy. Without expression or warning, he drew back the cane and struck the boy across the face. I watched as he again lifted the cane and struck the boy multiple times.

Townspeople, witnessing the beating, walked by without uttering a word of protest or even pausing to view the spectacle. The young man attempted to sit up by pushing himself up into a sitting position, but the old man was relentless. Seeing his blows had not done sufficient damage, he lifted the cane and swung it. The wooden walking stick struck the boy's forehead, sending his body flying backwards as it hit the wooden deck with a thud.

The savagery of the beating was too much to handle. As the old man lifted the cane to continue his beating, I felt the muscles in my legs tighten, and I, seemingly involuntarily, began to stand erect.

"What the hell are you doing?" Simon whispered as he frantically pulled me back into a sitting position. But it was too late.

The old man, noticing my sudden movement, looked at me as he wiped his blood splattered cane on the boy's tattered shirt.

"You got a problem boy?" he asked, his slurred words smacked of contempt and disgust.

I sat motionless as my chest began to slowly expand, my breathing becoming deeper as I struggled to control my emotions.

Simon, recognizing my transformation spoke, "No Massa. He ain't got no problem. He just feelin' sorry for the boy, considerin' he a cripple and all. He ain't got no problem. No sir.'"

The old man continued his laser-like focus without acknowledging Simon's plea.

"I can't hear you boy," he added while continuing to hobble toward us. "Did you have something you wanted to say?"

I looked on, unable to hear his words, my chest and hands beginning to slowly tighten. As he took each step, I began to visualize numerous ways I could instantly bring him to his knees. A quick punch to the throat or a low kick to a knee could both permanently immobilize him. Before I knew it, he was standing on the elevated deck looking angrily into my eyes.

My nose wrinkled as his breath painfully emitted a combined smell of alcohol and rotten flesh. Grabbing my arm, he calmly yet forcefully repeated his slurred threat, "I see someone is going to have to teach you to mind yo business boy."

As he lifted his cane my fist tightened in preparation for the fatal blow when Ms. Carter interrupted.

"Mr. Norris. How dare you lift a hand to my man. You will release him immediately!"

The old man released his grip on my arm and looked at Ms. Carter then at Simon.

"By what authority would you strike another man's property?" demanded Ms. Carter.

"Your property here seems to be overly concerned about my retarded nigger. It looks like his lady owner hasn't taught him how to properly conduct himself in front of a white man. I should have known he was one of your uppity niggers."

"How I treat my 'uppity niggers' is none of your concern," she replied while looking down at the bloodied boy lying amidst the spilled goods. "And how you handle yours is of no concern of mine! Dante and Simon, please load up the supplies so we can leave Mr. Norris to his…business."

I looked over at Simon and watched as he slid the taser back under the buggy's wooden bench before hopping out and quickly loading the supplies. I looked around nervously before stepping down and assisting him. By now, a small group of townspeople had gathered to watch the spectacle. It was not until all the supplies were loaded that I noticed two of the slaves had managed to clean up the spilled goods and help the younger man to his feet. Despite the humiliating beating he had just endured, he looked up at me through squinted eyes and smiled. I returned the smile, but not before tears began to well up in my eyes. I turned away from Simon and Ms. Carter, wiping my eyes with the backs of my fists.

"What kind of a man would beat an innocent boy?" I thought while again wiping my face with my shirt sleeve. I climbed into the front seat of the of the buggy as Simon slid in next to me. Grabbing the reins and with a whip of the leather straps, the horses jolted forward.

"Head south out of town Simon. We can go the long way back and cross over boggy creek," explained Ms. Carter.

"Good idea. I think we've had enough excitement for one day."

***

We left town from the opposite side from where we entered and traveled in what appeared to be parallel to the town. After several minutes, we arrived at Boggy Creek. It was not quite dark, but the sun was quickly beginning to set when Simon announced a brief stop to rest and water the horses.

I took advantage of the break by quickly hopping down and walking down to the water's edge. Splashing cool water on my face, I used my open palms to wash away the dirt and dry tear stains. Simon casually strolled down to the water's edge and dipped a metal cup into the clear water. After taking a long drink, he offered the cup to me. I dipped the cup and quickly drank several cups of the cool water.

"What happened back there?" Simon asked. "I told you to keep your eyes down and mind your business."

"I don't know," I replied before pausing. "I thought I was prepared. I figured I would see some slaves being humiliated but I didn't anticipate anything like that." I paused to collect myself. "I have a cousin, Daryl, who was born with Down syndrome. He is s a couple of years older than me and kids have always given him a hard time. They have done some pretty shitty things to him and his classmates. When I saw that boy and his face, I saw my cousin and I just couldn't take it." I again splashed water on my face in an attempt to hide the tears welling up inside of me.

"I understand," said Simon as he tossed a rock in the creek. "Some of the things you're going to see here will make you sick to your stomach. Back home, it might be one person or a couple of bullies. But here, the majority of society is backwards, and it is going to take some time for them to change. You can't go punching every old guy in the throat."

I turned to look at Simon, "How did you know I was going for the throat?" I asked in amazement.

Simon laughed, "The guy was begging for it. Besides, that's what I would have done."

I let out a big sigh and immediately started laughing.

"It's going to take every ounce of your being to ignore that insult or to look the other way when you see an act or hear a negative comment," Simon explained. "But think about the millions of good people, both black and white, living here now. They do it daily. Like them, you are going to have to find a way to bottle it up. Push it deep down inside of you. Then, when the time is right, you are going to get a chance to unleash all that you have worked so hard to bottle up. Then, someone like that guy is gonna feel it. I remember when..."

Simon paused for a moment, looking at the tree line behind the buggy. Motioning for me to be quiet, he signaled for me to follow him back to the buggy.

"I remember swimming in a creek just like this as a boy," he continued while reaching under the buggy seat and pulling out his 9mm. With his index finger pressed against his lips he signaled for Ms. Carter to be quiet.

"Man, the hours we'd spend swimming and fishing,." Walking casually around the wagon he was now within an arm's length of the first row of trees lining the forest's edge. "The stories I could tell you," he continued.

As he got to the first tree, he pulled back the slide, making the distinct 'click' sound indicating a bullet was now loaded in the chamber.

"I'll give you three seconds to come out or I'll start shooting. One, two..."

"Wait! Don't shoot mister. We're coming out," said a soft voice from behind the tree.

Simon stepped back; gun still locked in on whatever was preparing to step out from the woods. Peering through the wagon wheel I watched as two young black girls emerged from the tree line. One appeared to be about my age while the other was several years younger. They were obviously scared and, judging by their clothing and condition, hungry and cold.

"We don't want any trouble Mister," explained the older of the two girls. "We're looking for the Apple Mountain Plantation and a Ms. Carter."

Simon smiled wide as he pulled the gun's lever. Releasing it, the bolt clicked loudly before popping out a single bullet. With an extended hand he caught the stray bullet, flipped the safety switch, and slid the pistol innocently into the waist of his pants.

"Welcome ladies," Simon said through a warm smile. "May I introduce you to Ms. Carter of the Apple Mountain Plantation."

The two girls stood motionless, frozen in disbelief as they looked up at Ms. Carter sitting above them on the carriage. Sliding down from the buggy, Ms. Carter opened up her arms and fully embraced the two now emotional young girls. Both sobbed quietly as they embraced the matriarch. I watched as even Simon stood misty eyed as the two young girls finally felt safe to release the emotions they had likely struggled to bottled up.

"My name is Jamaya and this is my sister, Briana," explained the older of the two.

We sat quietly as she began to wipe the tears from her eyes. Briana continued to cling to Ms. Carter, however Jamaya looked around nervously from under the wide brimmed hat. Although slender and petite, the extra clothing successfully camouflaged her identity. Rather than two young black girls walking along the tree line, a casual glance from an unsuspecting passerby would have likely seen a young man leading a sibling to or from an assigned chore. Pulling the hat off and holding it awkwardly in front of her, she continued.

"We belong to a Mister Theodore Lewis of Alabama. It was almost a week ago Sunday that we left," she began while speaking softly. "Our sister, Debra, was teaching us some arithmetic when Master Lewis's stepsons came calling. They'd been pawing at Debra for weeks but Mr. Lewis' only son, Thomas, set them straight. Almost beat one of them to death on account of things he had been saying and the way he'd been acting toward Debra. But this time, Thomas had gone to town for supplies and they knew it. They beat on the door of our house, demanding she allow them to come in. We were all scared, so she made the two of us go out back before she'd let them in,

'I'll come looking for you once they're gone,' she promised.

After almost two hours, we went back to the cabin. By then, Thomas had returned, and judging by the condition of the room, something bad happened while we was gone. It was the next day that Debra decided it was time to leave.

"This will never end Thomas," she cried "and next time it's going to be one of them."

Thomas sat quietly before ultimately agreeing with her. It was that evening when we decided it was time to head north."

"We were all supposed to leave that night, but something happened. Richard, an older slave who told stories about the slaves who had successfully made the journey north, was picked to guide us. The plan was that we would leave first, then, in all the commotion, Debra and a few others would follow. We left Birmingham that night and made it as far as Huntsville. We kept out of sight that night and by morning found an abandoned house. It had only been a day and he had already began getting too friendly with Briana. I shouldn't have left her with him but I needed to find food and water. When I came back, I found that dog on top of her. That's when I introduced him to Bessie."

She pulled a large meat cleaver from her sack and held it out for us to see. "I swung for his head but caught him deep in his shoulder. While he lay on the ground screaming, we took flight following Debra's instruction to follow the North Star. Unfortunately, it was cloudy that night. That, combined with the darkness, lead to us quickly getting lost.

"We eventually found our way to Murfreesboro Tennessee. That was four days ago. Since then, we survived by stealing food and relying on the kindness of nice folks, both black and white. One slave mentioned a slave owner by the name of Ms. Jackie Carter near Franklin. About this time yesterday, we set out to find her when we discovered a poster announcing our escape and the reward."

"I saw a copy of that poster," I said interrupting. "Victor, in the stables, was reading a wanted poster describing two runaway girls."

"Somebody sure is going to a lot of trouble to find you two young ladies," added Simon.

"Well, it's of little consequence," said Ms. Carter, attempting to change the subject. "You two brave women are safe with us now. Please, hop in the buggy. It's nearly dark, but we will be home shortly."

Simon lifted the girls up into the buggy and positioned the supplies safely around them. He and I climbed in the front seat and encouraged Big Jake and Peanut to get moving. We traveled most of the evening until we came to the creek and started our way up the hill passing the Apple Orchard Plantation sign. Although it was not my home, it felt good to be back in the confines of the plantation.

# Six

# Abduction

I soared through the air while peering down at the barely recognizable court below. From the elevated location, everyone in the auditorium looked like ants scurrying around the parquet floor. Palming the ball, I descended on the rim like an eagle pouncing on its prey before slamming the ball through the iron rim. The force of the monster dunk colliding with the seemingly indestructible backboard caused the tempered glass to instantly shatter into thousands of pieces. The wooden floor cracked and splintered as I landed with a thud atop the glass shards. The crowd, momentarily silenced by my unsuspecting dunk, roared their approval.

Looking at the awestruck referee, I handed him the mangled rim before walking over to Jennifer, the head cheerleader. After a series of flips and summersaults, she landed, legs straddled around my waist and arms draped around my neck. I looked at her as our lips locked and......

"Wait, I don't play basketball," I thought as I began desperately feeling on the lumpy feather filled mattress beneath me. "This must be a... dream,"

Laying there, eyes closed, I began to feel a sensation or feeling that someone was watching me. Opening one eye slowly, I immediately saw her.  It was a smiling Yolanda looking down at me.

"Good morning!" she said with a large grin.

"Can I help you?" I asked while closing my eyes in an attempt to seem unmoved by the intrusion.

"Nope, just waiting for you to get up, but it looks like….I'm a little late," she said while pointing to my uncovered body.

"Uh, excuse me!" I said reaching for the blanket. "Have you ever heard of knocking?"

"I did, but you didn't say anything, so I decided to come in," explained Yolanda.

"How long have you been standing there?" I asked while frantically trying to get dressed under the blanket.

"Long enough… who is Jennifer? Is that someone you fancy?"

"No, well… kind of, Jennifer is…where is Simon?" I asked uncomfortably.

"He and Ms. Carter went for a ride. She gave me very specific instructions to keep an eye on you.".

"I don't think she meant for you to watch me sleep in my underwear," I replied.

"Why, are you embarrassed to have someone look at you in your under garments? I just couldn't imagine how that might feel," she replied with mock astonishment.

"Oh…because the night I met you, I…ok…I get it. Look, I am sorry about that. I feel like an idiot. It's just," I said, looking away, "I've never seen anyone as…as…pretty as you. Where I am from, girls don't…don't…well, they don't look like you. At least none that speak to me."

Yolanda smiled, unfazed by my confession.

"It's ok. Ms. Carter told me to take care of your breakfast then bring you with me while I see to my chores. Get dressed and I'll make sure everything is ready." Yolanda extended her hand.

"Truce?" she asked.

I looked at her extended hand for a moment before extending mine.

"Truce," I replied. As she turned to walk away, I noticed she was wearing another cotton dress however this one was form fitting, exaggerating her narrow waste and full athletic build. I watched as she gracefully walked out of the room and into the hallway. Swinging my legs over the edge of the bed I started to stand but realized I might need a few more minutes before I was ready to head downstairs.

***

After getting dressed I made my way down to the dining room. Once again, the halls were bustling with workers coming in and out of rooms. Some were carrying laundry and linens, while others carried cleaning tools and metal buckets. Entering the dining room, I found a table set for one but nothing or no one else was present. I walked through the large swinging doors and into the large kitchen where I found Yolanda busily preparing food and placing it neatly on a platter.

"Go sit down. I'll bring the food in there," she instructed.

Pushing through the doors, I collapsed into one of the chairs positioned neatly around the long wooden table. Yolanda followed with a platter and a small metal kettle. After placing the platter on the table, she poured freshly brewed coffee into a small ceramic cup.

"Eggs, ham, and biscuits? Did you do this?" I asked in amazement.

"Yes. Ms. Crabtree had some errands to run, so I told her I didn't mind doing it."

"Wow, this is really good. I feel like I haven't eaten in days...I mean weeks," I added while greedily cramming a biscuit into my mouth.

Yolanda smiled as she watched me devour the food.

"How did you learn to cook like this?"

"My mother, she used to do all of the cooking before Ms. Crabtree came."

"Wow, does she still work here? I'd love to meet her."

"No, she died three years ago while helping some children trapped in a burning building. She got the last one out before the building collapsed on her. Everyone said she was a hero."

"Wow. I'm sorry to hear that but she sounds like an amazing person."

"She was an amazing...no...a perfect mother. I wouldn't have changed anything about her. But Ms. Carter has been incredibly kind to me. I have known her as long as I can remember. After my mother died, she took real good care of me. Made sure I could read and write, even taught me arithmetic. I know it sounds weird, considering she's white and all, but it's like she's my mother."

"Trust me, I can understand more than you could ever imagine," I responded.

Yolanda smiled as she grabbed a cloth napkin and wiped the corner of my mouth. Gently grasping my hand, she began running her finger along my palm. Rather than the long neatly painted nails the girls at school wore, her hands were scarred while her nails were neatly trimmed but short.

"Your hands, they're softer than any I've ever seen before," Yolanda said, surprised.

I tried to pull them away, but she quickly grabbed them tightly.

"Don't be embarrassed," she said as she continued to rub her fingers across my open palms. "They're soft, not as soft as your feet, but soft," she said laughing.

"Oh man, I don't believe this, you saw my feet?"

"Yes, while you were sleeping. Besides these on your arms, you do not have any cuts or scars anywhere on your body."

Yolanda reached out to push up my partially rolled up sleeves.

"How did these happen?" she asked with a curious expression on her face.

"Oh…that…It was a friend's cat," I said while frantically trying to cover up my self-inflicted wounds.

"It must have been a mountain lion to make scars like that," she replied.

"Mountain Lion? You are funny. I have some scars that look like I was attacked by a grizzly bear," I replied, attempting to change the subject.

"Right here on my knee, I was riding…well… I fell down. And here on my finger, I was chasing my sister when she slammed the door on my finger. See…I have scars." I raised my hand to display the small scar on my hand.

"More like a grizzly bear cub. Those are baby scars. Look! This is a burn I got picking up a hot pot sitting over a fire. This was a cut I got while sharpening an axe, and this," she said, pulling up her dress and exposing her inner thigh, "This is one I got climbing over a wired fence. And this one…."

"Ok…Ok… you definitely have me beat on scars. Maybe one of us is a little clumsier than the other," I said before laughing.

"Maybe," Yolanda replied as she playfully pushed me. "Are you ready to help me with my chores?"

"Sure…let's go."

We spent the remaining hours of the morning and all of the afternoon zigzagging across the plantation as Yolanda checked the progress of several projects. Everything from those assigned to wash laundry, to those unloading the last of the supplies purchased the previous day. As we passed through the kitchen, Yolanda stopped to discuss some details with Ms. Crabtree.

I looked across the room and saw Jamaya chopping vegetables. Yolanda was still talking to the cook, so I decided to walk over and check on her.

"Hey, you're looking much better today," I said.

Jamaya turned around, revealing a smile from ear to ear.

Without the over-sized coat and the large hat, I quickly noticed she was kind of cute. In fact, looking at her more closely she was very pretty.

"Dante," she said while hugging me tightly. "Yes, I'm doing much better, thanks to you and Mr. Simon."

"It looks like Ms. Carter has you busy here in the kitchen."

"Yes, she assigned Briana and I jobs until we're ready to start heading north. I'm in the kitchen and Briana's out back helping with the laundry. She thought it be best if we worked separately so as not to attract any undue attention.

"Have you seen Ms. Carter this afternoon?"

"No, I haven't. Is everything ok?" I asked.

"Well,,,there was this man, I think his name was Jeb. He came by asking a lot of questions. Who we are and where we're from. I didn't know what to say, so I told him we're visiting with you and Mr. Simon. He kept asking questions until Ms. Crabtree ran him off."

"Hmmm…that's interesting. I was just on my way to see Ms. Carter. I'll be sure to let her know."

"Thanks Dante," Jamaya added as she again gave me another hug.

"Am I interrupting something?" Yolanda asked abruptly as she walked up.

"Uh, no. I was just catching up with Jamaya. I hadn't seen her since we made it back yesterday."

"That's nice," Yolanda said through a forced smile, "but I'm sure Jamaya needs to get back to work. Don't you girl?"

"Yes ma'am. I'm sorry," replied Jamaya as she lowered her eyes and began furiously chopping vegetables.

"Come on," Yolanda instructed while pulling me toward the door. "I want to show you something."

"Sure," I said as we walked away. I looked back at Jamaya and waved. She smiled briefly before quickly returning to her assigned task.

Yolanda led me out of the house and down the hill.

"You like her, don't you?" she asked with a tone that smacked of jealousy while at the same time bordered on accusatory.

"Who?" I asked confused.

"That colored runaway," she spat through that same forced smile.

I laughed. "I just met her yesterday, but what's not to like? They have to be two of the toughest people I've ever met. They left their home and family, escaped their owner, and fought off an attacker."

"Anyone can run! Some of us stay and fight to make a life here," replied Yolanda.

"Is that why you're still here, staying to fight for equality and justice?"

"Maybe. Ms. Carter lets me help teach the girls about cooking and taking care of the house. I have a job here. People know and respect me," she replied while talking to no one in particular. "I've thought about leaving, going north, but I'm not sure where I'd even go. The world ain't kind to black folks, especially black women."

"Do you have any family, maybe a father or siblings?" I asked.

"Since my momma died, I don't have any family. She told me my daddy was a runaway. He stayed here but eventually left when I was a baby. I don't know if he's dead or alive. Sometimes, I think about leaving to find him and any family that might be out there, but Ms. Carter is good to me, almost like a mother. She helps out anyone that needs it."

"Like Jamaya and Briana."

"Yes, like those two runaways."

"Why do you say it like that? It's like they've done something to you, but that's impossible because you just met them."

"I don't have anything against them, it's just...they're runaways. They probably worked in the fields picking cotton or rice. They don't know anything, and you can't teach them anything. White people look at them and think we're all dumb runaway slaves."

"I can't believe you're saying that. They are black just like you and me. Many, like Victor, want to learn. They just need a little help."

"You sound just like Ms. Carter. She thinks everyone wants to learn. She's always saying, "One day Negroes are going to be free. It is the responsibility of those that can, to teach those that cannot.' I just don't see any reason for field niggers to learn to read and write."

I thought about the upcoming Civil War and the eventual 13th Amendment that would free slaves, resulting in thousands migrating north. Or for some who might choose to stay behind and start their own communities or share crop with their former owners. I also thought about the deceit and manipulation that would result largely due to the fact that many blacks simply would not know any better.

"Ms. Carter is right. The abolitionist movement is changing people's minds and hearts. Have you heard of the book, "Uncle Tom's Cabin"?

"Yes. By Harriet Beecher Stowe. Ms. Carter read it to me."

"People like Ms. Stowe and Fredrick Douglass are making a difference and changing people's minds. The time is coming when people like you and I are going to be called upon. Where I am from, everyone..."

Yolanda, detecting the pause in my voice, looked at me as if waiting for me to finish my thought.

"Where I'm from.... life is very similar to everything going on here. Even though we are all black people, we look at and treat each other differently. But those differences should not separate us. It should help us come together."

Yolanda paused as if pondering my impromptu sermon.

"Ok...maybe. Maybe you and Ms. Carter are right. I just know most white people are going to fight with everything they got to keep black people on their farms," she expressed confidently.

We turned off the path and started walking through a small cluster of apple trees. I had seen the same trees just two days earlier, but almost overnight, they were fully in bloom. The aromatic buds filled the cool spring air.

Yolanda reached down and gently grabbed my hand.

"Sometimes, when I am having a bad day or I am thinking about my momma, I come down here. It is where I go when I want to get away. We used to come down here in the spring and have picnics. She'd teach me to read or tell me stories. Then, in the fall we'd pick apples and bake pies."

"As a word fitly spoken is like apples of gold in a setting of silver."

"What's that?" asked Yolanda.

"It's a Proverb, from the Bible. I remember reading it once," I explained.

Yolanda smiled. "A bible proverb? That is what I am talking about. Your bible quotes, the good you see in people, and your hands." She pulled my hand close to her and again ran her fingers along my palm. "Your baby soft hands. I've never met anyone like you before." She kissed the back of my hand, then my palm before leaning in, pressing her body against mine.

"You're special," she whispered. I looked in her eyes and for the first time, realized her long dark eyelashes were hiding beautiful hazel-colored eyes. Smelling the sweet floral perfume and feeling her soft body pressed against mine began to stir up feelings. Feelings much like those I had experienced the previous morning when we first met.

She moved my hands to where they were now cupping her backside before playfully running her index finger around my lips.

"Do you want to kiss me?" she whispered.

Images of Jennifer flashed in my mind, however having Yolanda there physically in front of me immediately numbed those thoughts. Looking in her eyes I nodded slowly.

The corner of her mouth curled into a tiny mischievous smile. Then, without warning, she kissed me. We stood there looking at each other for a moment as her playful smiled returned. She put her arms around my neck, leaned in and again firmly pressed her lips against mine.

For the next few minutes, we stood there, tightly wrapped in each other's arms until I heard a cough.

Spinning around I quickly found Simon and Ms. Carter standing nearby, awkwardly looking anywhere except in our direction.

"We were just… talking…talking about.…apples," I explained while awkwardly pointing to the blossoming trees.

I could instantly tell from Simon's expression that something was wrong. "What is it?" I asked.

"It's Jamaya and Briana," replied Simon, "They're missing."

***

The sun was starting to set, but I could tell we were getting close. Simon explained that shortly after he and Ms. Carter returned from their ride, they found a flustered Ms. Crabtree waiting for them on the porch. After apologizing for the delay connected with dinner, she explained that Jamaya had abandoned her job assignment. According to Ms. Crabtree, "She just disappeared."

Simon and Jackie both thought it was odd, so they went out back to see if her sister had seen her. The girls washing laundry reported that hours earlier Victor and Jamaya had come looking for the young girl. Apparently Victor's father had instructed him to bring Jamaya and Briana to the barn. From there he and Simon were planning to take the sisters into town.

Simon and Ms. Carter hurried to the barn only to find Victor there alone grooming the horses.

Surprised to see Simon, Victor explained his father and a new slave Jeb, took the girls to meet Simon in town. By then the plot was clear. Jim and Jeb were taking the girls to town, not to meet Simon, but to claim the reward. It was shortly thereafter that Simon and Ms. Carter found Yolanda and I in the apple orchard.

We decided we could more easily track the four on foot rather than on horseback. As a result, for the last hour we'd been running through the dense forest, leaping over creeks and dry riverbeds in pursuit of the girls and their abductors.

After traveling about 3 or 4 miles Simon lifted his hand and made a fist instructing me to stop. Although we took a knee, my chest swelled rapidly in response to the rapid pace we had maintained over the last hour.

Never a fan of long-distance running, I thought back to the intense cardio workouts Simon introduced to our regular regimen over the last two months and realized they had paid off this today.

I inhaled deeply and followed with a cautiously quiet exhale, then repeated the process several times while listening intently.

With my eyes closed, I concentrated on clearing out the indigenous noise, birds chirping, the creek's water gurgling as it flowed through the creek bed. I took another deep breath and exhaled slowly, clearing out those natural noises, and focusing on any foreign sounds, I opened my eyes, it was laughter.

The images were not yet visible, but the unmistakable sound of deep unbridled laughter filled the forest. Simon turned, and, judging by his expression, he'd heard the same sound. With a pointed finger swirling in the air, he signaled for me to circle around the location of the laughter. Pointing to his eyes then himself, he instructed me to be alert and wait for his signal. I started moving slowly to the right, making sure not to inadvertently sound an alarm to the abductors.

Making my way around them, I positioned myself on the opposite side of Simon. From my new vantage point I could now make out the scene unfolding in front of me.

The girls were sitting behind a large fallen pine tree. I could barely make out the tops of their heads, but from Simon's viewpoint, he could almost certainly see the girls as they squatted behind the tree while Jim and Jeb sat on top of another fallen trunk.

"Praise the lawd! A fifty-dollar reward. Twenty-five dollars each," Jeb exclaimed as he slapped his knee.

Jim, not amused by Jeb's calculations, paused as he looked at him.

"Nigger yu's a fool," spat Jim. "You can't read o write. Hell, you ain't no more than a dumb runaway yourself. She not gonna pay you nothing. Old man Norris is gonna pay her, then she gonna pay me! But considering Ima jenrus man," he continued, "I'll give you twenty dollars."

Looking down at the two girls, he smiled and added, "And I'll even let you pick which one we enjoy first."

Jeb looked up at Jim, studying him while he considered the proposal. After a few tense moments, his smile returned.

"You got yurself a deal," he replied while shaking hands with Jim. Looking down at the two girls he smiled as he pulled a long knife out of his boot. "Which one of you girlies want Uncle Jeb to show you a real good time?"

Jamaya stood up, wielding a baseball-bat-sized log. Swinging the log loosely, she issued a warning, "You come any closer to either of us, and I'll keep swinging until one of us ain't moving no more."

Jeb turned around and looked at Jim before both erupted in laughter. Ramming the metal blade into the fallen tree trunk he looked at the younger of the two girls with wide excited eyes.

Extending his hand to the young girl he smiled as he reached out to caress her but before he could get close, Jamaya, fulfilling her threat, swung the log making full contact with the back of his head sending dozens of rotten splinters falling to the forests' floor.

The force of the blow left the large man temporarily stunned before toppling to his knees.

Jamaya quickly returned to her sister's side, huddling just out of my line of sight.

Based on the force of the blow I was confident it would, at a minimum, leave him unconscious for a few minutes. Jeb, apparently stunned by the blow, remained on his knees for a moment before he began to laugh. What began as a low chuckle of sorts, quickly turned into a deep sinister laugh.

"It looks like this yella nigger is playin hard to get," Jim said before joining in the laughter. Jeb stood, shaking off the fog caused by the strike. Turning toward the girls, he smiled as he began to take off his tattered flannel shirt.

Jeb was not a young man but his scar-covered back reminded me not only of the beatings he had endured but the reality of a life of hard physical labor. I instantly began scanning his body for a weakness before focusing on his leg. Despite his size and obvious strength, I noticed as he approached the girls that he was walking with a noticeable limp.

Tossing his shirt aside, he pulled the boot knife from the fallen tree.

"Now, don't you go bein no dam fool," Jim quipped as he snatched the knife from him. "Old man Norris and his girlie ain't paying for no dead runaways. Besides, we don't need no knife for little baby girls," he said before slamming the knife deep into the fallen tree. "I got something that's gonna work much betta."

"I heard you gentleman were looking for me," Simon announced calmly as he strolled into the clearing, hands out and palms up.

The two men, caught off guard by the impromptu entrance, nervously looked at each other with confused expressions.

"Hello Simon. Yessir, we sho was looking for you. Wes headed to town to get some new clothes and shoes for these here youngins. We were waiting on you but Misses told us to get to town before it got late," Jim explained as he slowly began walking toward Simon.

"Is that so Jim. Ms. Carter and I found Victor. He told us you made him bring those girls to you. What are you planning to do, turn them in? You're gonna send those girls to a life of death for two hundred dollars," Simon asked.

"What the hell is he talking about, Jim?" screamed Jeb. "You said the reward was fifty dollars, and you were going to give me twenty," screamed a now irate Jeb.

"Shut up you dumb nigger. Can't you see he's lying, trying to make us turn on each other? And you," he said, turning his attention back to Simon, "you just a smart-ass ol house nigger. Running Ms. Carters errands like a little dog. I got news for you. I ain't never going back to that place!"

"What about your son, he looks up to you. You're all he has," replied Simon.

"That stupid nigger ain't no kin of mine. Sure, I laid down wit his momma, but he wasn't mine. I shoulda killed him... like

I'm 'bout to kill you," he said while pulling out a small knife from the waist of his pants.

Jeb, seeing Jim pull out his knife, began feeling around in his boot in an apparent attempt to locate his blade.

Then, without warning, Jim charged. Simon stepped back, watching the futile swings aimlessly slice through air before identifying an opening. Grabbing Jim's hand, Simon twisted his wrist prompting his upper torso to lean forward just low enough for Simon to unleash a powerful front kick. Jim's head snapped back in response to the impact. Crimson blood oozed from the center of his face as he sat there momentarily dazed by the blow. Not letting up the pressure, Simon delivered several quick jabs to his face. The sound of raw flesh colliding echoed through the peaceful forest. Still holding his wrist, Simon fell backwards and placed Jim's fully extended arm between his legs. Jim screamed in pain as Simon leaned back and pulled the arm in an unnatural direction. The bone and muscle silently breaking in response to Simon's hyperextending armbar.

Jeb continued scrambling for his knife until he too heard Jim's momentary silence followed by bloodcurdling screams of agony. He looked on in silence as Jim writhed in pain cradling his unnaturally bent arm, unsure if he should or could help undo the visible damage inflicted.

That was my cue. Running into the clearing I vaulted over the fallen tree, landing feet first on the large man's knee. Bone and cartilage cracked as Jeb's leg buckled under the force of my lunge.

Jeb screamed in pain before falling to the ground clutching his contorted leg.

Crouching in a defensive position I sat patiently waiting for a counterattack.

Laying there in pain Jeb cursed and screamed as he attempted to stand before again collapsing to the ground. Reaching into a small leather pouch dangling from a strap around his neck he took a pinch and placed the brown colored substance between his cheek and the back side of his mouth. With bloodshot eyes peering through me he clutched the tree next to him and, defying logic, slowly began to pull himself upright.

Although not fully erect, he was still a massive figure standing in front of me. In an attempt to finish off the now injured man I charged, once again focusing my attention on his weakened leg. Despite his injury, he easily brushed off my attack and returned a wide arching blow to my temple. The hit sent me falling sideways away from the girls still huddling by the fallen tree.

Seizing on my miscalculation, Jeb immediately collapsed on top of me. I could feel his large hands reaching for my neck, but each time I was able to twist free from his grip. After multiple attempts, he eventually succeeded in wrapping his large, calloused hands around my throat.

I fought furiously to try and pry his fingers loose, but it was futile. With his grip tightening, brown colored saliva dripping from his devilish smile, and his hot breath radiating off my face, he stared into my eyes and appeared to enjoy the spectacle of my life slowly slipping away. I continued to fight however my body slowly began to weaken as I struggled to breathe until I noticed Jeb's expression instantly change.

Eyes once enraged and focused, now doubled in size, while his mouth opened partially as if to say something, but no words came out. Those once powerful hands quickly loosened their grip, allowing me to inhale deeply. Then, those same inflamed eyes slowly rolled back in his head before he took one last gasp. With a blank stare, his body slumped as he collapsed on top of me.

I immediately began pushing against his lifeless body, intent on sliding from under his weight. Once my upper body was free, I rolled his body from atop mine. Peering up I could see, standing behind him was a stoic Jamaya.

The blank expression on her face prompted me to look down at Jeb's lifeless body. It was then that I located the knife he had been desperately searching for. Wedged deep in his back, midway between his shoulder blades, amongst the raised gnarly and scarred skin, protruded his boot knife.

Placing her foot on his bare back, she grabbed the long narrow blade with two hands and pulled it from his lifeless body. After wiping the bloody blade on his flannel shirt she tucked it in the fold of her dress and scampered back to her sister.

I walked over to Simon who was now standing over the crying and whimpering Jim.

"What do we do with him?" I asked.

"Take the girls and start heading back to the plantation," replied Simon.

"Why, what are you going to do?" I asked.

"Take the girls, start heading back, I'll catch up," Simon said without looking at me.

"He's gonna kill me boy! Please don't let him kill me," Jim whimpered.

Looking at Jeb's lifeless body then at Jim laying on the ground cradling his contorted arm, I realized Simon was right, it was time to head back. With that, I gathered the girls, left the clearing, and began the trek back to the plantation. As we walked through the forest we continued to hear Jim's frantic screams for mercy.

The pleas got more and more frantic until suddenly the calmness of the forest returned.

We continued in that silence on the same path for the next two hours. Simon eventually caught up with us as he resumed navigating us through the dark forest while walking in silence. At that point, there was nothing that really needed to be said. We knew what had just happened.

I immediately recognized there was mercy to be extended to white people. After all, an argument could be made that they didn't fully understand their actions. The beatings, the violence, those abuses had existed for hundreds of years. But for a black person to knowingly betray, assault, and attempt to enslave another black person, it went beyond any consideration for mercy. After all, how could they ever again be trusted? After his crime and ultimate admission, he could not stay amongst his people. And there was no court or judicial system for treacherous slaves. There was no alternate solution, he had to die and surprisingly, I was ok with it.

My thoughts then turned to Jamaya and her sister. I watched as she walked closely alongside Briana tightly clutching her hand. If I did not know it before, I knew it now, they were in danger. If their captors hadn't known about their whereabouts, it wouldn't be long until they were located. They needed to keep moving north.

Thinking through the day's events, I also thought about Victor. He had spoken proudly of his father and the trusted position he had earned with Ms. Carter. How would he take the news of his father's denial and later execution in connection with his betrayal?

My mind raced with questions, then stalled as I struggled to find sufficient answers.

# Seven

# Due North

By the time we got back to the plantation the sun had long since set. Looking out over the valley surrounding the plantation I watched as once again, small fires illuminated the small slave homes.

Walking past the main house we escorted the sisters to their cabin. Each home was designed with three small bunk-styled beds to accommodate several individuals or a large-sized family. The building occupied by the girls was empty allowing them to utilize the entire cabin's space. As Jamaya tucked Briana into her bed, Simon focused on building up the dwindling fire for the night. I watched as she gently pulled the blankets up over her sister and whispered what I imagined was a prayer or words of encouragement.

She had been strong over the course of the last week. Listening to her older sister, fleeing their home, defending her younger sister and even, in the end, defending me, all took an immense amount of courage. I had recognized something special about her when we first met however now I looked at her with even more admiration.

Jamaya walked across the room and lit the oil lamp sitting on the window ledge. I watched as the soft light of the lamp shined gently on her caramel-colored skin. A single tear fell from her eye as she quickly wiped it away.

"What's wrong?" I asked.

"Nothing. I'm fine," she replied, turning her back to me.

"Really, you can trust me," I said.

"I just can't help but think there might be others out there. People trying to take us back to Alabama. What if more come? What if they come back or someone else comes?"

I had not thought about that. Certainly, by now everyone had connected the wanted posters with the two girls. What would stop them from coming in the middle of the night?

"What if I stayed with you tonight? I can sleep in a separate bunk and I'll be sure to leave before anyone sees me in the morning."

"Are you sure? I don't want to cause any problems with you and Ms. Yolanda. I'm just worried about my sister."

"It's not a problem. And Yolanda and I are just friends. Besides, you saved my life," I said with a smile. "I kind of owe you. Let me talk with Simon."

I went outside to update Simon and he immediately agreed it was a good idea.

"The likelihood of an abduction attempt tonight is fairly small," explained Simon, "but I'm sure they will sleep better knowing someone was close by. Take these." Simon handed me his switchblade style knife and a small taser. "You be sure to get some rest," Simon said with a smile. "We need to talk about getting those girls moving north as soon as possible."

"What are you implying?" I said pushing him.

Simon laughed, "Just get some sleep. That's all."

"You be sure you get some rest," I replied as he started his way up the hill.

Simon held up his hands as if saying, "You got me."

I laughed as I turned and walked back into the shack, "Get some sleep?"

By the time I returned, Jamaya had already climbed into the bed above Briana. I turned off the lantern and began stoking the fire. Shifting the logs, I could faintly see the two girls lying peacefully in the beds across the room.

I stood over the fire, warming my hands until the warm flames reminded me how desperately my body needed rest. Collapsing into the bed farthest from the girls I kicked off my boots and tightly clasped the knife in one hand and the taser in the other. Leaning back I thought about the day's activities. The abduction, the fight and the eventual killing of the two men. I played over in my mind the expression Jeb displayed the moment his life ended and that last gasp of air as his body slumped lazily against mine.

I'd seen movies and played video games depicting death, but nothing seemed to compare with being present when a man took his last breath. Then I thought about Jamaya and Briana.

What might have happened to them had we not caught them in time? If Simon and Ms. Carter had not found Yolanda and I in the orchard, they definitely would have made it to town.

"Oh my god, Yolanda!" I thought. With all of the excitement I had forgotten about her. The time we spent throughout the day, the kiss, she was probably looking for me right now. How would I explain this evening?

My mind wondered for the next few minutes, thinking about the day and what it might take to get the girls to safety. I had momentarily drifted off to sleep when I heard a thud. Something had fallen on the wooden plank floor.

Clutching the knife in one hand and the taser in the other, I slid from the bed and crouched next to it while surveying the room. Pausing long enough to allow my eyes to adjust to the dimly lit room, I could see a slim figure walking slowly toward me, the long nightgown flowing with each step. The figure stopped in front of me and I immediately recognized it was Jamaya.

I started to speak, but she gently pressed her index finger to my lips. Untying the string on her nightgown it fell innocently to the floor before climbing into the bed. Pulling me towards her she kissed me softly.

"Hold me," she whispered.

Thinking about the evening we had just experienced and the fact that this was likely the last moment I would spend in her company, my arms moved, almost involuntarily, as I held her tightly.

As the night proceeded, we both explored each other in ways I had only seen in movies or read about in books, but it was not like many guys described in the locker room. It was...different. Laying there in each other's arms we talked as we watched the fire dwindle down to where only a few embers faintly glowed in the fireplace.

Before I knew it, the orange glow of the morning sun slowly began to peek through the small windowpane. As quickly as the night had begun, it had quietly ended with me lying next to a peacefully sleeping Jamaya. Slipping out of the bed I carried my boots to the doorway and slipped them on.

There in the doorway I watched Briana and Jamaya resting quietly. I thought about the evening and wished I could climb back in the bed for just a few more minutes but the plantation would soon be up and hard at work, and the last thing Jamaya needed was to be seen with me leaving her room.

After a brief pause, I turned and stepped off the small porch. The sun was just starting to peak over the hillside. The result was a series of lingering shadows I could use to discreetly navigate my way back to the big house atop the hill. Halfway to the house I walked through the large field dividing the house and the smaller slave quarters. There was little activity in those early morning hours however I noticed several workers busily constructing a wooden structure. I paused long enough to watch as log by log, they appeared to be constructing something, possibly a building. It was odd however I continued navigating my way toward the house.

From atop the hill, I looked down and could better see the structure. It looked like a wooden pyramid with smaller brush and branches wedged in-between each log. "What could they be doing with that?" I thought before turning toward the house. A quick climb of the few steps and I was able to peek through the kitchen window.

The house was already busy with individuals bustling through the kitchen and dining room areas. I opened the door and took a deep breath. "Act as if you belong here," I thought as I closed the door behind me.

"Good morning," I mumbled as I passed Ms. Crabtree and a team of workers pounding dough into small balls. Walking around the large fire, I exhaled before pushing through the swinging double doors. After stepping into the dining room, I immediately saw her. It was Yolanda. She was sitting at the far end of the long table watching me as I entered the room.

I immediately cursed my luck for coming in the wrong entrance however, I quickly realized either way I was busted. She had strategically sat far enough in the room where had I entered through the front door, she would have seen me and by facing the swinging door she didn't have to move an inch to spot me. I quickly decided the best course was to play it cool.

"Good morning," I said through a nervous smile. "You're up early. Having problems sleeping?" I asked jokingly while reaching out to touch her hand only to be quickly rebuffed.

"How do you know I ever went to sleep?" she asked sarcastically. "Maybe I was so terrified that you and Simon were chasing two crazy men in the forest that I stayed up all night waiting for you to come back. Then, you could probably imagine someone that terrified might be surprised to see one of you walk up to the house by himself," she added, her voice becoming more and more intense. "And it's perfectly reasonable to imagine how someone might feel like a fool for crying over someone she thought was dead, only to discover he was very much alive."

"You stayed up all night waiting for me?" I asked confused.

"Of course I did, and I look like a fool. I waited all evening and when Simon came walking up to the house, all of us thought you were dead. "Then Simon tells us you're fine. Just answer me this, did you sleep with that... that...runaway?"

"Yolanda, you don't understand. They were frightened and worried. I just stayed the night to make them feel safe. I didn't stay with the intention of...."

"I was wrong about you. You're just like all these other good for nothing niggers!" she yelled through tearful eyes. "And you're a liar!" Yolanda stood and, while wiping her eyes, quickly stormed out of the dining room.

I stood there confused as to what just happened. "Should I run after her and explain what happened?" I thought. I kept looking at the door thinking she might come back and give me the chance to explain. After a couple of minutes I started to walk away when I heard footsteps in the kitchen. Turning I found two young girls peeking through the swinging doors. They giggled before quickly ducking back into the kitchen.

I smiled at the thought of how foolish I must have once again looked. Lingering for a moment longer, I realized the conversation could have ended much worse. Rather than push my luck, I slipped out of the dining room, made my way to the shared bedroom, and opened the door.

As I suspected the room was empty. Both beds were made up with no sign of Simon. Collapsing in the bed, I began to reflect on the last few days, the things I had seen and some things I have to take care of when I got back home.

Being away from my family had given me time to think about my family and relationships. Suddenly, the things that seemed to normally occupy my thoughts Jennifer, Marcus, even the things Justin and I frequently talked about, all seemed small in comparison to the challenges people here were facing. For better or worse, I had changed. I would eventually get back home and settle back into school, but I knew at that moment things for me would never be the same. My mind wandered until I once again drifted off to sleep.

***

"Hey Casanova, you gonna get up sometime today?" I opened one eye, not sure who might be staring down at me but smiled as I saw Simon sitting on the bed across from me.

"You're a sight for sore eyes," I said rolling over.

"Long night?" Simon asked, fighting back a smile.

"Not funny," I said. "And where were you this morning? I could have used a little help."

Oh…you must have bumped into Yolanda. I tried to get back in the room before you got back."

"No biggie, it wasn't your fault. She was staking me out. Either way I came into the house, she was ready for me. It was kind of creepy. I tried to explain, but she was not interested in hearing anything I had to say. What about you? It didn't look like you made it back last night either."

"Yeah, I stayed with Jackie, I mean, Ms. Carter last night," admitted Simon.

"What's up with you two? The feeding each other and those looks. What's the deal?"

Simon laughed, "Jackie and I have been seeing each other for a couple of years now. We can occasionally get together back home, but when we are here, there are some obvious challenges. So any time we can spend together when I'm passing through, we make it work."

"Wait, how do you guys communicate back home?" I asked.

"The same way you and your friends communicate, text messages and phones," Simon said, shaking his head.

"Look, as much as I would love to spend more time here, we need to get those girls moving north. They are not safe here. Jackie is throwing an End of Winter party to help create a diversion."

"What's that?" I asked.

"Several times a year local plantation owners allow their slaves to attend community galas or parties."

"Oh, that's why they were building the bonfire?" I asked.

"Yes. They will build the bonfire, have food and dancing. It is a perfect time for us to slip out. I figure we will head up to Kentucky and take them as far as Louisville. We have a contact there that will let them spend a day or two before helping them get to Indianapolis. Once we get them settled, we'll make our way back here, spend the night, then head back to Atlanta."

"Sounds like a plan. What do I need to do?" I asked.

"It's one in the afternoon now. Go to the stables and have the boy get the horses ready for departure. Once the fireworks begin, we'll make our way North."

Simon picked up his saddle bag and placed the taser and knife back into the deep pockets as he scanned the room for any remaining items. "For now, just blend in, mingle with everyone." We started walking down the long hallway as Simon continued his instructions. "We don't want to alert anyone to our plans." We stopped in front of a bedroom door on the opposite end of the house. "I'm going to go say my final goodbyes before we leave," Simon explained while pointing to the door. "Remember, blend in. I'll see you downstairs at the festival," he said as he slipped into Ms. Carter's room.

I mentally played back the instructions Simon had just given me. "Blend in, mingle, and get the horses ready." My thoughts quickly turned to Victor. I had thought about him as we made the walk back to the plantation last night. How was he handling his father's death and was he aware that that he had denied him during his failed kidnapping attempt? I knew it would be an awkward conversation, but it had to happen. I turned and started making my way to the stables.

It was late afternoon, and the plantation was busy with activity in anticipation of the upcoming celebration. Fearful that I might bump into Yolanda, I kept a safe distance from the revelers as I made my way down to the stables. My plan was to try and make peace before we left however, I had not quite found the words. As a result, for now, I thought it best to avoid the conversation.

Opening the large wooden barn door, I found Victor hard at work tossing hay into stables.

"How's it going?" I asked as he stabbed a large pile of hay and aggressively tossed it in the stall.

"You mean since my father used me to kidnap those two girls? I'm fine," he said through a forced smile.

"I was just wondering, because if I were you, I don't think I'd be fine," I replied. "I didn't know him, but I gather you and your father, like most, were close?"

"You're right Dante, you didn't know him! He worked hard and taught me a lot. He could shoe a horse or train a pony faster than any man I've ever known," he replied while leaning against the pitchfork. Looking out into the pasture he paused before continuing, "But he was also a dishonest man. I watched him do things…things I knew were wrong. And I looked the other way. I knew he was lying when he told me to bring the girls to the stables. I guess…" he said, pausing. "I guess I hoped this time was different. But when I saw Ms. Carter this morning, I knew nothing had changed."

"What did she tell you?"

"That he had kidnapped those girls, and if it weren't for you and Simon he would have turned them in for that reward." Victor turned to me, tears welling up in his eyes. "Were you there, when he died?" he asked.

"Not exactly," I said. "But I was close by."

"Did he say anything? Anything about me?"

I thought back to Jim's final rant. Comments denying Victor as being his son as well as disparaging comments about his mother. "Nothing," I said. "He mumbled several things before he died but nothing about you," I said confidently.

"It doesn't matter now anyway," Victor said as he resumed shoveling the hay into the stalls.

"Ms. Carter promised me I can stay as long as I want. She even told me I could take over my father's house and tend the barn and stables."

"I'm glad to hear that Victor. You're a good man," I said, extending my hand. "Better than your father."

Victor stopped working and looked at my hand then shook it, "Thank you Dante. How are Jamaya and Briana holding up? I'm sure the whole thing's been pretty tough on them."

"Yes, it was, but they're ok. They're pretty tough. That is actually part of the reason I stopped by. They are still in danger. As a result, Simon and I are taking them to a safe place tonight. We need you to get Misty and Blaze ready by dusk, but we don't want to alert anyone. We'll meet you in the apple orchard, just after the celebration begins."

"Of course, I'll have them ready. I just hate to see you guys leave so fast. I was hoping we could read some of this here newspaper," he said holding up a tattered document.

"I'm not gone yet. Do you want to go over some now?"

Victor smiled, "Yes, sir. I'd like that a lot!"

***

I weaved my way through the crowds on my way to the forest of small apple trees. After spending time with Victor, I sat and watched the crowd jubilantly dance around the fire. The combined sounds of the banjo and fiddle was something I would have never listened to at home but the melody and tempo was oddly familiar and comforting. Although I am not a dancer, the happy and upbeat music almost prompted me to join in the festivities.

Walking around the celebration, I reached the top of the hill, turned, and looked back at the fire and the group of slaves celebrating. Despite the horrible things I had seen and experienced in just those few days since my arrival, I decided I was going to miss the plantation. The people, their strength and optimism. I turned and started walking past the big house when I heard a voice.

"Now you're just gonna leave?"

I instantly recognized the sarcastic tone before turning to find a smiling Yolanda leaned against the railing of the front porch. "You come here and humiliate me with that nigger and now you just leave?"

"Look Yolanda," I said, walking toward her, "I didn't mean any disrespect to you. Like I tried to explain to you this morning, it's not what you think."

"It doesn't make any difference now," Yolanda said, interrupting me abruptly. "You gonna marry that runaway? Maybe have a bunch a little white babies? You think you're white? Better than the rest of us darkies?"

"What are you talking about?" I replied. "We're just trying to help them. After tomorrow, I will never see them again. It's over."

"That's where you're wrong, this is far from over," she spat through heavy breaths. "Safe travels, Dante," she added through a smirk before going inside the house and closing the door.

I stood there, shocked and confused by her comments. And the threat, what did she mean 'It's far from over'?" I watched the door, waiting for her to come back on the porch and elaborate on her warning until I heard the sound of horses approaching. Turning, I found Victor coming around the corner with Misty and Blaze in tow.

"I'll take those," I said, hopping over the rail and reaching for the reins.

"They're all yours." "They've been fed, watered, and are ready to go. It is almost like they knew they were about to leave."

I laughed. "They're both pretty smart. It wouldn't surprise me," I said while extending my hand to Victor. "You're a good man. It was nice meeting you. I look forward to coming back one day and seeing the progress you've made."

"Thank you sir, I mean Dante," Victor replied before shaking my hand. "Be well and travel safely."

I pulled myself into Blaze's saddle and grabbed Misty's reins. With a gentle kick of the heels, I sent him into motion.

Following the path down the hill, just inside the orchard, I found Simon standing next to Ms. Carter, Briana and Jamaya. Simon whispered something into Ms. Carter's ear and, after embracing her tightly, tossed his saddlebag over Misty and walked over to Briana. Kneeling down in front of her, he asked, "Are you ready?" She smiled and nodded her head.

In one swoop, he lifted her up, climbed into the saddle and placed her safely in front of him.

Looking down at Jamaya, I smiled and said, "I guess you're stuck with me." She smiled and quickly climbed into the saddle behind me. After adjusting herself in the saddle she wrapped her arms around my waist and rested her chin on my shoulder. I watched as Ms. Carter quickly wiped tears from her eyes.

"Thank you for your hospitality," I said riding alongside her.

"You're welcome," she replied before clasping my hand tightly. "Take care of my friend Dante," she whispered. "You be sure he gets home safely."

I immediately recognized the sincerity and feeling behind her words as I shook my head. "I promise," I replied while squeezing her hand tightly. I turned to find Simon had already maneuvered out of the trees and was heading to the hillside creek. I pulled the reins and nudged Blaze into a gallop.

# Eight

# Declaration

We spent several hours hugging the tree lines as we made our way north. During the course of the night, we had on two occasions been instructed by Simon to stop and take shelter in the forest. We sat quietly as first two riders rode toward us, followed by another set of three moments later. Neither group appeared to notice us, but we cautiously watched from the shadows as both groups rode hard as if they were in a hurry to reach a similar destination. After waiting several minutes to ensure no other riders followed, we resumed our journey north. By the time we crossed the Kentucky border, the first glimpse of morning light began to illuminate the night sky. Just before dawn, Simon announced we would retreat into the forest and rest up before continuing the next leg of the journey.

Over the course of the evening, the cool night air had been tolerable as we traveled in the open night sky but sliding out of the saddle under the dark green canopy was a reminder that the shadow cast by the trees made the morning temperature considerably colder. We walked through the forest until we found an suitable campsite. Several large granite blocks created a natural semi-circle amongst the towering trees. Then, just a short distance away a slow-moving creek flowed quietly behind us.

"We'll spend the day here and start making our way later this evening," Simon explained. "Dante and Jamaya, you two find some firewood while I show Briana here how to cool down the horses. We have some cold ham and bread but if you see anything," he added while pulling a rifle from his saddle and tossing it to me, "we should be far enough where no one would hear any shots or think anything of it."

I took the rifle and a burlap sack and Jamaya and I started our firewood search.

Although we had ridden together the last nine hours, we had exchanged only a few words. She'd wrapped her arms firmly around my waist and gently rested her head on my shoulder. I enjoyed hearing her breath softly as she drifted in and out of sleep behind me. Now, in the early morning hours, we walked awkwardly together, pausing occasionally to pick up fallen pieces of timber.

"Look Jamaya," I said, "about the other night."

"Dante stop. You don't have to say anything," she replied as she leaned in and kissed me quickly. "I may only be 17 but I've seen a lot. Nothing happened last night that I didn't want to happen."

I smiled as she pulled away, gently wiping her bottom lip. "That's such a relief. I felt bad thinking I'd somehow taken advantage of you at a time where you really just needed a friend."

"That's sweet of you Dante but maybe I was taking advantage of you," she said laughing. "Did you ever think of that?"

"When you say it like that it makes me feel cheap."

"I wasn't sure you would stay," she added.

"What do you mean, why not?"

"Because of your girlfriend," she said sarcastically.

"My girlfriend?" I replied. My mind raced as I quickly thought through our previous conversations. "Had I inadvertently told her about Jennifer? She must be thinking about...do you mean Yolanda? She is most definitely not my girlfriend.

I told you, I met her a day before I met you."

Jamaya bent down to pick up a small log and placed it in the sack. Her lips wrinkled while one eyebrow raised as if contemplating my explanation.

"Seriously. Simon and Ms. Carter gave us instructions to complete some chores before we left. That was the only reason we were together when we saw you." I thought back to how rude Yolanda had been to Jamaya.

"Speaking of which, I'm sorry about how she treated you. She is...troubled. You know, losing her mother and all. Ms. Carter has taken on a mother type role for her and I think somehow it's skewed her view of the world."

"Troubled? She acts as if she's better than the rest of us. I have seen blacks like her my whole life. They live and eat better than others and somehow they think they are superior," she added while bending over to pick up another log. "Any time a black person spends time with white folks, things change."

"I don't know. I have met a lot of good white people and some I have grown close to, like Ms. Carter. She is a good Woman," I replied.

"Yes, she is. Mr. Lewis, my old Master and his son are good people too. They took care of my sisters and I. It's just when they get involved with black folks when the trouble starts. I see Ms. Carter making eyes at your friend Simon. I've never seen a white woman look at a Negro like that," she explained through wide eyes.

Hearing Jamaya speak about the strangeness of a white woman displaying feelings for a black man made me think about my mother. The looks or comments she and my father receive, whether from family or strangers, still surprised me. Then I thought about the looks and comments Jennifer and I got while in the mall or at school. Over 150 years had passed and we're still acting like it was the 1860's.

"We'll you better get used to it," I said before slinging the sack over my shoulder. "Once you get up north, you're going to find things are little different from down here."

"What, they love black folks up north?" she asked sarcastically.

"No, there are problems everywhere, even where I'm from. But people up north are starting to understand the problems. And in the next few years, my guess is somebody's going to figure out how to start correcting some of them." I could see the wheels spinning as she processed my words.

Before she could ask the inevitable question, I changed the subject. "So, where are you eventually going? What are you and Briana going to do?" I asked.

"Indianapolis. We have an Auntie there, Eva Sue. She used to work on the plantation next to us. Masta Lewis tried to buy her but her owner, Mr. Cook, wouldn't sell. So she ran away. We're going to find her and when I save enough money, I'm going back to Alabama to get my sister."

Turning towards me, she stood on the tips of her toes, leaned in closely and playfully asked, "You gonna help me bring my sister north Mister West?"

"It would be my pleasure Ms. Lewis," I said with a smile.

Giggling, she gave me another quick kiss before pausing suddenly.

"Shhh," she said, pressing her finger against my lips while simultaneously reaching for the musket rifle. Confused, I resisted but reluctantly released the barrel as she began systematically prying each of my fingers from the barrel. I curiously watched as she first loaded the powder followed by the lead ball into the musket barrel. Looking into the dense forest she slowly began to walk in a low squat-like waddle before again pausing abruptly. With her long cotton dress bunched neatly between her legs she sat quietly in the brush. Then, without warning, she slowly lifted the rifle and pointed it towards the empty grass ahead and pulled the trigger.

The resulting explosion echoed through the towering trees leaving the small clearing cloudy with gun smoke.

Excited, Jamaya jumped to her feet and began tromping through the dense dew-covered brush. After a brief walk through the brush she reached down and pulled up a turkey. The wild bird was much larger than the birds mom purchased annually from the local butcher.

Holding the trophy above her head, she proudly held the bird by its feet, letting the wings hang limply in front of her.

"How did you see that from way over here?" I asked.

"I didn't. I heard it. Then, once I knew what I was hearing, it was easy to find it. Haven't you been hunting before?"

"Of course I have," I said through a forced smile.

I thought back to the last time I had seen an animal die. It was last summer, right after I'd found my cousins pellet gun in the attic. I was using some old coke cans for target practice when I saw a squirrel hopping in the trees above me. Against my better judgment, I lined the squirrel in my sights and pulled the trigger. The pellet must have gone straight through because the squirrel jumped at the impact then sat motionless while clinging to the branch. I watched as it sat there breathing heavy, blood dripping down to the deck below. I knew it was dying but I could not bring myself to put it out of its misery.

If it had not been for my sister strolling through the side gate while chatting on her phone, I would probably still be there watching it bleed out. She looked up at the dying squirrel and motioned for me to give her the gun. While continuing her conversation she loaded the pellet and began to quickly pump the lever. After a brief pause, she lined the squirrel and pulled the trigger. The squirrel instantly went stiff before falling to the deck with a thud. I grimaced at the gruesome sight. Handing me the gun, she opened the sliding glass door and disappeared only to quickly reappear with a trash bag. Without saying a word, she scooped up the dead carcass and tossed it into the trash can.

"Do you have a knife?" Jamaya asked. "Dante, do you have a knife?" she repeated.

Snapping out of my momentary trance, I reached into my pocket and pulled out the knife I had confiscated from Andy. Before I could ask what she was doing she had already began pulling feathers from the bird's chest. She tossed a clump of long bloody feathers towards me prompting me to grimace at the sight.

"What the hell is that?" I asked in disgust.

"It's the beard," she replied surprised. "You don't keep the turkey's beard where you're from?" she asked while pushing down on the bird's legs, creating a crunching sound as the joints and bones dislocated.

"Not usually," I said as I watched her make surgical cuts on each of the breasts. Peeling back the skin she continued the incisions until both breasts were extracted. Tossing the two hunks of meat on top of the burlap bag, she wiped her hands on the wet dewy grass and looked up at me.

"Do you want to carry the meat or the wood?" she asked while flicking feathers and flesh from her fingertips.

I felt my stomach churn and my mouth water as my body warned of an imminent heave. After a deep breath, I reached for the bag of wood. "I'll take the wood," I said while fighting to repel the smell of bloodied flesh, "It's kind of heavy."

Arriving back at our make-shift camp we found Simon and Briana sitting close to a small fire. I dropped the wood and collapsed to the ground.

"What's wrong with you?" Simon asked.

"He's apparently never seen a turkey skinned," Jamaya said with a smile as she walked past the fire on her way to the creek. Dipping the two large turkey breasts in the creek, she yelled out, "What kind of boy's never kept a beard?" Walking back to the fire, she continued dissecting the breasts into four strips then carefully pierced each with a long willow branch. After wedging the branches between several large rocks, she gently leaned the skewers just out of the fire's reach.

"When we were little we'd go hunting with Master Lewis and his son. They would always do the hunting, but they would let us fetch the turkeys. Then, after we cleaned and cut up the meat, they'd give us kids the beards. We would keep them and make stuff out of them, necklaces, or charms. All the kids looked forward to it. I can't believe you didn't do that."

I sat puzzled thinking of an explanation for my ignorance when Simon spoke up.

"Dante is from a city in Georgia called Atlanta. In the city, boys don't get to do much hunting and trapping. Not like you and me country folk," he said with a smile. "It's going to take a little while for that meat to cook. Why don't you two ladies get some rest? Dante and I will keep watch."

Jamaya led Briana past Simon and I, not before pausing briefly and rubbing her hand along my arm.

"Thank you," I said looking at Simon. "She tossed that thing at me and I didn't know if I should run or step on it."

Simon laughed. "It's funny. We used to do the same thing growing up as kids in Maryland. Turkey beards, deer antlers, rabbits' feet, we kept them all. Sometimes my Master's brother would bring his dogs up from Virginia to hunt coons. We would skin them and if we were lucky, he would let us keep the hide or the tail. I guess you and your friends didn't do anything like that in Decatur or Buckhead."

"Nope! The closest we got to shooting stuff was first person shooter games." Simon laughed as he started poking the fire with a large stick.

"Where do you think those riders were headed?" I asked.

"I don't know but I've been thinking about it. Remember this is war time. It's April 15th, 1861, the year of Lincoln's inauguration. By now, more than half of the southern states would have seceded from the Union. War officially started three days ago and it will not take much longer for word to spread via telegram. Those riders could very well be militia groups anxious to get into the fight. I was hoping to be back home by now but we've got to get these girls to the next stop by tomorrow morning. Get some rest. I will keep watch. We'll pull off at sunset."

***

The second leg of our ride north was more treacherous than the previous night. Every hour we were forced into the woods to allow riders or men on foot to pass in their march south. They came now in larger groups of five or six men of all ages armed with old musket rifles. We crouched in the woods and listened as they laughed and sang songs while marching. Despite the repeated stops, we arrived outside of Louisville just before dawn in a small town called Shepherdsville. Walking through the gates of the 'Gables Plantation,' we were greeted by a busy farm bustling with workers preparing for the day.

As we dismounted, an older black man stood stoically as he reached for the reins.

"Good morning Simon," announced a voice from behind us.

We turned to find a wiry older woman sitting on a horse. Dressed in pants and work boots, her salt and pepper hair was tucked neatly under a wide brimmed straw hat. Her voice was feminine, but it had a rough scratchy tone as she spoke. Had she not spoken, I would have sworn she was a man.

"It's good to see you," she said while dismounting. "You picked a hell of a time to come up this way."

"Hello Mrs. Stewart," Simon responded while extending his hand and shaking hers. "We passed several men headed south. Looks like they are gathering in Tennessee. What's going on?"

"It's official. The Confederates fired on Fort Sumner three days ago. It looks like we are headed for Civil War. President Lincoln called for volunteers today. My eldest son will be on the next train to Washington to offer our support."

She then turned her attention to me. "I received a telegraph from Jackie. You must be Dante," she said extending her hand. "And you two must be Jamaya and Briana. I have heard a lot about you three. Ladies, I have a place for you until Friday. My son and I will be delivering a shipment of mineral water to Indianapolis that evening. Lord willing, you should be safely in Indiana by Saturday afternoon.

"Alma," she said, turning to an older black woman in an apron, "can you please escort these two young ladies to the basement and ensure they have food and a change of clothes?"

"And you two," she continued turning back to Simon and me, "we have an apartment attached to the barn.

Thomas here will show you to your quarters and see to your horses."

"Thank you for your hospitality Mrs. Stewart. We will get some sleep and rest our horses, but plan to be gone by nightfall. We need to get back before this war escalates," Simon explained.

"I understand. We'll speak before you leave," she replied before turning and climbing back on her horse.

Jamaya squeezed my hand before following Mrs. Stewart to the basement. I followed them until they disappeared into the large house.

Turning to Simon I asked, "Are you ready?"

Simon nodded as we started walking toward the barn.

"Is Mrs. Stewart a Conductor?" I asked.

"No. She is an abolitionist though. Originally from Indianapolis her business manufactures a mineral drink here in Louisville. They bring it up to various distributors, some of which are favorable to our cause, especially if there is a little financial incentive. We don't usually pass runaways through these parts unless we have special cases that need to cross safely and quickly."

"What about us, what's the best way for us to get home?" I asked.

"I've been thinking about that," Simon said, opening the door to the small cabin. He reached into his saddle bag, pulled out a small map, and laid it across the table.

"We're here in Louisville. When we leave, rather than going back through Nashville, we will swing around like we are going through Chattanooga. That will create two possible challenges. Heading east will put us in Cherokee territory. They will not take kindly to us crossing into their lands, so we will have to move quickly. Then, there is the war. The first battle will not happen in Tennessee for another year, but there is strong support for the Confederacy. Tennessee was second only to Virginia regarding the number of battles fought within their borders. So, although they are technically neutral, it is not going to be pleasant if we run into any of the Tennessee Militia. If we are lucky, we will be back to Georgia in three days. But for now, let's get some sleep. We're going to need it."

***

We spent the last part of the day preparing the horses and getting rations ready for our departure. I spent most of the morning and early afternoon catching up on sleep. After putting the last few items in Blaze's saddle bag, I turned, surprised to find myself face to face with Jamaya.

"Going somewhere?" she asked.

"Yes," I replied awkwardly, "We're planning to leave at sunset. I'm thinking any moment now."

She wrapped her arms around my neck and smiled as she looked at me. Looking in her eyes, I could see a tear beginning to well up before she blinked, sending the single teardrop rolling down her smooth caramel colored cheek. I gently wiped it away with the back of my finger.

"What did you go do that for?" I asked while playfully butting my head against hers.

"Because I'm an idiot," she said smiling. "Falling for a boy I've known for less than a week and that I'll never see again."

I had been anticipating a conversation before we departed however, I was not quite sure how to convey what I was feeling. From the moment I met her, she had been so tough and independent. Having her now, in near tears telling me she fell for me, left me speechless.

"Listen Jamaya, I have to tell you something."

"Don't say anything. I know I sound silly and you probably don't feel for me the way I feel for you but I do care for you. From the moment I saw you in the kitchen, to the moment you saved Briana and me, I knew you were special. Now you're gonna go back to your big city and all those pretty girls. Just don't forget about me and the time we spent this week."

Tears were now streaming down her face, prompting my eyes to involuntarily well up. The idea of leaving Jamaya and Briana behind with a looming war and all of the devastation the country would soon experience left me perplexed and conflicted.

"Take this," she said, pulling the simple silver wedding band from her right index finger. "It was my mother's. She gave it to my sister, and she gave it to me."

She slipped the ring onto my pinky finger. "For luck. And maybe it will help you remember…us," she added while wiping tears from her eyes. "And don't go giving that to one of your fancy city girls," she added with a laugh.

I watched her, presumably for the last time as she looked at me. With her head cocked slightly to the right, her mouth closed tightly as she fought back tears.

"Travel safely," she added before kissing me quickly. With that, she turned and scurried back to the large brick house.

I paused for a moment, looking at the door, somehow expecting it would re-open and she would come back however, after several moments I found myself standing alone and in silence. Looking down at the crudely made wedding band I began to slowly twist the metal ring on my finger.

"You about ready to head out?" asked Simon as he approached from behind.

Quickly rubbing my eyes with the backs of my fists I replied, "Just waiting on you," before turning around and making eye contact with Simon. "All packed up and ready to get back to the ATL. I've been dying for some mall pizza."

"Pizza? Of all of the good food in the city you're thinking about mall pizza?" Simon asked with a laugh.

"I've been thinking about a really good burger, extra onions, maybe some fries. That's the first stop for me."

Simon and I spent the next hour tormenting ourselves as we thought about the best food spots in downtown Atlanta. Before I knew it, midnight had come and gone.

# Nine

# Escape

Leaving Louisville, we were careful to hug the same tree lines we had used while heading north. But once we approached the state line, we started to veer off course as if we were heading to Chattanooga. As we left the security of the tree line we paused briefly to examine the large vastness in front of us. The rolling hills and open prairie seemed to go on for miles before disappearing into the moonlit horizon. On either side of the open landscape, large clusters of trees peppered the expanse where, if necessary, we could use the thick forests for cover.

"All of this was formerly Cherokee land," Simon explained while pointing over the fields in front of us. "There are still tribes out there that remember the Cherokee-American wars of the 18th Century. Native Americans collaborated with the British to end the American Revolution. Hundreds, maybe thousands, are still occupying these lands. We'll want to move as quickly as possible to reduce the likelihood of running into them," he added before nudging Misty forward.

"Besides...." he added. "The sooner we get back, the quicker we can get that mall pizza" he added with an exaggerated frown.

"Actually, your burger isn't sounding that bad," I replied with a chuckle. "Anything beats this hardtack."

Simon simulated painfully eating the hard-baked cake before pretending to load a broken piece of the cake into his shotgun barrel.

We laughed while leaning forward into our saddles and nudging Misty and Blaze into a faster trot.

The next hour was spent riding at a steady gallop in an attempt to cover the terrain more quickly. The flat ground eventually gave way to a series of low rolling ravines that created natural barriers from the cool night wind. Approaching the lowest point we could see nestled into a flat riverbank, a large blazing fire. We stopped immediately, not sure if the fire's owners had detected us when we heard the click of a revolver's hammer.

I reached for the gun tucked in my saddle bag when a voice spoke out from the darkness.

"Nigger, you move one muscle and I'll blow you clear off that horse." The voice stepped out of the shadows holding the gun pointed squarely at me. "Jimmy, Colt, over here. I got a couple of niggers on horses," he yelled.

Stepping into the moonlight, I could see he was an older man with tattered unkept clothing. Judging by his balding gray hairline, he was probably in his late 60's.

"Now, what would bring two niggers' way out here on a night like this riding two fine looking animals? What are ya, thieves or runaways?"

Before I could reply, Simon spoke up.

"Neither boss. We just delivered some hausus and cows for old man Johnson in Louisville. We's headed back to our Massa in Chattanooga. He expecting us to be back by noon or he gon' be mighty angry with me and the boy here. I's got a tag showing we's official." Simon reached for his saddlebag, prompting a stern warning from the old man.

"Easy boy. You try something funny and I'll shoot yo black ass dead."

Simon, slowly reaching in his saddlebag, pulled out the Georgia slave tag and held it out innocently in front of him. The old man cautiously reached for it and inspected it closely. For a moment, I worried that he would recognize the Georgia seal, however I remembered a fact Simon shared with me, "1 in 4 Americans during the 1800's was illiterate." So by that estimation we had a 25% chance this guy couldn't read a Dr. Seuss book.

"You boys shouldn't be out this late. War is brewing and you's liable to get yoself killed walking up on the wrong man this time of night." The old man walked up to Simon and began to give the slave tag back when his two companions walked up.

Neatly groomed and considerably younger than the older man, both men approached with a youthful air of confidence.

"What do we have here?" said the younger of the pair. "Two niggers on horses, at night, and in the middle of nowhere."

"It's ok Jimmy. They just delivered some livestock to old man Johnson in Louisville. They're headed back to Chattanooga," explained the older man.

"Old man who?" said the other young man. "What are you talking about, Earnest? There ain't no Johnsons in Louisville buying livestock. Don't nobody buy anything in Louisville without me knowing about it. Who are you boys?"

"They's slaves from Chattanooga Jimmy. I just read it from this here pass," the old man said while holding up the slave tag.

Jimmy walked up to Simon and inspected him suspiciously. "Give me that," he commanded before snatching the leather patch from the old man. "You know you can't read," Jimmy barked while examining the tag. "Now, unless you boys don't know the difference between Georgia and Tennessee, I'd have to say you're pulling my old friend's leg."

Jimmy tossed the tag to Simon.

"That pass is from the state of Georgia and its over two years old. Hell, it's probably stolen like these horses. Now, you boys wanna tell us who you really are and what you're doing out here?"

"Well boss, truth of the matter is…"

I could see Simon reach behind his back and slowly pull out his 9mm pistol. Sliding the firearm to his side, he rested it on his lap with the business end pointing directly at the group's leader.

Simon continued to add vivid details to his story while surveying the small group of men. As far as I could tell, the old man was the only person with a weapon, but I wasn't sure. Watching Simon I could tell he was analyzing the situation while preparing his next move. His story began to lag until the leader could not take it any longer.

"Enough of yo lies boy," he snapped while pulling out a revolver. Holding the gun loosely pointed in our direction he continued, "Tell me," he said, pulling back the hammer, "what yur doin' out here." Seeing the pistol was all the confirmation Simon needed.

"Sorry boss. You wouldn't understand even if I told you," Simon replied before exposing the 9mm.

The distinct 'clack-clack-clack' rang out through the silent night sky as the full clip rained down on the unsuspecting group. The trio, obviously caught off guard by the offensive attack, stood motionless before frantically scrambling to avoid the onslaught. I cringed as the first few bullets inflicted maximum damage to the young man's chest. His partner, apparently grazed by one of the bullets, staggered away from the clearing before disappearing into the thick brush.

The old man was equally unlucky. Hit by the series of shots he lay motionless atop a small bush. Still clutching his pistol with trembling hands, he slowly lifted the barrel. While struggling to hold the firearm and with a blank fearful stare, he squeezed the trigger sending a small flame and black smoke exploding from the barrel.

Undeterred by the single shot, Simon calmly reached behind his saddle and pulled out the double-barreled shotgun and returned fire. The boom of the high caliber shells rang out loudly, leaving me temporarily deafened by the blast. The resulting high-pitched buzz reverberated throughout my eardrums as I struggled to follow Simon's direction.

Recognizing my temporary impairment, he raised his voice to what I imagined was a loud roar.

"We can't afford for any of them to get away. Finish him off," he said, pointing to the old man. "I'm going after the other one." Simon slid out of the saddle and quickly disappeared into the darkness.

Slipping out of the metal stirrups, I too dropped to the ground and cautiously walked over to the old man. A quick scan of his lifeless body confirmed he had taken a few bullets to his shoulder, but the real damage had come at the expense of the last shotgun blast. Blood oozed from the gaping holes torn into his chest and abdomen, soiling his dirty under-shirt, the bushes and grass around him. Looking up at me, his eyes called out as if begging for help, yet no words were spoken.

Pulling the pistol out of my saddlebag I pushed the barrel firmly against his forehead. His eyes widened as he glared through the tops of his eyelids, focused intently on my trembling hand gripping the firearm. I thought about how close he had come to killing Simon and how, in the end, he'd had resolved to let us go. Had it not been for the young man's intervention, we would have been long gone.

Rubbing my index finger on the trigger, I tried several times to pull the lever however I couldn't do it. Standing over him I contemplated his life when I heard a gun go off. The sound of the blast echoed loudly in the night. Time seemed to stand still as I began frantically looking around for the source of the gunshot.

Looking down at the old man, I could see his breathing drift from heavy, to soft, to virtually no movement.

"He's gone," I thought while sliding my index finger off the pistol's trigger. My hand, seemingly exhausted from the brief contemplation of taking a life, fell lazily to my side. Peering into the direction of the last gunshot, I waited patiently for any signs of life. After several minutes, I called out, "Simon! Simon! "

After several minutes of painful silence, I began walking briskly toward the commotion. With the pistol firmly in hand, I combed through the high grass and dense underbrush until I could see the silhouette of the brightly burning bonfire. Approaching the flame, three horse silhouettes could be seen, all tied up nearby with bed rolls laid out around the make-shift camp sight.

With eyes now adjusted to the brightly glowing flames, I quickly discovered the recipient of the last gun shot. There, lying just inches from the raging fire, was the third militia man Simon had pursued. The heat from the flames was already causing the cotton fibers in his overcoat to smolder. What was left of his neck and lower mandible confirmed the final lethal shot had come from Simon's shotgun.

Looking closely at the size and build, I instantly realized he couldn't have been much older than me. His neatly pressed uniform and overcoat were now soiled and bloodied as he lay motionless in silence. The grim sight instantly reminded me that over the next several years, thousands of young men, just like him, would face the same eventuality. In places like Antietam, Gettysburg, Vicksburg and dozens of others, young boys will have considered themselves fortunate to have been able to hastily dig graves to house the remains of fallen comrades who died during the bloody battles.

Simon took a knee and began rummaging through the dead man's pockets. Pulling out a piece of paper, he held it up close to the fire and examined it.

"Death to King Lincoln and his tyranny," he read aloud.

"They're definitely militia," Simon said while tossing the paper into the fire. The paper burned quickly before Simon began kicking dirt on the flame and smoldering overcoat. The once bright fire quickly extinguished as Simon started walking back toward our horses.

"We've got to get out of here and avoid any more of these militias. These lands are relatively flat, anyone within a few miles had to have heard the gunfire. By morning, the country-side is going to be crawling with them."

Simon grabbed the barrel of his rifle and turned toward me. As he turned, he collapsed onto one knee, while gingerly holding his left arm close to his side. Reaching to help him up I immediately discovered the warm liquid had already saturated his left side.

"You've been shot!" I said kneeling to his side.

"I'm fine," he said, standing. "We've got to get out of here. The old man, did you finish him off?" he asked.

I looked over to where the old man was just lying and discovered he was gone.

"He was just right here, bleeding from multiple gun shots. He couldn't have gotten far," I explained while frantically searching through the brush.

"No!" Simon said. "We don't have time. We've got to get to those woods." Simon pulled himself up on his horse and I hopped into Blaze's saddle while nudging him to follow behind the now galloping Misty.

Moment s later, shots rang out. Bullets whizzed overhead before colliding with trees in front of us. Looking back, I could see the silhouettes of several individuals hastily climbing atop horses while preparing to pursue us.

"Several riders behind us Simon," I yelled over the sound of our galloping horses, however Simon continued riding focused solely on reaching the security of the dense forest.

After several minutes of carefully navigating through walls of trees, I prepared to dismount when Simon shook his head.

"I don't know how long I can walk and we need to move quickly," he whispered loudly. "Follow me and keep quiet. The worst might still be ahead of us."

Climbing back atop Blaze and moving deeper into the woods, we carefully navigated our way through the tall pines and thick hardwoods. Simon had effortlessly navigated us from the moment we stepped through the portal, but now, as I looked around the dark forest, I began to question whether or not we were randomly changing directions.

"What if his wounds are fatal?" I thought. "Are we lost? If so, how could I ever navigate my way out of this…this…place?" I squinted in an attempt to focus on Simon and his movements. He had been quiet since we entered the forest, but I could tell by the way he slumped in his saddle that the gunshot wound was taking its toll.

Darkness was now merging with the thick fog as it began to slowly roll in through the trees. The horses naturally weaved through the thick brush, stepping through and over bushes and fallen branches. But for me, I struggled to keep my eyes on Misty as she carefully navigated in front of me.

In the silence of the forest, I could hear Misty and Blaze's hooves gently slosh through the forest's soupy floor while small branches snapped, and water splashed as they waded through slow moving creeks. Those sounds echoed throughout the forest until an unfamiliar sound caught my attention.

A laugh followed by voices caused me to sit upright in Blaze's saddle.

Simon, apparently oblivious to the sound, continued forward through the thick fog. It was not until I snapped my fingers in quick succession that he pulled back on Misty's reins. After pointing to my ears then eyes, I directed his attention to the thick cluster of trees ahead.

We paused there in the middle of the forest while the blanket of fog slowly rolled away from us leaving the trees directly in front of us open and visible. Now clear, the soft light of the night sky revealed the source of the robust laughter. Standing no more than 40 feet from us was a small group of militia men looking directly at us.

The group of men stood silent, obviously shocked to find they were not alone in the forest, but equally surprised to discover they were looking at two Negroes on horseback. In that split-second, Simon alone recognized the small window of opportunity and seized the moment.

"Charge!" he grunted.

Prodding Misty, she instantly leapt into a gallop, easily covering the 40 feet in two or three strides. Before they could respond her large frame trampled the first group of the militants. Screams filled the air as she skillfully destroyed everything in her path.

With his reinvigorated 9mm, Simon led the charge against the remaining group of men. The barrage of shots sent men scattering while others fell, unable to evade the quick succession of bullets. Blaze and I, attempting to follow Simon's charge, pushed forward through the remaining soldiers.

In an attempt to evade his slashing hoofs, soldiers scrambled in all directions. Firmly grasping his reins, I turned him quickly, causing his large frame to spin wildly as he eagerly looked for more bodies to trample. With no one left standing, I pulled back on his reins and prepared to move forward when a tall slender militia man defiantly stepped in front of us. Holding an old musket fixed with a bayonet, he held the weapon nervously in front of him.

With a commanding nudge Blaze bolted forward into a trot which quickly turned to a strong gallop.

I watched in disbelief as the soldier closed his eyes and blindly lunged with the bayonet. Blaze cried out in agony as the metal blade pierced his upper leg, prompting him to rear back on his hind legs. The momentum instantly threw me from the saddle and sent me crashing to the forest floor. Looking up through dazed and starry eyes, I could see Simon turn around as if waiting for me to follow. Stumbling to my feet I looked around expecting a confrontation but no one was left standing. If they had not suffered from Misty's hooves or the rounds Simon was able to unleash, the remaining soldiers frantically scrambled for their lives.

Wrapping the leather straps tightly in my hands, I prepared to climb into the saddle when I noticed the slender man with the bayonet was lying in front of me. Now empty handed he began a frantic backwards crawl while staring at me in between quick scans for an escape route.

Picking up the bayonet and holding it firmly in my hands I followed him as he continued his desperate crawl. Pausing, I stood over him and stared directly into his eyes. I could clearly see he was an older man, perhaps in his late 60's. Other than a contorted leg, I couldn't see any visible signs of injuries sustained during the confrontation. He glared up at me as he surprisingly poke.

"What the hell are you doing out here boy?" he spat.

I thought back to the old man I had spared just hours ago and the bullet he had fired at Simon. The merciless beating of the young boy administered by old man Norris and the damage the militia and eventually the Confederate army would soon inflict on millions of people. It was then that I began to feel the anger that Simon warned me about.

"You are going to have to find a way to bottle it up. Then, when the time is right, you are gonna get a chance to unleash all that you have worked so hard to suppress. It's then that someone will feel it."

Standing over the man, I held the bayonet directly above him, prepared to unleash the rage, the rage that had been building for years. His eyes widened as he looked at the blade just inches from his chest. My heart, equally terrified with holding a person's life in my hands, pounded as I lifted the rifle into the air. My hands trembled, surprisingly anxious to thrust the blade deep into his chest, when I thought about my mother.

I had been in this world for nearly a week. Meeting new people while narrowly escaping danger however, it was not until this moment that I thought of her.

My breathing slowed as I envisioned her, tearfully standing nearby, shocked at the thought of me holding a gun. I could vividly see tears streaming down her face as she looked on in horror. Standing next to her was my father. Never one to share his emotions, he stood next to her silently looking on, the shame evident on his face. Then I thought about Dr. Stillwell and his hypothetical question, "What would you do if someone tried to forcibly seize you?" I looked down at the man who was now looking up at me helplessly.

"I'm going home," I replied as I began to lower the bayonet tipped rifle. Peering over my shoulder I could see Blaze had calmed down but the small gash on his upper leg continued to slowly ooze crimson colored blood. Fully lowering the rifle, I started to walk away when the old man spoke.

"Get back here nigger! Don't you turn your back on me!" he spat while fully propping himself up on his elbows. "Give me that horse. You're not going to leave me out here."

Looking back, I turned the rifle upside down and slowly allowed the rifle to slide downward until I was left holding just the barrel. Walking back to the soldier I stopped in front of him and looked down in disgust.

"You help me get up boy," he commanded "or by god help me I'll beat you until you wish you were dead."

Grabbing the rifle firmly with both hands, I smiled before swinging the stock backwards and quickly accelerating until the butt slammed squarely into his face. The sound of bone and cartilage crushing under the force of the rifle rang out as blood erupted from his nose and mouth. Surprisingly, he briefly stayed upright, momentarily dazed by the blow, before collapsing backwards.

"My name is not boy, it's Dante," I replied before tossing the rifle at his feet. Grabbing Blaze's reins, I pulled myself into the saddle and trotted over to Simon and Misty.

"I took care of it," I announced while approaching the slumping Simon.

"Simon! The coast is clear," I repeated, but again he sat motionless, slumped lazily against Misty's neck. Grasping his hand, I frantically felt along his forearm searching for a pulse. With his hand in my palm, I rested my index finger on his wrist and stood silently as the calm of the forest returned. He had a pulse, but it was weak.

I called out again desperately, "Simon! What should we do? Which way do we go?" But again, he sat slouched in the saddle.

Digging deep in his saddle bag, I pulled out the map he'd closely examined earlier that evening. He was confident in his chosen route however now, I wasn't so sure. After entering the forest, we had seemingly gone in circles and now, with the emerging morning light, I could just now begin to make out the landscape around us. Scanning the wall of trees surrounding us, I could see a slightly worn path ahead of us, yet reflecting on both Simon and Blaze's injuries, I questioned how much longer either could continue.

Refocusing on the map, I closely examined the distance between where I estimated we were and Atlanta. It wasn't far, though questions raced through my mind.

How could I get him the rest of the way with his injury? And once there, how could I get help and explain the bullet wound?

I continued to scan the map when gunshots shattered the silence. Standing motionless, I listened as another round of bullets again tore through the branches above me, littering the ground with leaves and limbs. With one last glance around us, I pulled on the reins and scurried down the path and with Simon clinging to life, we went deeper into the forest.

***

We continued down the worn dirt pathway winding through the forest. Twice in two hours, we ran into what appeared to be dead ends however, in both instances, we got off the path only to find our way back on the same gently worn trail. It was the third time, when the forest did not offer an alternate route. Walking for the better part of the morning, we made a repeated semi-circle pattern intent on finding the dirt trail that would eventually lead us out of the dense forest. On the last sweep, I pulled on Misty's reins in an attempt to redirect the convoy when Simon slid from the saddle. Dangling from the stirrup, he laid partially suspended in the air. Lifting his leg, I twisted his foot in the leather stirrup until we both collapsed to the forest floor.

Exhausted, I looked up at the gray overcast sky. It had been foggy the previous night, but now the distinct smell of an eminent rain permeated the air around us.

"We're never going to make it," I thought while looking over at Simon. His chest was rising and collapsing slowly, but it was obvious that he was becoming weaker. Looking over at Misty and Blaze, I watched as they grazed patiently on a small bush next to a slow-moving creek when I heard the voices.

My body tensed, anxiously listening for confirmation of the source of the conversation. Despite my focused attention I could not make out the words, but I had no doubts on the source, it was the militia.

Hopping to my feet, I looked around for an idea of where to run, but all directions appeared to be the same. Each offered the possibility of escape however, with an injured horse and Simon's inability to ride, the odds seemed stacked against us. Scanning the landscape, I searched for any possible escape route when I saw it.

About 30 yards away, I could see a small grotto or cavern cut into a wooded hillside. Grabbing Simon by the top of his jacket, I used a fireman's pull to drag him toward the hillside cave.

Initially the pine needle filled soil helped as I struggled to pull Simon's large frame across the forest floor. Unfortunately that quickly changed as a light drizzle set in. Climbing the now slick hillside while searching for stable footing seemed to be an impossibility. Adding to the challenge were the voices. Eagerly searching for us, they too were making large sweeping circles in an attempt to locate us.

Reaching the top of the hillside, I stepped into the small cavern and pulled Simon in just in time to hear the patrolling voices pass by.

"They had to have come this way. You two go that way, I'll back track."

Ducking out of sight, I breathed silently, fearful that something as simple as a deep breath of air would be enough to alert our pursuers to our location.

"What about Blaze and Misty?" I thought. "Surely they're in view."

When I could no longer hear the voices I stood, partially erect, and scanned the clearing where they had been grazing. I slipped back into the cave, confused by their absence. I could feel my chest start to quickly expand as my breathing became erratic.

"What would I do if they're gone?" I thought. "I can't carry Simon, and what about the food and the map?"

Closing my eyes, I took a deep breath and quickly stood erect. From the outside of the cavern, I scanned the area for any signs of life but when I examined the dense brush, I noticed movement on the other side of the clearing. Squinting firmly, I watched as the objects moved slowly through the afternoon mist until I was sure, it was Misty and Blaze.

As if anticipating the need to hide, they moved, not with Simon and I, but further into the forest. There they waited patiently while the militia completed their search. Collapsing to the cavern floor I laughed quietly at their cleverness. I had known from the moment I met Misty that she was smart, but not even I could have imagined she would initiate a well-timed version of hide and seek. Rolling over onto my back, I looked up at the rocky root covered ceiling. It was not an ideal resting place, but considering the rain and militia search party, I was more than happy to have a place to hide.

After several long yawns, my eyes began to blink uncontrollably. The muscles surrounding my eyes began to tighten as I struggled to keep my eyelids open. While rubbing my eye sockets with the backsides of my fists I aggressively fought the feeling of sleep quickly overtaking me.

Lying in the dimly lit cave, I watched as the water dripped from the earth suspended above us. With every drop that splashed on the rocky soil next to me, I seemed to become more and more entranced, unable to fight the sleep that was quickly overwhelming me. After one last yawn, my eyes closed, and I was neither willing nor able to resist.

***

Thunder clashed sending shock waves throughout the rocky cavern floor. The mini seismic tremor jolted me out of my sleep while prompting the dirt ceiling to litter the cavern floor with dirt and rubble. Moments later, a bright flash of light illuminated the night sky followed by another jolting round of thunder. In that brief moment of light, I could see Simon sleeping peacefully next to me.

Resting my hand on his chest, I could feel him breathing slowly as his chest rose then fell. Relieved, I looked out of the cave's entrance. Despite the sun's slow ascension on the horizon, I looked on as the torrential downpour dumped buckets of water over the unsuspecting forest.

"It will be morning soon," I thought. "Now what? I'm lost and Simon's hurt. Even if I knew where to go, how could I get him there? Is this how it ends? Dying at the hands of some zealous 19th century militia or starving to death somewhere in Tennessee?"

"My thoughts quickly switched to Jamaya and the simple ring she'd placed on my finger. I twisted the band as I examined it closely. "I would have loved to see her just one more time," I thought. "Just a few moments to tell her how much I appreciated the time we spent together and how I wished we could have met under different circumstances. I wish she could have met my parents and Trisha," I thought, laughing. "They would have gotten along well. Both of them are feisty and no-nonsense."

Thinking of the two of them reminded me of stories my father told me about his mother.

Before she was a Bible thumping Christian, she too was a no-nonsense lady. I smiled as I thought back to the story of the would-be-thief that attempted to rob her Chicago apartment back in the 50's. By the time the police arrived, the guy was begging for medical help. It turns out my grandma unloaded her Beretta through the bedroom door. He was lucky to have only been grazed by two bullets. It was her toughness that would later inspire my father to join the police force.

"What would grandma do?" I thought. "If she were here now, what would she tell me to do?"

"Stop all that damn crying boy!" she would shout. "Say a prayer, then give him something to work with."

"Say a prayer, then give him something to work with," I repeated as I wiped away the tears beginning to well up in my eyes.

Clutching Simon's hand, I closed my eyes and did something I had not done in years.

"God," I said aloud. "I know it's been a while since we spoke, but I'm not sure where else to turn. Grandma always spoke highly of you. She told me stories about how you helped people in the past...well, I need your help today. Truth is, I have spent most of my life hiding. Hiding from people...I do not know...maybe even hiding from myself or who I am. I have been afraid. Afraid of what others might say or do, afraid of disappointing my parents and teachers. But over the last few months, things have changed. I am not afraid anymore. I don't care what people think and I don't want to hide anymore. And a lot of that has to do with this man. I made a promise to get him to safety. A lot of people are depending on his survival. I am not sure what you have in store for me, but I need to help him. But neither of us can do that if we die in this hole. I know you probably hear it a lot, but if you can see fit to get us out of here, I will owe you. Not that I have anything you need, but I promise I'll do all I can to make this mess right."

Sitting there, quietly sobbing, I paused as silence once again returned to the forest. The downpour had stopped, and the forest was once again peaceful. Opening my eyes, I blinked as the sun peered over the dense tree line, illuminating the now cloudless sky. The only remnants of the downpour were residual drops of rain dripping from the rocky cliff above, and the clean refreshing post rainfall aroma.

I paused, listening for any signs of life, when I heard Misty's distinct neigh. Propping myself up on my elbows, I looked down the hill and could see both Misty and Blaze patiently waiting at the bottom. Amazed, I thought, "Certainly he hasn't answered my prayer that quickly, has he?"

Then, right on cue, I felt Simon squeeze my hand. "I think they're ready to go," he announced.

"Simon! I thought you were..." I replied while searching for the correct words.

"Nope. Not yet," he grimaced. "But we need to get back to the Apple Plantation. What time is it?"

"I'm not sure, but the sun is just now coming up."

"Travel away from the sun," he whispered through clenched teeth. "Once it is overhead, follow it.

We've got to get to the plantation," he repeated while clasping my forearm.

Climbing out of the cavern, I tightly clutched the back waistband of his pants while half carrying him down the hill. Now upright, I temporarily leaned him against Misty while examining the distance between him and the empty saddle. Calculations flooded my mind as I sought a simple solution to get him in the saddle when Simon, as if reading my thoughts, grabbed the saddle horn and lifted his left foot. Momentarily shocked by his sudden burst of energy, I quickly lifted his foot into the empty stirrup and with our combined strength, pulled him into Misty's saddle. With one hand tightly gripping the saddle horn and the other tucked gingerly against his blood-soaked side, Simon slumped in the saddle and rested safely against the crest of Misty' neck. After securing him in the saddle, I swung on top of Blaze and grabbed both reins. With a gentle nudge, he jumped into a start and began the soggy navigation through the water-soaked forest floor.

***

We spent the next two hours painstakingly navigating through the forest.

Per Simon's instruction, we kept the sun to our backs but by late afternoon, the sun overtook us as we continued our western trek. With the exception of the occasional anxious grunt or neigh by the horses, we traveled in virtual silence. During the latter part of the morning we heard gunshots in the distance however, we saw no signs of civilization until we reached the top of a small bluff. Mostly clear of trees or brush, it gave us the brief opportunity to see several hundred yards around us. Unfortunately, that same visibility was given to a small group of militia men who spotted us while we were inspecting the bluff.

A volley of shots rang out from the tree line prompting us to retreat down the hill and into the safety of the forest. The sun was beginning to set, but judging by its position, we still had several hours before we were again faced with complete darkness. Focusing beyond the sound of the hoofs colliding with the ground, I could hear yelping hounds combined with shouting voices as the militia signaled, they were getting close. Blaze navigated through the large pine and oak trees, moving left and right while pausing numerous times to go around fallen or impassable obstacles. I looked back and watched Simon swaying in the saddle as Misty maintained the urgent pace.

Excited by the chase, the hounds howl and barks echoed through the forest until they began to quickly fade. A new equally intense sound slowly began to overpower the dog's blood thirsty yelps.

It began as a low rustling, but as we continued, that low roar began to drown out all of forest's natural sounds. Struggling to decipher the source, I listened more and more intently until the mild roar was now unmistakable, it was a waterfall. Emerging from the trees and underbrush, we stepped into a large clearing. The rocky cliffs towered above us like a series of stadium seats while the water crashed over the cliff's edge creating thick blankets of foam covering large portions of the clearing. The water below was feeding into two separate bodies of water while each fed smaller rivers on either side of us. It was then that I fully understood my error.

In my haste to avoid the shots and hounds, I had unknowingly led us into a large clearing or marsh completely surrounded by the watery cliffs and two rivers. Other than wading into the waters or turning to fight, there were not any other options. There would be no escape.

I pulled Simon from the saddle and collapsed behind a fallen oak tree. Resting my fingers on his wrist, there was definitely a pulse, but the slow flow of blood reminded me he was fading quickly. Examining the wound, I tore my shirt and began using the material as make-shift gauze when I heard them approaching.

Muffled commands were being ordered as bodies quickly rustled through the bush as they moved to comply. Pushing the gauze firmly against Simon's wound, I rested him gently against the tree trunk while I slipped the rifle from the bed roll attached to the saddle. Pulling back the arm, I locked a round in the chamber and firmly pushed the bolt in place.

Up until now, I had managed to survive without taking any lives. The bounty hunter, Old Man Norris, Jeb, and Jim, even the militia men we had encountered the previous night. Despite the cruelty and violence, I had decided early on that I was not a killer. But at some point, in the middle of the night, something had changed. It was at that moment that I decided whoever stepped in my line of sight would be the first to witness my resolve. I sat patiently as I heard branches snap under the weight of the approaching militia force.

Laying back, I held the rifle pointed in the direction of the footsteps. With my finger resting on the trigger, I waited for an unsuspecting militiaman to step into the clearing. My hand tensed in preparation for pulling the trigger when a whistling sound filled the air. The high-pitched screech was quickly followed by dozens of similar sounds. As the noise intensified the advancing Militia began to fall to the ground shouting and writhing in pain. Propped up on my elbows I peered over the tree trunk and into the clearing. Several militia bodies laid lifeless with arrows lodged deep in their torsos. Others, clinging to life crawled or ran from the onslaught desperate to disappear into the security of the thick forest's foliage.

Scurrying back to the fallen oak tree, I scanned the forest and waterfall in search of the source of the volleyed cluster of arrows. Just as I located the individuals the roaring of the waterfall was temporarily muted by the screaming battle cries of several dozen Indian Warriors. Scaling down the steep cliff face they splashed through the foamy marsh in pursuit of the fleeing militiamen. Arrows flew and axes swung as they charged those unwilling or unable to flee from the onslaught. I could hear the weapons connecting to the unsuspecting troops as their screams and pleas for mercy quickly faded until the only remaining sound was the water once again crashing against the river below.

With a deep breath, I pulled the gun in close and pushed myself closer to the trunk looking to secure protection from the battle when a familiar voice called out to me. Peeking over the trunk, I smiled as I instantly recognized him. It was Mohe.

"Dawntee," he said with a smile and an extended hand.

I reached up and grabbed his hand, relieved to identify my rescuer. He continued to make short quick expressions that I struggled to understand until I made out the word Simon.

"Yes, he's here, he's injured," I said walking around the tree while pointing to Simon and his injury.

Mohe's expression immediately changed as he knelt down and began inspecting him. After a brief examination, he stood up and began giving what I imagined were instructions to his clansmen who quickly responded to his requests.

"What are you doing?" I asked. "Wait…he has a wound."

I grabbed at the warriors who were beginning to take off his overcoat and shirt before Mohe stopped me. Sensing my concern, he spoke calmly to me, "Tohiyusdv. Tohiyusdv" he repeated.

"I'm sorry…I don't understand Mohe, what are you saying?" I asked frantically. "What are you saying?"

Mohe, placing his hands on my shoulder, looked me directly in the eyes and repeated the phrase, but this time more calmly, "Tohiyusdv."

Looking over his shoulder he yelled out another phrase that was equally foreign to me, "Onacona!"

The warriors too began looking around as if searching for something until moments later the crowded clearing began to part and an older male warrior emerged from the throngs of soldiers.

"Hello Dante. My name is Onacona. It's a pleasure to meet you."

Standing there I stood shocked looking at the older Cherokee warrior. Small in stature he moved gracefully as he walked toward me while navigating through the brush and over the large fallen oak tree.. His salt and pepper colored hair was pulled back into a ponytail and those loose hairs hanging alongside his face perfectly framed his wrinkled bronze weathered skin.

"Tohiyusdv. It means be calm," Onacona explained. Bending down he examined Simon's blood-stained shirt before lifting it up briefly to inspect the entry wound.

"He has lost a significant amount of blood and there doesn't appear to be an exit wound. Someone needs to retrieve that bullet. We do not have the equipment to do it properly. The nearest town is probably Knoxville. If we head out tonight we could maybe be there by morning."

"No. We've got to get him back to Franklin and Ms. Carter," I replied.

"You don't understand Dante. Simon needs professional care. Franklin does not have the necessary facilities or doctors. We must journey to Knoxville."

"I understand but I promised someone I'd make sure he gets back safely. If we can get him there, Ms. Carter will be able to help him."

Onacona stood there examining me for a moment before shrugging his shoulders, "Ok...we will travel to Franklin. Let's get him stabilized and ready for the journey to Franklin."

Before I knew it the warriors had converted the clearing into a makeshift campsite. Smoke filled the glade while several Indians huddled around small fires chatting and laughing while they sorted through the items left behind by the militiamen.

Sitting across from Simon I watched as the soldiers took off Simon's shirt and began cleaning away the mixture of dried

blood and dirt. Once clean they began caking on a yellow powder before firmly wrapping a long swath of material around his
midsection and tying it firmly.

"What is that I asked?"

"My people call it Plumajillo however I believe the white man
refer to it as Yarrow," explained Onacona before deciding on
one of several small apples and taking a bite. "It helps to stop the
bleeding while fighting infection,"

"Is it safe?"

"Of course Dante," Onacona explained. "My people have been
using it for thousands of years. Centuries before the white man
arrived on these shores. We do not have drug stores and elixirs
like your doctors and infirmaries. Mother earth has provided us
with everything we need. You just have to know where to find
it," he added before popping another small apple into his mouth.

"How do you speak English so well?"

Onacona smiled while finishing up the last bit of apple.

"I was a translator for the English in the Second American
War, the War of 1812. The majority of the indigenous people of
the Americans fought with Tecumseh and his alliance. After the
war ended and the British and American troops made a treaty, it
left us with no lands or alliance. As a result, I took my horse and
went back to live with my people near Knoxville," replied Onacona.

"Shit! I forgot about Blaze, my horse. He was injured by a
bayonet. I got to find him."

"Tohiyusdv Dante." Onacona replied. My people are dressing
his wounds. The blade must have broken because it did not fully

penetrate his torso. His wound is being cleaned and he and the other horse are being cared for."

"Everything is going to be ok Dante. Get some rest. We will leave as soon as Simon is ready to travel."

In that moment, I exhaled. Leaning back against the tree stump I took another deep breath and, despite my best efforts to fight against it, my eyes closed, and I quickly fell asleep.

It felt like minutes later I awoke to the feeling of heat radiating on my face. Opening my eyes I discovered I was face to snout with Blaze. His oversized lashes blinked curiously while his brown eyes peered at me as if saying, "what are you waiting for?"

"Looks like someone is ready to go?" expressed Onacona.

"How long have I been sleep?"

"Just a few hours. The sun will be up soon. Simon is all loaded up and this guy here has been patched up. Mohe and I are ready to escort you and Simon back to Franklin."

I hopped to my feet and began examining the wound on Blaze's lower torso. Where dried blood covered most of his leg just hours earlier, it was now clean with just a small incision barely visible through his dark brown fur.

"What did you do?"

"Not much. The wound was not deep. Looks like a piece of the bayonet broke off so it did not do much damage. We cleaned up the cut and treated it with some Yarrow. We'll take it easy this morning, but he should be fine in a day or two," explained Onacona.

"Amazing," I muttered to myself while rubbing Blaze's chest and lower neck. "I just knew he was a goner."

"Nope. If Mother Earth made anything more beautiful, she kept it for herself!" exclaimed Onacona while rubbing Blaze's hindquarter.

As if agreeing with him, Blaze lowered his head and gently nudged my hand, begging for a scratch between his ears.

Standing there examining Blaze I looked over my shoulder and discovered Mohe atop a Stallion. He was a beautiful Appaloosa with large brown spots covering his mostly white body. His long dark colored mane flowed gently in the morning breeze, giving him a majestic appearance. He stomped nervously, seemingly signaling his readiness to depart and start the journey. Mohe smiled and waved at me, while calmly stroking the anxious creature.

"Osiyo Dawntee. Hel-lo Dawntee!"

"Hello Mohe," I replied.

It had been almost a week since I had last seen him. At the time he was in pretty bad shape however in less than a week he looked much better. He had put on a few pounds and looked, what I imagine was, more like himself. Adorned in his traditional Native American garb of a leather top and bottom with matching turquoise and beaded necklaces, he looked strong and powerful sitting atop the beautiful horse.

Although not himself, Simon sat upright on Misty. Wrapped tightly in a red and black colored blanket he looked weak and slightly pale, but he was alive. With that slight half smiled he looked down at me and gave a barely recognizable wink.

"Inena!" proclaimed Mohe.

Looking at Onacona inquisitively he laughed. "Mohe says, "It's time to go!"

With that, I climbed into Blaze's saddle and fell in line beside Onacona.

It was just before dawn when we started navigating our way through the forest. Several Cherokee warriors rode ahead of us but by the time we made it to open terrain it was just Mohe, Onacona, Simon and I that remained. Once free from the deep concentration of trees we started making our way west.

Onacona and I talked about a lot of things while traveling. He explained how they had amazingly found Simon and me. Several of the warriors were in a hunting party the previous evening when they heard a series of gun shots. Two of them saw Simon and I rushing to the forest and did not think anything of it until they mentioned it to Mohe.

According to Onacona, "It's not every day you find white men chasing two colored men on horseback. Mohe had already explained his encounter with two colored men earlier in the week and wondered if it was possible that it was the two same men. We tracked you from the cave you were hiding in that night and caught up to you the next morning."

As he explained his unlikely story of randomly stumbling across us I wondered if that was mere coincidence or some help from the big guy upstairs. I laughed to myself thinking about what my 80-year-old grandmother would say, "Praise him!"

I shared selective things with Onacona about me and my journey with Simon and how I had become his student. And we also talked about the many different people, both good and bad, we had met in our journeys.

By the time he had finished telling me more about his childhood and memories from his battles during the American Indian

War we were crossing the creek and entering the gate of the Apple Mountain Plantation.

Wading through the stream, we made the short climb up the hill toward the big house.

Approaching the large house several workers paused as Simon and me, complete with our two Cherokee escorts, made our way to the front porch. One of the young boys, recognizing Simon, took off running to the front door and began yelling for Ms. Carter. Almost immediately Ms. Carter bolted down the stairs and began demanding to know what happened.

I contemplated explaining the sequence of events, but all I could say was, "He's been shot, on his side. He's lost a lot of blood."

Ms. Carter and several onlookers quickly grabbed Simon and gently lifted him off the horse.

"Quickly, please help me carry him inside," instructed Ms. Carter.

I turned around to thank Mohe and Onacona, but they were nowhere to be found. In the commotion, they had slipped away, descending back down the hill. I thought for a moment about following them but realized there was no use. Mohe had done exactly what he'd promised.

Sliding out of Blaze's saddle, I followed the group carrying Simon as they delivered him upstairs and laid him gently on Ms. Carter's bed. In the chaos of our arrival, I had not noticed Yolanda had rushed in with towels and a wash basin. She looked at me and smiled briefly as she put the supplies on the table.

Standing at the foot of the bed, I finally got a good look at him. I knew the blood loss had been bad, however seeing his complexion set off a new wave of warning flags regarding his ability to overcome the injury.

"Excuse me everyone. Please, I need everyone's attention!" shouted Ms. Carter to the crowded room of well-wishers.

"I do appreciate all of your help however Mr. Simon desperately needs some rest. He will have the best possible care and we expect a full recovery, but in the meantime, I need everyone to give him some time to rest. I promise I will provide updates shortly."

The onlookers and servants paused for a moment, not quite sure how to react to Ms. Carter's request.

"Please, I need everyone to leave immediately," she repeated more firmly. "I do appreciate all of your help, and I will update you on Simon's status just as soon as we assess his condition."

With Yolanda's help, the crowd slowly began to disperse. Seeing the final onlookers begin to file out I too began to exit when Ms. Carter grabbed my hand.

"Not you Dante. Please stay," she asked.

Looking around at the others, I walked back to the bed and uncomfortably watched Simon's chest slowly rise and fall as he struggled to breathe.

Ms. Carter continued to escort the last person out of the room before she paused to speak with Yolanda.

Whatever she said appeared to catch Yolanda off guard as her expression immediately changed. Ms. Carter hugged her tightly and again spoke to her softly before Yolanda surrendered the last of the towels and exited the room.

Closing the door behind her, Ms. Carter leaned over and locked the door with a key dangling from her neck. Her attention then switched to a large foot chest at the base of the bed and, using the same key she unlocked it. After rummaging through its contents, she pulled out a pair of jeans, a T-shirt, and a pair of sneakers.

"Please help me get him changed into these," she said before tossing me the clothes and locking the chest. "We don't have the tools or technology to give Simon what he needs. I've got to get him back to the future or he's not going to make it."

I grabbed the clothes and began stripping off Simon's tattered and bloodied clothing. Pulling off the blood-stained shirt, I watched as blood slowly oozed from the makeshift bandage applied by Mohes men. Using one of the towels left by Yolanda, I patted the wound then quickly helped him get dressed. Looking back, I was surprised to find Ms. Carter had already changed into a pair of jeans and an oversized brown T-shirt with matching boots.

Removing the necklace and key, she held it tightly in front of me. "I need you to hold onto this key," she explained before placing it firmly in the palm of my hand. Refocusing on a large piece of furniture in the corner draped in a dust cover, she pulled the cloth from the structure, exposing a large wooden armoire.

"I need you to keep the bedroom door locked. Do not let anyone in. Once we get back, I will be able to open the door from the inside. You'll need to keep the staff calm, especially Yolanda." Ms. Carter's expression immediately changed.

"She's been different lately. In the last few years she has had some pretty traumatic things happen to her. Since the accident, she's never quite been the same." Keep a close eye on her.

Despite his weakened condition, Simon held his weight surprisingly well while walking alongside Ms. Carter.

Opening the door I asked, "Should I go in with you?"

"No. We just need to get through the portal. Once there, we can call an ambulance. I have friends who work at a nearby hospital. If all goes well, we should be back in a day or two."

Clenching his forearm, I helped Simon step gingerly into the armoire while Ms. Carter stepped in behind him. "Remember, be careful," she whispered before gently closing the door.

Standing there alone in the bedroom, I stared at the large cabinet, seemingly waiting for the door to swing open.

The reality of once again being alone in a foreign place without the ability to get home began to slowly cross my mind. After several minutes of staring blankly at the cabinet, I looked down, exhausted from the near brush with death and exhaled loudly. Looking down at the wooden planked floor, I noticed several drops of blood splattered on the floor leading to the armoire. I immediately thought about Simon's wound and the amount of blood he had lost during our escape. Using the blood-stained undershirt, I quickly wiped up the small pools of blood before collapsing onto the bed.

After a wide yawn, I looked up at the plaster patterned ceiling and again began to wonder about Simon and Ms. Carter. Had they found help in time? And if so, when would they return? Refocusing on the wooden cabinet, I kept watch on the door they had just gently closed. Waiting patiently, my eyelids began to close before slowly sending me into a deep sleep.

# Ten

# Manipulation

I sat up, startled, and disoriented by the darkness and the aggressive knocking.

"Hello. Ms. Carter, can I bring you some food?" Yolanda asked as she frantically knocked on the door.

Rubbing my hand on the lacy bedspread, I instantly remembered I was in Ms. Carter's bedroom.

"Um, I think we're ok for now Yolanda. Thanks," I replied nervously.

I sat quietly as she stood silently on the other side of the door before turning abruptly and stomping down the long hallway leading to the staircase. Reaching for the glass kerosene lamp, I twisted the flint striker until the lamp slowly began to brightly illuminate the room. Holding the light next to the large armoire, I searched for any sign that Simon or Ms. Carter had returned however, a brief examination of the cabinet and doorway confirmed the obvious.

Holding the lamp at eye level, I made a semi-circle scan of the room while reviewing its full contents.

From the window I could see the bright flames glowing in the fireplaces of the small slave quarters dotting the plantation's landscape. Seeing the homes and thinking about the people inhabiting them reminded me of Ms. Carter's instructions, "Keep everyone calm."

"How the hell do I do that?" I thought. "I've got to get downstairs. Let them know everything is ok."

Placing the lamp on the dresser, I pulled the necklace and key from around my neck and unlocked the door.

Stepping into the doorway and peering down the long hallway I patiently waited to ensure the hallway was empty. Once comfortable that I was alone, I stepped into the corridor and locked the door behind me.

Judging by the eerie silence and the candle lights flickering on the sconces lining the wall, it had to be well past midnight.

A quick walk down the stairs, through the dining room and into the empty kitchen confirmed my suspicions. The room was empty and cleaned spotlessly however the aromas from earlier that evening lingered in the wide-open cooking area. The smells, combined with the aching feeling in my stomach, quickly reminded me that I had not eaten in the last day or two. Just as I began rummaging through the wooden ice box, a familiar voice made me pause.

"I prepared food for you hours ago."

"Hello Yolanda," I replied nervously without looking at her directly. "How are you?"

Turning, I could see her standing in between the wooden swinging doors. Draped in a long cotton housecoat with arms crossed, she strolled into the kitchen, eyes fixed squarely on me.

"I knocked several times," she continued, "but no one responded."

"Oh, I'm sorry. Simon was resting, and Ms. Carter...she was...well...taking care of him," I explained awkwardly.

"How is he?"

I thought about Ms. Carter's comments and tried to listen beyond the question.

"He's doing much better. Ms. Carter asked me to bring some food up, maybe some broth for Simon and whatever I could find for Ms. Carter and I."

Yolanda sat staring through me for a moment before responding.

"Of course. Let me put a tray together," she replied while opening the pantry doors and the same wooden ice box. "Whatever happened to those girls you were so obsessed with?" Yolanda asked while casually placing food on the tray.

"Jamaya and Briana? I'm not sure, but I hear they are far away from here," I replied while reaching for the food tray."

Yolanda stood, examining me closely before reaching for my hand.

"That's a beautiful ring," she exclaimed while clutching my wrist and running her finger along the smooth exterior of the band occupying my pinky finger. "I swear it looks identical to a ring I recently saw around the neck of a runaway slave girl."

"That's funny," I replied while attempting to pull my hand away from her surprisingly strong grip, "I didn't notice."

After partially balling up my fist, I pulled my hand away before grabbing the tray of food.

"I'm going to drop this off to Simon and Ms. Carter. If you need anything, I will be spending the evening in the guest room. Maybe I will see you tomorrow," I said with a smile.

"If I don't see you sooner," she replied with a mischievous smile.

The smile stayed plastered on her face as I slowly backed out of the room and disappeared through the dining room's swinging doors. Walking briskly, I made my way up the stairs to the large bedroom.

After placing the tray on the dresser, I sat on the bed looking at the large platter of food staring back at me.

"How could I possibly dispose of that?" I wondered out loud as I looked around the room. "Can't flush it or throw it out."

Looking at the plate of food, I instantly thought about the extreme eaters I had seen on TV. "Dip and stuff," I thought.

Wrapping the slices of ham and cheese in the thick hunks of bread, I dipped them into the warm broth and shoved them into my mouth. I repeated the extreme sandwiches until the platter was empty. Once finished, I grabbed my saddlebag and the empty tray. Walking into the hallway, I left the tray on the bare wooden floor, carefully locked the door, and made my way to the small guestroom.

Even though it would soon be daylight, the small guest room was still pitch black. I reached in my back pocket for my phone and briefly panicked until I remembered I had left it back at Simon's shop. Feeling my way through the room I found the small oil lamp on the dresser. With a twist of the flint striker the lamp began to glow. A slight adjustment of the metal dial intensified the brightness until the room was brightly lit. I tossed the bags on the opposing bed and collapsed in the bed I had occupied a few days earlier.

Looking up at the ceiling, I wondered how long it would take for Simon and Ms. Carter to return. What if Simon did not make it? My mind began to race as I thought about the possible outcomes when I heard the creaking sound of the old floorboards. I reached for my bag, preparing to pull out my knife, when Yolanda stepped in the doorway.

Rather than the bland cotton robe she wore in the kitchen, she was once again draped in the sheer nightgown she had worn the first morning we met. However this time, she was not shy about me seeing her. Holding a small candle smoldering on a silver candle tray and with the hallway's oil lamps illuminated behind her, everything was now fully exposed.

"You know," she whispered as she sauntered into the room, "the last time we were alone, we got interrupted. This time, it's just you and me," she said while placing the candlestick holder next to the bed.

"I was hoping we could try this again," she explained while swinging her leg over my body and seductively resting on top of me.

"Yolanda," I said.

"No more talking," she said before kissing me.

This time, I knew Simon was not going to interrupt us, nor would any thoughts about Jennifer. Over the last few days, I had all but forgotten about Jennifer and the time we had spent over the last two months. I did, however, think about Jamaya. I knew I would probably never see her again, but the time we spent together was somehow different...special.

Yolanda, as if sensing my mind was elsewhere, again kissed me, this time more sensuously, intent on forcing me to focus solely on her. Despite my repeated efforts to resist, in that moment, she was successful.

***

I awoke to find I was once again alone, this time in the small guest room. After spending much of the waning evening hours with me, Yolanda had at some point slipped out of the room. Those early morning hours had been enjoyable but beyond that, we did not have much to talk about. Lying next to her in the dimly lit room I had groped for the right words, but it had proven difficult. As a result, waking up to find her gone was a relief.

Getting up, I hurried to Ms. Carter's room and found a new tray of food had replaced the empty tray I had eaten the previous night. After unlocking the door, I quickly carried the tray inside and looked at the spread: eggs, ham, biscuits, and coffee.

"Everything three people would love to eat," I thought while shaking my head.

After a deep breath, I sat down and prepared to repeat my extreme eating regimen.

Piling the ham and eggs onto the biscuits, I made a dozen mini sandwiches. Inhaling each, I washed down the breakfast sandwiches with a quick gulp of coffee. After the last biscuit was cleared from the platter, I finished off the small pot of coffee and dipped my hands in the ceramic wash basin. With a quick splash of water on my face, I unlocked the door, placed the tray outside and stepped into the hallway. Pulling the metal skeleton key from the leather chain around my neck, I inserted it into the door and twisted it quickly. With a satisfying "click" I placed the leather string and key back in my shirt, and after a quick tug on the bedroom door, I turned and started making my way downstairs.

Scaling down the stairwell, I walked through the kitchen, pausing briefly to smile at the morning crew busily preparing the day's meals. From the back porch I could easily see well over a mile in the distance. Down the hill and across the field, the large barn towered above the small shacks and structures dotting the countryside.

"Victor," I thought. "I've got some time to burn, maybe I'll check on him."

Stepping off the porch, I grabbed an apple from a large basket sitting on the back deck. Tossing it in the air I caught it and began vigorously polishing it against my thigh as I started the trek down the hill toward the barn.

Passing the small wooden cabins, I smiled at those families already busily engaged in their day's activities. Although it reminded me of the families in my own neighborhood (those out on a Saturday morning cutting the grass, washing their cars, or chatting casually with their neighbors while children of all races threw footballs or rode bikes), I quickly reminded myself that it would be another 100 years before their great grandchildren would even have the hope of owning their own homes in a community of their choice. And that because of the pending war, many of them might not live long enough to even see a glimpse of that hope.

As I approached the last cabin, I noticed a young boy, maybe 9 or 10, playfully swinging what appeared to be a leg of a wooden chair. Before each swing, I watched as he reached into his overall pocket to pull out a small stone. After a quick inspection, he would toss the rock in the air and, without missing a beat, swing the wooden leg and make contact with the stone. The collision would result in the stone sailing into the brush nearly 40 to 50 yards away. Pausing, I looked on as swing after swing, he sent each stone sailing into the field.

Recognizing he now had an audience, he went deeper into his pockets and pulled out a slightly larger stone. This time, tossing the stone in the air, he swung but more powerfully. The familiar 'pock' sound of a solid object hitting wood rang out as the stone sailed twice the distance before disappearing into the thick apple orchard on the other side of the field.

The confidence and swag he exhibited after the 'grand slam' made me laugh out loud. He, like most of the boys in my neighborhood, had the natural ability that I lacked. Even at his young age, he was already showing power and impressive hand-eye coordination. Born at a time when the upcoming postwar baseball craze would consume the nation, he did not know it yet, but his color would ultimately exclude him from fully being able to capitalize on those natural gifts.

"What's your name?" I asked

"John Paige, sir," he replied.

"Paige," I repeated. "That's a good name," I replied before tossing him the apple. "You got a nice swing. Keep it up and it might make you some money one day."

The boy looked at me, momentarily confused by my obscure prediction, before taking a bite of the apple.

Continuing to the stables, I opened the door only to be surprised by Yolanda leaving the barn.

"Good morning," I said cheerfully.

"Hello, Dante," she responded coldly. "Did you get a chance to have breakfast? I was sure to have a tray delivered to Ms. Carter's door."

"No. I didn't eat anything, but it looks like Simon and Ms. Carter cleaned their plates. The food from last night and today was completely gone. I'm sure that has to be a good sign for Simon."

"So, he's back to himself…eating normally?" she asked inquisitively.

"No, he sipped the broth and coffee. Ms. Carter must have eaten the ham and eggs." Yolanda's expression instantly changed.

"Dante, Ms. Carter is a vegetarian. She would have never eaten ham and eggs," she replied before turning abruptly and continuing her march toward the house.

"Wait, I'm not sure who ate what. What difference does it make?"

"Because you're a liar!" she replied turning toward me. "They're not even in that room, are they? Where did they go?" she shouted while pushing me backwards. "Why are you lying?"

"Of course they're in the room. Where else would they be?" I replied while trying to remain calm.

Yolanda paused as if thinking about the question before turning abruptly and resuming her march toward the house. Thoughts flashed through my mind about pursuing her, but I paused while searching for answers to her questions.

"What should I say?" I wondered as she continued her focused hike toward the house.

"Let her go. Besides," I thought while clutching the key dangling from the chain around my neck, "As long as I have this, she does not know anything. What harm could she do?"

Walking into the barn, I found Victor scooping feed from a large barrel into smaller buckets.

"Hey Dante!" exclaimed Victor. "I wasn't expecting to see you this soon. I heard about Simon, is he ok?"

"Yes, I think he's going to be fine," I replied. "How's it been going with the reading? Have you been practicing on that poster?" I asked pointing to the empty spot on the wall. "Where did it go?"

"You know….a funny thing happened the morning after y'all left. Old man Norris came by here looking for Ms. Yolanda. They didn't know I was in that stall there listening," he said, pointing to an empty stall next to the post where the poster was originally hanging.

"He was asking where the girls were, but Ms. Yolanda didn't know. She just kep' saying, 'They left last night….I don't know…they left last night!'

I was going to speak up, but something told me to keep quiet. I hope that was ok, I ain't never much cared for Old Man Norris. He has a real mean streak in him. I try to avoid him whenever he comes up to sell Ms. Carter some of his livestock."

"No Victor, you did just fine. Sometimes it's ok to keep things to yourself. That is odd, why would Yolanda be speaking to this Old Man Norris?" I thought out loud when I noticed Victor looking at my chest.

"What is it?"

"That key on your necklace," he replied.

"Yeah, what about it?" I asked.

"It got wax on it," Victor replied while pointing to Ms. Carter's key hanging from the leather necklace.

Pulling the key in closer, I examined it closely. "You're right, it does have wax on it. How did that get on there?" I asked while flicking a small piece of wax from the large skeleton key.

"I make all the keys here for Ms. Carter," Victor explained while he resumed shoveling the feed. "Matter of fact, Ms. Yolanda was just here having me pour a new key for her. Said she broke the handle, so we had to use a wax mold to make a new one.

My heart sank as I finally realized where the wax had come from.

"She used me," I thought. "She manipulated me to get to the key and now she's heading to the house to open the door, and the…."

"I'm sorry Victor, I have to go," I said before bolting out of the barn. Running in the direction of the house I looked across the field and could faintly see Yolanda strolling up the hill toward the big house. I switched to a full sprint in order to close the gap while trying to stay out of sight for fear that if spotted, she might bolt for the house.

Passing the slave quarters, I squinted against the bright morning sun to see Yolanda approaching the big house. The only terrain left was the slow climb up the hill, and she would be on the back porch leading to the kitchen. As she started up the incline, I could see someone step onto a nearby porch and call her name. When she turned, I could instantly tell she had spotted me. Without responding, she instantly broke into a full sprint.

Although I was still 50 yards behind her, I sprinted up the hill and closed the remaining gap. Unfortunately, I was too late. Reaching the house, she leapt on the porch, ran through the door, and slammed it quickly behind her.

I too jumped on the porch and attempted to turn the handle only to find she had fastened the crude metal lock from the inside. Looking through tearful angry eyes, she stared at me coldly. Then, turning abruptly, she darted through the kitchen, disappearing through the swinging doors leading to the dining room. I motioned for one of the workers to open the door, but all eyes focused downward, refusing to leave any impression that they had crossed the vindictive Ms. Yolanda.

Hopping the rail, I sprinted around the house, through the front door, up the stairs and down the long hallway. Rounding the corner, I paused when I saw Yolanda standing frozen in Ms. Carter's opened doorway.

My mind began to race as I thought of possible explanations for Simon and Ms. Carter's absence. How could I explain the unexplainable?

Stepping through the doorway, I stumbled backwards when I saw him. There, sitting upright in the undersized bed was Simon. Calmly puffing on a cigar while Ms. Carter sat nervously in a small wooden chair beside him.

"Hello Yolanda," Ms. Carter said before standing and hugging her tightly. "Are you ok? You seem to be out of breath."

"No ma'am…I'm fine. Just wanted to see how you and Mr. Simon were getting along," she replied while looking back at me and nervously attempting to hide the hastily poured skeleton key.

"Dante," Simon said, extending his hand to me.

"Hey Simon. How are you feeling?" I asked, looking nervously at him and Ms. Carter.

"I'm well," he replied. "It sounds like it might have been worse had it not been for you."

I smiled. "Thank Mohe. He came through for us both. I thought we lost you."

Simon smiled, "Not with some sissy .22. When it is my time, it is going to be a man's gun or his hands," he explained before blowing smoke into the air and grimacing at his overconfidence.

"I'm glad to see you're doing better Mr. Simon," Yolanda explained while slowly backing out of the bedroom. "I guess I'll let you get some rest and maybe come up and check on you later."

"That will be fine. I look forward to speaking with you Yolanda," added Ms. Carter.

Yolanda left the room, closing the door gently behind her. After a couple of minutes, I opened the door and peered around the corner to make sure she had left the hallway. Closing the door, I turned to Simon and Ms. Carter, "We need to talk."

I used the next hour explaining how Yolanda spent the previous day, and most of the evening, manipulating me in an attempt to break into Ms. Carter's bedroom. Holding up the wax-caked key, I explained the epic race back to the house and my surprise to find her and Simon had returned.

Simon and Ms. Carter sat in quiet disbelief as I explained the details Victor shared regarding the conversation between Yolanda and Old Man Norris about the runaway slaves.

"And now that I have had a chance to think about it, I do remember Jeb and Jim talking about two people paying for the reward," I said.

"You know Dante, now that you mention it," explained Simon, "I remember that same conversation. Something about her paying Jim after Mr. Norris gave her the money. In fact, right up until the end, Jim was saying something about, "She's the one you need to worry about..." and "they're going to get away with it...""

"Wait…. are we saying what I think we are saying?" I asked. "Could Yolanda really be that 'she' they were referring to?"

"I'm afraid to say it's very possible," said Ms. Carter. "Mr. Norris controls most of the livestock for the county, so I occasionally have to buy feed or supplies from him. He is hands down the most brutal and racist man in Franklin. It wouldn't surprise me to find out he was behind the kidnapping attempt. Now that I hear Yolanda was having secret meetings with him, it is very likely she was involved.

Before you two arrived last week, she was becoming increasingly hateful, even cruel to some of the workers. I tried to get her to take a low dose of Lithium, but she refused and now she's not responding to conversations I have been trying to have with her. Then, after you left, she was especially angry. For some reason, she really hated those girls. It saddens me to say it but nothing would surprise me."

"Lithium, what's that for?" I asked.

"Her condition. I believe she, like her mother, is Bipolar. Her mother battled the disorder right up until she died."

"From the fire. Yolanda told me her mom died after getting trapped in a fire while rescuing some kids. Not true?"

"No. I believe Yolanda started that fire and there were no children," explained Ms. Carter. "Her mother was one of the original slaves freed when I took over. It was during one of her episodes that she got pregnant with Yolanda. The father, Fredrick Wilmington, was another free slave that lived with them here on the farm. We both tried our best to help her. I would bring medications from the hospital and he would care for her during those difficult times, but eventually she refused to accept our help. He eventually moved north and purchased a few acres outside of Buffalo New York. I took her and Yolanda in but it didn't change, in fact it got worse. It got to the point where she wouldn't stay here at the house. On any given day you'd find her in any of several cabins with god knows who."

"On the day of the fire," she continued, "Yolanda was 13. She was there, at the cabin begging her mother to come home. She had been living with a man for over a month. According to Yolanda the cabin was dirty, and she wanted to help her clean it but needed to boil some water. She said she started a fire that quickly got out of control. It ended with her mother and the other man being trapped in the house. Both of them died in the fire. Old Man Norris was the magistrate at the time. He alone determined the fire was an accident. The poor girl watched them burn alive. Yeah...she's been through a lot and if she's involved with Old Man Norris and this kidnapping attempt, there is no telling what she's capable of."

"What do you think we should do, talk to her?" I asked.

"That's a good place to start, let's go down to her room," said Ms. Carter. "We'll show her the key and see what she has to say."

Simon flipped the bedspread back in preparation to slide out of the bed.

"Where do you think you're going?" Ms. Carter asked.

"I'm going with you to speak with Yolanda," Simon responded.

"Are you sure?" she asked.

"I was shot not killed," Simon snapped followed by a quick wink. "Which way are we headed?"

We followed Ms. Carter down the long hallway, passing the guest room until we arrived on the opposite side of the house. Ms. Carter knocked gently on the door.

"Yolanda. I need to speak with you honey." We stood quietly waiting for a response before she knocked again. "Yolanda, I know about the key. It's ok. We just need to talk about it." Turning the handle, she discovered it was locked.

"Dante, would you please try your key?" Simon asked while taking a step backwards and gently pulling Ms. Carter close to him.

"My pleasure," I responded. Taking a step back, I unleashed a simple front kick right next to the door handle. The doorframe instantly cracked and splintered as the door swung open wildly. Ms. Carter looked at Simon and shook her head as she stepped into the room, prompting a satisfied smile from Simon.

Ms. Carter stood in the doorway examining the room from afar. After a quick assessment, she came to her conclusion, "She's gone."

"What do you mean 'she is gone?" You barely looked around?" Simon asked.

"A painting of her mother as a child always sits on her desk. And she keeps a sweater on the back of this chair. It is one I made for her just after her mother died. They're both gone."

Ms. Carter moved over to the large, mirrored vanity and gently sat on the floral-patterned cushion. Opening the drawer, she sifted through the contents before gasping loudly.

"I can't believe it!" she cried out while holding up items recovered from the vanity. "My jewels, a silver hair pin and brush. I have been missing these for months. In fact, she and I just discussed these very items a few weeks ago. I suspected she had stolen them, but she insisted an older woman, Janice, from housekeeping was the thief. I knew she was lying but I allowed her to push me to accuse someone else."

"What happened to her?" I asked.

"I had her work assignment changed from housekeeping to outside laundry. I feel horrible," she said out loud while examining the stolen items. "How could someone you love like your own child betray you over and over again?" she asked.

"Like you said, she's troubled," Simon replied. "People do the oddest things when they're suffering from an illness or feeling desperate. If she did run, do you have any idea where she might go?"

"I'm not even sure I know her anymore. If she is involved with Mr. Norris, she could be anywhere. He has homes and buildings all around the county. And as a free woman, she can come and go as she pleases."

Moments later, a young girl popped into the doorway. "Excuse me ma'am. Ms. Crabtree wants you to cum to da kichen. She say it a umurgency."

The four of us hurried downstairs, rushed into the kitchen, and burst through the swinging doors, The kitchen looked like a hurricane had blown through. Flour and sugar were thrown on the floor along with shards of broken dishes.

"And that's not all," exclaimed a tearful Ms. Crabtree. "The moneybox you gave me for buying food items is empty. It's all gone. It was Yolanda, Ms. Carter. I walked in when I heard the dishes breaking and found her throwing things and screaming. It was like something evil just came over her. I tried to calm her down, but she struck me. She put some food in her bag and ran out the back door. That's when I sent Tonisha to come find you."

Ms. Carter silently surveyed the damage then turned to her staff. "I'm sorry you had to see this Ms. Crabtree. Yolanda is going through something right now. We are going to help her, but for now, I need your help. Please pass on to all the staff that effective immediately, Ms. Yolanda is no longer permitted in the house."

"I'm going away for a few weeks and I'm leaving you in charge of the house and its day-to-day operations. I will speak with Mr. Gleason, he will manage the plantation and outdoor staff. If you have any problems, please discuss them with him. For now, I need you to pack two days' worth of food for three. Tonisha, sweetie," she said, turning to the young girl, "please tell Victor that we need the small carriage up front. We will be leaving immediately. Have him use our horses and to strap Mr. Simon's horses to the back."

Ms. Carter smiled as she turned to Simon and me, "I think it's time I got you boys home."

***

The ride home was uneventful. We passed several militia groups along the way however, having Ms. Carter made us seemingly invisible to all onlookers. Riding mostly alone in the rear of the wagon, I sat quietly in the rear watching Misty and Blaze follow lazily behind us. Rubbing my hand along her face and down to her muzzle, I looked at my reflection in her large brown eye as she looked at me inquisitively. Protected by the long black lashes, she blinked rapidly as she gently shooed away the small gnats buzzing around her. Maintaining laser-like focus, her glare seemed to confirm she, too, was ready to go home.

Having reached her prime, there were certainly things and people she had encountered in the last decade of her life. Things that were memorable while others were likely not so memorable. "If only you could talk. I bet you've got some stories to tell," I concluded while giving her a good scratch behind the ears.

She quickly nodded her approval while Blaze leaned in for some affection.

"I didn't forget about you," I added while rubbing under his chin. "I know you've both seen a lot in the last decade. No one should have to see some of those things, man or animal!"

Climbing back to the front of the wagon and grabbing the reins from Simon I began thinking about Jamaya. By now they had certainly reached Indianapolis. Had they found their family? Were they safe? Then there was Yolanda? What had caused her so much pain that pushed her over the edge? And had she been involved with the attempted kidnapping?

Finally, I thought about my family. I couldn't believe it but I had really missed them. Being away and around people who did not know their families or those who were missing family members made me appreciate mine even more. I smiled as we made the last turn and the large plaster rock slowly came into view. There were times in the last week where I was not sure I'd ever see that stupid, and at the same time, beautiful fake rock.

It had been a week since Simon, and I embarked on our journey to sell some horses and replenish Ms. Carter's supplies. The two months prior to that was spent mentally and physically pushing myself, never imagining I would be forced to utilize those newly acquired skills.

Over the course of the eight weeks, I had learned so much about myself. Not only had I uncovered some vulnerabilities, but I also discovered I was stronger than I had ever imagined. Pressing the button, the fake, plastered rock swung open revealing the narrow path leading through the woods. With a tug of the reins, I guided the horses up the narrow trail leading to Simon's compound.

"Home sweet home," I said, hopping out of the wagon and unstrapping the horses. After opening the pasture Gate, I watched as Misty, Blaze, Big Jake, and Peanut bolted into the pasture, seemingly moving with a little more swiftness now that they were back in familiar surroundings. Walking back to the house, I found Ms. Carter and Simon sitting on the porch, now in modern plain clothes.

"Are you ready to head back to modern day Atlanta?" Simon asked, smiling.

"Oddly enough, I think I am."

We walked into the small cabin and opened the door of the armoire. After opening the portal door and peeking through, I stepped through the inner door and held it open.

"We're going to open the front doors," Simon said, "We'll let you get changed."

Walking back into the work area, I picked up my cell, 5:45 PM. In just 34 minutes, I had 3 missed calls from Jennifer. Of all the things that had run through my mind, Jennifer was not one of them. I took off the tattered clothing and put on my jeans and T-shirt. After buttoning my jeans, I pulled on the waist and realized they were fitting kind of loose. A quick glance in the mirror and I realized the activity over the last week must have caused me to lose a few pounds.

"I wonder if anyone will notice," I thought as I walked toward the front of the store where I found Simon and Ms. Carter finishing up with a customer. Standing in the entryway I waited as Simon gave handling instructions for the client's newly refurbished bag. After several minutes, the customer, satisfied with the explanation, turned, and walked into the mall.

"I guess we are done for the day," I said, looking at Simon and Ms. Carter.

"Yep. What are your plans?" asked Simon.

"Me, I'm heading home. I'll probably chill out for the rest of the night, maybe get some pizza or grab a burger," I said smiling.

"Well, you deserve it. I owe you Dante," said Simon.

"No you don't," I said. "I'm still repaying you for saving my butt."

Ms. Carter came from behind the counter and looked at me through tearful eyes. "I asked you to take care of him, and you did. Thank you, Dante," she said while hugging me tightly.

"No problem Ms. Carter."

"We're family now Dante. Please call me Jackie."

I smiled, "Of course, Jackie. You two enjoy the weekend and I'll see you after school Monday."

Swinging my bag over my shoulder, I started walking toward the escalator. Pausing before stepping on the quickly moving steps, I looked at the two of them standing in the store's doorway. Who could ever imagine this odd cosmic relationship? A former slave from the 1800s and a white woman from downtown Chicago. I smiled at the thought as I stepped onto the escalator and started moving to the upper floor. I gave one more wave before they disappeared from my view.

# Eleven

# Refined

After a brief ride on the city bus, I paused as I made my way into my subdivision entrance.  Looking at the pool and playground where Justin and I hung out virtually every summer for the last 12 years brought back good memories. Comparing that life to the experiences of many that lived years before us, especially those I recently met, made me feel incredibly blessed and fortunate.

A brief walk down my street and up the driveway brought out a quick smile as I turned the handle and walked inside. My father, as was his custom, could be found sitting in his favorite recliner watching the game somewhere between partially awake and aggressively snoring. Anticipating his reaction, I quietly grabbed the remote sitting on the arm of his chair.

"What are you doing, I'm watching that," he said through closed eyes.

Laughing at the expected response I collapsed on the couch and replied, "Ok, then who's winning?"

"Hawks just scored. They're about to start overtime. Coach Pierce needs to take out that Bazemore, he's playing awful tonight," he responded without opening an eye.

I held back a smile as I sat intensely listening to his in-game analysis. When I noticed him starting to fade, I headed into the kitchen to check on my mom and Trisha.

Although Trisha was technically the cook, mom was usually in the kitchen assisting her. They had recently decreed Friday evenings as 'Trisha cook night' after my sister insisted, she needed experience cooking before going off to college. As a result, we'd spent the last three Friday's eating interesting meals prepared and served by Trisha.

"Hey." I announced casually while walking past her toward my mother.

Unimpressed with the cool greeting Trisha gave me an exaggerated kiss on the cheek followed by her customary pinch of my cheeks. To her surprise I returned the kiss before walking over to my mom.

"Hey mom," I said while giving her a huge bear hug.

"Eww…..you're skin and bones. It's like hugging a sick Snoopy Dog!"

"That's Snoop mom, Snoop Dogg"

"Snoop Dogg. You know what I meant, you are too skinny," she added with a laugh. "What have you eaten today?"

Uh….I don't remember??"

"Well sit down I don't remember" she commanded while rummaging through the refrigerator and placing sandwich fixings on the island. "I swear since you've been working it's like you're getting skinnier and skinnier. Dinner is going to be a few more minutes," she added while looking over her shoulder and pointing at Trisha who was now furiously stirring a pot on the stove, "so you are going to eat a sandwich."

My mother started constructing the sandwich when she noticed the ring on my finger.

"What's that on your finger Boobie, I mean Dante?" she asked.

"Oh, it's just a ring. I got it from a friend."

"I bet it's that Vietnamese girl with the pretty hair. The one he's always texting," exclaimed a smiling Trisha.

"No it's not Jennifer's. It was a friend's but she just moved to Indianapolis.

"Indianapolis. That's pretty far. Why is she moving there?"

"Her parents, they're having a tough time so she's moving in with her aunt."

I don't recall meeting her. We're you guys close?"

"No, she didn't go to West View. I actually just met her earlier this week We had a chance to hang out while she was moving."

"That's nice. I'm glad you're making friends. Seems like if you're not texting that girlfriend of yours, you're in your room playing games with Justin," she added while sliding the turkey sandwich over to me.

Taking a bite, I looked down at the ring and thought about Jamaya.

"Mom, have you ever had a long distance friendship? You know, where you like wrote or talked long distance?"

"Of course. I have a lot of friends from middle school that I still talk to. In fact, I had a friend in Baltimore, her name was

Melanie, we had known each other since we were 8. Man, we did everything together until her father got transferred to Tucson. We wrote for several years, right up until high school, but eventually we lost touch.

"Do you ever think you'll see her again?" I asked.

That's what's funny. Your dad and I were in New Orleans a few years ago. It was during Mardi Gra, thousands of people flooding the streets. I was buying one of those Hurricanes. You know, the drink with the rum, lemon juice, and passion fruit syrup, well anyway, we got our drinks and when I turned around, we literally bumped into each other."

"Who did you bump into?" I asked.

"Melanie, my friend from Baltimore. Turns out she was on vacation there with some girlfriends. And get this, we were staying in the same hotel! Can you imagine that? What are the odds? The next day your dad went out on a fishing charter and Melanie and I spent the entire day catching up. That was three years ago. Since then, a day hasn't passed where we haven't talked or texted at least once."

Wow, I thought as I started doing random calculations on the actual odds. Sensing my mind wondering Trisha looked at me and rolled her eyes.

"The question was rhetorical Boobie! The answer is it doesn't happen.

"No...it happens. Every so often the universe has a way of re-connecting people and places. Just when you think you'll never see someone again..poof."

I sat there eating my sandwich thinking about my mother's miraculous story of reuniting with her childhood friend. Is that possible? I mean, it's statistically possible, not probable, but anything is possible. Sitting there twisting the ring on my finger I watched my mom sample my sister's concoction before instructing her to add some seasoning to the pot. My mother looked back at me and mimed throwing up before my sister caught her and retaliated by dashing her with the saltshaker.

Watching them confirmed how much I had missed having them around. So...for the rest of the evening, I did not think about Simon, Jennifer, or the armoire. For that night, I simply enjoyed spending time and reconnecting with my family.

After sleeping most of Saturday and Sunday morning, I got a Snap from Justin. Laying their swapping messages, I thought again about telling him where I had been and the related experiences. And each time, despite the fact that we had told each other every secret since I could remember, I realized it was a bad idea. Being captured by bounty hunters, evading capture from militia men stirred up by the Civil War, and ultimately being rescued by Cherokee Warriors. Unlike those I met while traveling with Simon, Justin would understand.

We had often theorized about how science supported time travel and imagined what we would do if we were ever able to travel back in time. People we would like to meet, places we would like to travel however, the more I thought about the burden and responsibility associated with knowing about the discovery. The more I thought about it, the more I realized I could not do that to him.

As a result, rather than stepping through the portal and exploring Simon's ranch and horses, we spent the afternoon like most high school juniors, hanging out at my house playing Call of Duty.

The next day I made my way to school. The previous night I'd laid in bed thinking about Jennifer. I hadn't thought about her in several days and that bothered me. I felt like I had to tell her something, but what? How could I explain any of it? My conscious continued to nag at me throughout first period. Once the bell rang, I began the unfamiliar walk to 2$^{nd}$ period gym class.

Although the route was familiar, I rarely used the hallways during the normal three-minute in-between class transfer period. However, since my return, many things had changed. It began when I started working for Simon, coupled with the time I'd spent over the last week at the Apple Mountain Plantation. For a lack of a better term, it changed me.  In the past, my goal was to avoid confrontations, to blend in. But now, although I was not looking for a confrontation, I wasn't hiding from it either.

Casually walking in the locker room, I dropped my gym bag just as the tardy bell rang. The small musty locker room was once again packed with kids of all sizes and ages. Some standing around laughing and joking while others, like Justin and I in the past, worked diligently to get dressed and into the gymnasium as quickly as possible. Locating an empty locker I started to unload my stuff when I recognized a familiar face. It was the kid from the office. I had only seen him briefly while waiting for Mr. Johnson, but as I focused, I was certain it was him.

I started to walk over to speak with him when a towel came flying across the room. The soiled wet towel collided with the unsuspecting kid, prompting Marcus and his gorilla friends to erupt into laughter. I paused, certain he would find a way to slip out of the crowded locker-room, but rather than run, he stood there quietly.

Picking up the towel he looked at it and slowly began rolling it into a ball. Without saying a word, he took the wet towel and threw it across the room. The moist towel flew, almost in slow motion, across the room before hitting Marcus in face with a splat.

The sound of the collision seemed to reverberate throughout the locker room. This time, the entire locker room erupted into laughter as a stunned Marcus stood draped in the soggy towel. My eyes bounced back and forth between the kid and a now enraged Marcus. Without warning, Marcus charged at the kid. I had already taken a few steps in his direction, which left me directly in his path.

Watching his strides, I took one additional step and intentionally collided with Marcus. Although the contact was minimal, it was just enough to redirect his momentum. Rather than colliding with the kid, he crashed headfirst into a wall of lockers. The room again erupted into laughter as Marcus stood bloodied and disoriented. Looking at the kid then at me, he wiped his forehead with the back of his shirt sleeve, leaving behind a crimson-colored streak. Refocusing his gaze on me, he started in my direction when a loud whistle instantly silenced the raucous crowd. All eyes instantly turned to the entrance where Coach Brown stood, hands on hips with his whistle hanging from his roped necklace.

"I don't know what the hell you men are doing in here but you've got exactly two minutes to get dressed and in that gym. Please do not try me," barked Coach Brown.

Turning to Marcus he pointed a finger and continued his threat. "Mr. Marcus, that goes double for you and your boys. Clean that shit off your face and get in that gym!"

Marcus, still nurturing his bloodied wound, glared at me briefly before storming into the gym.

Coach Brown repeated his threat one last time before turning and making his way to the gymnasium.

Once the coast was clear Justin slipped back into the locker room and began to wildly wave his arms while making gorilla sounds. I couldn't help but laugh at his stupidity.

"What the hell were you thinking?" he asked. "You walked in at the same time as those damn gorillas. You should have been dressed ten minutes ago."

"Yeah, I know. I'm tired man." I opened my locker and started getting undressed. "Tired of being afraid, tired of people, just tired dude. And I'm especially tired of being afraid of Marcus and those damn idiots."

"So, you're tired huh? Tired of people, tired of being afraid of Marcus," Justin asked. "Are you tired of taking those damn steroids?"

"What are you talking about?" I replied.

"Those and that," Justin said pointing to my torso and arms. "Dude tell me you're not shooting that stuff in your butt. Because if you are, I completely want in!" he said while pulling down his shorts and exposing his bare butt.

"Man you're stupid," I said, closing the locker door and pushing him. "I've been working out...after school."

"I need to get in on that workout and tighten up my abs a little bit," he replied while pulling up his shirt and rubbing his stomach.

"What you need to tighten up is that fade," I said, while grabbing at his head.

"Man my barber is sick, I gotta find somebody to hook it up," he replied while leaning toward the mirror.

"For now, we better get in the gym before crazy ass Coach Brown comes back in here with that damn whistle," I replied.

With the exception of Marcus's constant scowl, the hour and a half passed without incident.

I met the kid, Jonathon, who had just escaped the altercation with Marcus. In speaking with him, I confirmed he was in fact upstairs the afternoon I got jumped. After hearing Marcus and his friends approaching in the stairwell, he hid in a maintenance closet until they passed. Once out of danger, he found the security guard and alerted him that something was going down on the top floor. I was not surprised to hear that despite being new to the school, he had already reached his limit with Marcus.

As we worked out, Justin and I explained our long history with Marcus. Looking across the gym, I could feel his eyes glaring at the three of us. And my experience with Marchs assured me he could not let it go. It wasn't over.

***

The lunch bell rang triggering the mass exodus to the cafeteria or whatever nook or cranny kids could find to eat lunch. I made my usual trek up to my locker then downstairs to meet up with Justin. The entire time, I twisted the ring on my pinky finger while again thinking about Jamaya.

By the time I made it down to the cafeteria, the large lunch-room was in full swing. Lines had dwindled down to a few stragglers picking through prepackaged items which meant most everyone was finishing up lunch or sitting around talking. Making my way through the crowds in route to our normal meeting spot I looked around nervously, not for Marcus, but Jennifer. I'd resolved to end it however I wasn't yet confident about how or what to say. As a result, I thought it best to avoid the conversation.

In doing so, I skillfully found groups of people that I could blend in with while walking through the lunchroom. That was until I once again stumbled into him. While bouncing through the crowds I turned and literally bumped into Marcus. He and his gorilla friends were sitting awkwardly in front of the table where we routinely met for lunch. I paused as he arrogantly plopped on the table.

Since gym class earlier that day I'd been preparing for this moment. I assumed Marcus would find me or Jonathon, the new kid, and would demand his pound of flesh. I'd literally dreamed of the moment, maybe even subconsciously I'd been looking forward to it, however my moment of reflection the previous night while spending time with my family had offered some new perspective.

Real lives had been lost and people had suffered. I understood it happened many years ago but for me, it was happening right now. It was happening to people I now called friends and somehow, it seemed silly wrestling on the floor and throwing punches with a kid at my school. Seeing Marcus' fat butt sitting on the table attempting to bait me into a fight seemed not only stupid but embarrassing. Looking past Marcus, I spoke directly to Justin.

"Hey, you ready to head upstairs?"

Always seeking to be the focus of everyone's attention Marcus propped his feet up on the adjacent table, blocking our exit.

"How you gonna come in here and walk by me like I'm not even sitting here? That's very rude Mr. West? I know you're mommy taught you better than that," he added which prompted his goons to bust out in laughter.

"Look dude. I don't know how all of this got started but it's time to squash it. I don't have any beef with you. Let's end this bro," I replied while extending my fist.

"It started because you're a little Bitch!" he barked before pushing my fist away.

I looked at him, his friends, and all of the kids standing, poised for a response. Any excuse to legitimize what happens next I thought.

"You don't get it dude. And what's sad is, you aint never gonna get it."

"Let's go," I said to Justin while motioning for him to climb over his extended legs. Hopping up from the table Marcus grabbed my shoulder and spun me around. Before I could fully turn, he reared back and swung a punch/push with his right. Anticipating the punch, I had just enough time to deflect the blow with my left forearm. Visibly agitated by the miss, he quickly countered with another large haymaker but this time, I saw it coming. At the last possible moment, I dodged the blow allowing his wild swing to sail innocently above me. The empty swing, combined with his lack of control, left him grossly off balance. As he staggered forward, I expedited his fall with a firm push. He tried to catch his balance but it was too late. His large frame clumsily collided with a thud on the cold linoleum floor.

By now the lunchroom audience was beginning to grow. Chants of 'Fight, Fight, Fight' were beginning to reverberate throughout the auditorium. Phones were out as kids extended their devices above the crowd, determined to get a quick recording they could upload to their stories. However, despite the jeers from the crowd, I was determined to avoid the confrontation.

Dazed, Marcus sat up on his heels before standing erect. Looking around nervously he stood motionless, seemingly confused by what just happened.

"I'm not doing this with you dude. It's over!" I repeated to Marcus. Turning my back I motioned to Justin and said, "Let's go."

Before I could fully turnaround Marcus lunged. It wasn't a disciplined forward attack I'd practiced with Simon rather it was a wild exaggerated temper tantrum. A tearful Marcus suddenly charged. With arms flailing and eyes closed he lunged. Determined to avoid an outright confrontation I once again stepped aside allowing his momentum to crash into a table.

Food, milk, and everything imaginable flew in the air leaving Marcus drenched in the days lunch special. The crowd erupted in laughter as kids with phones got closer as they narrated their video or snapped quick pics of the schools notorious tough guy.

Justin, standing next to Marcus, laughed, and innocently joined in on the jeering. A visibly upset Marcus looked at the undersized Justin and angrily shoved him. The force of the push caused him to fly across the lunchroom floor. Not letting up,

Marcus charged, not me, but Justin. Falling on top of him he raised his hand intent on landing a blow on the scrappy little guy squirming beneath him. Seeing my undersized childhood friend wriggling under the oversized Marcus triggered something in me.

Grabbing his clinched right fist and placing it between my arm and left hip, I unleashed a series of quick jabs to his face. Dazed he looked up at me while trying to both stand and free his clenched arm from my grasp. In what I could only imagine was a desperate attempt to free his arm he swung a wild haymaker with his freed left hand. The punch landed innocently on my shoulder but the attempt to punch me further enraged me.

Taking his right hand I grabbed his wrist and fell backwards. With his extended arm between my legs I leaned back. Frantically struggling to free his newly incapacitated arm he used his strength to pull his fully extended arm back to a ninety-degree angle, but I too was determined. Placing my foot on the side of his face I crossed my arms over his wrist and leaned back. I could feel his powerful resistance pulling his arm away from me, but his powerful bicep was no match for the full strength of my legs and upper torso. Slowly inching backwards, all the while pulling his arm back to full extension, Marcus began to scream.

"No...no...no. I give, I give," he shouted.

Callous to his cries for mercy I fully arched my back until I felt the pop. Marcus instantly screamed out in pain as I pulled his arm in an unnatural direction.

The crowded lunchroom gasped at the grotesque sight while Marcus screamed in pain as the hyper extended arm laid limp on the lunchroom floor.

Releasing his contorted arm I rolled over and leaned in close and covered his mouth. Marcus' eyes darted around desperately terrified at what was coming next.

"I told you. Whatever this is, it's over," I explained in a clear, no-nonsense voice. "This shit ends now! Understood?" Marcus quickly nodded his head repeatedly in agreement. Standing up and turning around I was surprised to find the audience had grown. By now, the entire lunchroom had created a semi-circle around Marcus and I until the crowd began to quickly part.

It was Vice Principal Johnson. Always quick to stop cafeteria disruptions he was fighting his way to the front of the mob.

Looking down at a tearful Marcus holding his contorted arm he asked, "What the hell is going on in here?"

Marcus wiped away his tears and looked up at me then Mr. Johnson.

"Nothing sir. I must have s…s…slipped," he stammered.

Mr. Johnson looked at me then again at Marcus. "Then get up!" he instructed. "You and you," he said, pointing at two of Marcus's friends, "Help him up and get him to the nurse's office. The rest of you, finish up your lunch and clear out of here."

Mr. Johnson stood there, giving directions, while ensuring his orders were followed. As the crowd thinned, he looked around, seemingly surveying the situation. "Slipped and fell huh Mr. West?" he asked, without looking.

"I believe that's what he said sir," I replied.

Mr. Johnson, who had just two months earlier challenged me by saying, "They aren't going to stop bullying you until you take a stand," looked at me then watched as Marcus gingerly walked out of the lunchroom.

"Thank god for slippery surfaces. Fortitudine West…. Fortitudine," he said to no one in particular before turning to walk away.

"You kids finish up and get to class," he barked to the throngs still standing around before he too, disappeared into the crowded lunchroom.

After my mix-up with Marcus, things began to change almost instantly. Sitting in our usual lunchroom hallway, we watched as word of my "Deebo -Ice Cube" moment spread. The ensuing conversations prompted people I had never met to come up and speak to me.

"Yo Dante…Marcus just got knocked da F- out!"

Justin and I would just laugh and smile as person after person stopped in passing to engage in chit chat about Marcus' meteoric fall from grace. As the lunch period continued it was apparent that more people than I knew were also impacted by Marcus and his friends.

We continued eating lunch until that familiar baritone voice bellowed out a greeting.

"Good afternoon Mr. West. Are you men enjoying your dinner break or are you now talking about Gigamites?"

"Yes sir," I replied while fighting to suppress a laugh at his attempt to talk tech. "We were just finishing up our lunch and talking about some new software."

"You young people and your technology. There was a time when radios and electric typewriters were cutting edge technology. Now, one of your intelligent phones can do more in ten minutes than an entire 1950's office could dream of doing in a day. Times are definitely changing…. Speaking of letters, I read your end of semester essay on Pre-Civil War Slavery, and I must say, I found it profoundly refreshing. Your grasp of the subject seemed to transcend modern historical assessments and takes on insightfulness normally found in eyewitness journalistic writings. You effectively captured the pain of the 19th century slave while at the same time communicated their hopes and aspirations. It's almost as if you traveled back in time and personally interviewed those subjects you referenced," he said, looking over the top rims of his glasses.

"I wish!" I replied nervously. "Truth of the matter is I read a lot of the Slave Narratives and researched many of Dr. Gates's references."

"Yes. I guess traveling back in time is a little farfetched," he replied while still peering over his glasses. "Well, job well done. Perhaps we might spend some time next week and discuss some of those references. In the meantime, Archie Grimke, a former colleague and owner of the slave mannequins currently adorning my classroom, will be in town this week. His family owns Gateway City Antiques in Charleston. He will only be here briefly, so I would like for you to meet him. I am sure he will enjoy sharing some of his experiences with you. Good day, Mr. West," he added while walking away, gingerly shifting his weight between his good leg and his trusted cane.

"What was that all about?" asked Justin.

"I'm not sure," I replied, looking at my phone. "But we better wrap it up. The bell's about to ring."

***

The final bell rang, and I made my way to the city bus stop. Walking out of the main entrance, I stopped to watch Marcus, now wearing a sling and a borrowed West View High T-shirt leaving the school. Moving slowly, he gingerly climbed into a waiting car. Before the door could properly close, the driver sped away. I thought back to the number of times my father had spoken with his parents and how each time the conversations had little to no impact.

As the city bus pulled up I stepped in, dropped my change in the ticket machine, and collapsed in the seat behind the driver. I thought back to my history with Marcus and wondered if this incident might finally change how he interacted with Justin and me. Did he understand that I did not want to keep fighting with him or did this incident simply represent a continued, rather than a different, chapter?

After a quick glance at the silver ring I again began spinning it gently around my finger. The bus pulled into the mall but inexplicably stopped short of its usual stop. Looking out the window, I could see the mall entrance was filled with emergency vehicles with flashing lights.

"Looks like we're not going any further folks. If the mall is your stop, this is it," explained the bus driver before pulling the lever and opening the doors.

Grabbing my bag I hopped out and started making my way into the mall. Despite the long week I shared with Simon and Jackie, I was looking forward to working today. Those hours and days with Simon, Misty and Blaze had become the highlight of my day. However, this afternoon I was especially anxious to share the details of my confrontation with Marcus.

Simon had been my instructor however over the last few months, he had become a trusted friend.

Once on the escalator I immediately heard unusual commotion coming from the ground floor. As the metal stairs reached the bottom I realized the reason for the emergency vehicles.

In addition to a dozen officers and EMT workers, the Shoeshine Store was roped off with yellow cautionary tape. I ran toward the entrance only to be stopped by two plain clothes police officers.

"That's my boss's shop, I gotta get in there!" I yelled.

"Sorry kid, this is an active crime scene," replied the officer. "No one is allowed in or out."

"Dante," I heard over the bustling sounds of the mall and emergency personnel.

Looking above the crowd, I could see Simon standing next to the entrance waving at me frantically. Breaking free from the officer's grip I darted under the yellow tape and ran to the stores entrance.

Despite the loss of life and beatings Simon had witnessed, not to mention his own near-death experience, I had yet to see him even so much as shed a tear. However this time, I could tell he was visibly shaken.

"What happened?" I asked. "Are you ok?"

"It's Jackie," he said. "She's been shot. They don't know if she's going to make it."

# Epilogue: Prowler

The intruder peered through the kitchen window scanning the room for any signs of life. Once convinced the workers had long since left for the night, the prowler gracefully leapt up on the porch rail then crouched, cat-like, before pausing briefly to gather their balance. Then, with surprising agility and strength, they jumped, grabbed the edge of the wooden shingled roof, and in one singular motion, pulled themselves atop the wooden thatched roof.

The view from above the kitchen was breath taking. The lanterns were lit and brightly glowing in the small wooden homes dotting the countryside. The intruder paused, reflecting on the impact this new war would have on the residents of this small plantation, but quickly dismissed the thought.

"It's time I worried about me," they mumbled aloud.

After a quick glance in the window, they pulled a small knife from a back pocket and gently slid the slender blade through the window seal. Unlatching the lever they opened the window and with a graceful spin over the window ledge, slipped through and landed quietly inside. Maneuvering through the darkness while cautiously feeling around the room, they found a small glass lantern next to the bed. After a quick strike of the flint, the oil lamp quickly ignited.

The bright orange flame softly illuminated the room as the light reflected brightly through the glass lantern. Holding the lantern in the air, the prowler turned slowly while surveying the room and its contents. Starting with the small vanity, they began to quickly open and close the drawers. Pushing past jewels, coins and anything appearing to be of value, they continued, focused on their search. Although not clear as to what they were searching for, they were confident they would know once it was located.

Not finding anything, they reached deep into the neckline of their cotton shirt and produced a crudely made skeleton key. Rubbing a finger along the metal device, they continued to hold the lantern close to any item resembling an opening.

After several attempts to locate a hole they turned their attention to a large object neatly covered in the corner. Having been in the room numerous times, they didn't recall ever seeing or opening the structure. Placing the lantern on the window ledge, they pulled off the cloth exposing an immense wooden armoire. On the front, etched deep into the smooth wooden surface, was an image of a lantern. Gently rubbing their fingers along the etched lines, they stopped at the cabinet's keyhole. Grabbing the key, they inserted it and gently turned until they heard a 'CLICK'.

As the intruder pulled the key out of the door it slowly swung open. Lowering the lamp into the cabinet, they were surprised to find the closet empty. Resting the lantern on the closet floor, they rubbed their hand along the seams while examining the door and the cabinet's bottom. Looking at the floor of the cabinet, they noticed several small stains on the surface. Lowering the lantern closer to the ground they confirmed several distinct marks on the smooth wooden surface. After gently rubbing a finger over the spot they held it close to the lantern. Rubbing the fluid between their index finger and thumb, they examined it closely and were shocked to discover the solution was in fact, blood.